Window

on the Square

Whitney

1.

MY FIRST summons to the house in Washington Square came to me inscribed in an imperious feminine hand on rich cream notepaper. Apparently a friend had recommended me as dressmaker to Mrs. Brandon Reid. The note stated that Mrs. Reid would be pleased to receive me on Saturday, if I would come to her residence at eleven o'clock in the morning.

The name of Leslie Reid had a familiar ring to my ear. Had there not been some scandal a year or two before? Something to do with the death of her first husband and her eventual remarriage to his older brother? The details escaped me. In any event, they had no bearing on this work I needed so badly.

How anxiously I went to my appointment with Mrs. Reid that Saturday. The business of dressmaking was my mother's, built up painstakingly in the ten years and more since my father had died in the fighting at Shiloh. Now, with the sudden, shocking death of my mother and young brother beneath the hoofs of a runaway horse only six months before, I was left to continue my mother's work. I lacked her skill and interest in dressmaking, however. A fact that was all too evident to the ladies who had come to her for so long and were now reluctant to trust their wardrobes to a girl of twenty-two. I had a single order to complete and then I would not know which way to turn for my sustenance.

Autumn leaves were drifting from the trees in Washington Square and lay in golden swirls on every walk, crackling beneath my feet with the crisp sound that spells October. With increasing doubts of myself, I approached the row of red brick houses that faced the square, their tiny garden plots fenced in fancifully with wrought iron. The Reid House had marble steps and balustrades mounting to a columned doorway of the Greek revival period. I had often admired these handsome homes.

As I waited for an answer to my ring, I lifted my face to the hazy sunlight, letting its mild warmth flow through me. Grief had left me cold for so long, it seemed. The butler who opened the door did not warm me with his manner. He was high of nose and stiff of neck, and a glance at the unfashionable cut of my mourning must have told him that I was beneath his notice. He ushered me into a small, elegant sitting room and went away to announce my presence.

I had always enjoyed glimpses into the homes of the wealthy. Thanks to my mother's reminders and my memories of our own home, these surroundings neither abashed me nor made me envious. If my father had lived, I would have grown up in our big, rambling house in New Jersey, where he had been a professor of history.

Thus I looked about me at the teardrop chandelier, the French gilt furniture, and fine paintings, and found interest in them. I was fond of such evidence of good taste and elegance, and there was nothing about that bright small room to warn me of the blight that lay upon the rest of the house. Over the mantel of Italian marble hung a large oval mirror, gilt-framed, and I suppressed a feminine impulse to leave my chair and look at myself. After all, I did not want to be caught primping and I knew well enough how I looked.

4

Mourning did not become me. My coloring was too dark, my hair too black. Only the blue of my eyes must have lent contrast to the unhappy picture of sorrow I offered. My dress I had made hurriedly, with no time for the pains I must give to the gowns of my mother's clients. While it was drawn into a bustle at the back, it lacked the fussiness of present styles— a fussiness I decried and would not put upon my own person. The basque bodice fitted my figure well, with a neckline that ended in a touch of white ruching at my throat—since I could not resign myself to unrelieved black. The skirt was the current overdrape, with plain black showing beneath. In my ears I wore tiny gold earrings, and my hat was an old one of my mother's, small and rather flat, tilted forward over my bangs. Its black veiling I had put back upon entering the house.

So lost was I in this inventory of my appearance—sans mirror—that I heard no step in the doorway. I was staring at black-gloved hands clasped about my black reticule when a voice startled me.

"You are Miss Megan Kincaid?"

I rose at once, being here for purposes of serving, and faced the man who watched me from the doorway. Having once gazed, I could not look away. Seldom had I seen eyes so coldly gray and appraising. They were set in a face leanly handsome, somber, the brows dark and winged beneath high brushed dark hair. The nose was strong and faintly crooked, with a marked hump of bone at the bridge, the mouth full-lipped, or it would have been were it not pressed into so straight a line. He was a man in his early thirties perhaps, though he might have been older. I felt unaccountably drawn and yet a little repelled at the same time. Later I was to know that Brandon Reid often had this effect upon those who met him for the first time. Particularly when they were women.

"Yes, I am Megan Kincaid," I managed and wondered why

5

I should feel suddenly nervous in this man's presence. After all, I had come here to see Mrs. Reid and no one else.

"I'm sorry," he said, coolly courteous. "My wife is indisposed this morning and unable to keep her appointment with you."

My face must have betrayed my disappointment, though I tried to hide it at once. I straightened my shoulders proudly, having discovered that it is often by the set of one's shoulders that inner despair is revealed.

"I am sorry Mrs. Reid isn't well," I said. "Perhaps I may see her another day?" With that I moved toward the door to indicate that I meant to take nothing of his time.

He did not, however, move out of my way, and I was forced to come to an awkward halt a foot or two from him. His gray eyes had never left my face except for the moment in which they flicked over my person, as if still measuring, still weighing. Then he stepped abruptly out of the doorway.

"If you will come with me, please," he said and turned toward the stairs.

What this meant I did not know, but his manner of authority was not to be disregarded. I followed as he led the way, aware of his distinguished height and carriage.

The houses of Washington Square are apt to be narrow and fairly deep, but this house seemed of greater width than most. The staircase was graceful in its upward curve around a central oval. My hand on the black walnut banister, I glanced up and saw the oval glass skylight three stories above. There was no landing, but a continuation of wedge-shaped steps around the graceful turn, mounting to the second floor. The wallpaper was a dark figuring of raspberry upon cream, with the darkness predominating. The gas fixture on the wall lighted our way with a greenish-yellow, faintly hissing glow. Above, the hall was as gloomy as the stairs.

The man who conducted me led the way to closed double doors at the front of the house, flung them open, and stepped

6

back to permit me to enter. Still commanded by his manner, I went past him into a great square library. Here there was brightness again, for the dark green draperies had been drawn back from windows that made up one wall of the room. Pale sunlight set the glass aglow and lessened the dark severity of the room.

On each side of the double door, on each side of the mantel and chimney, and covering the remaining wall were shelves of books. My heart quickened a little at the sight. I could remember such a library from my childhood and I could remember my pain when from time to time since his death my mother had sold my father's books. But this room had some foreignness of ornament that I did not look at closely just then, my attention being mainly for the man who had brought me here.

Mr. Reid drew a chair before the handsomely carved mahogany desk and seated me. Then he took his place in a larger chair behind the desk, still watching me in his curiously intent manner.

"Tell me about yourself," he said, and I heard the rich, deep timbre of his voice, warmer and more winning than his cold, grave manner. Again my face must have betrayed bewilderment, for he added quickly, "I have good reason for asking."

By now I had lost much of my earlier poise. I felt younger than I wanted to feel and I did not like to be measured and studied as this man seemed to be studying me. I had come here to offer myself as a dressmaker to his wife. Why should he question me?

Nevertheless, I began somewhat stiffly to tell him how I had taken over my mother's work and mentioned the name of a client who had stood by me and found satisfaction in my efforts. I did not get far with this recital because he stopped me with an impatient wave of his hand.

"No, no—I know all that. What I want to hear about is

7

you. Tell me about your background, about your family life."

More bewildered than ever, I managed a brief account of where we had lived when I was a child. Of my father's death in battle during the war, and of the way I had learned to help my mother.

"Your education?" he asked curtly.

I mentioned the well-approved seminary for young ladies which I had attended at home, and explained that my parents had tutored me besides.

All these things he listened to with the same slight air of impatience, so that I wondered why he bothered to ask. When I fell silent with nothing more to tell, he picked up a carved ivory paperweight from his desk and weighed it from palm to palm.

"Have you any special interests?" he asked. "Is there any subject that particularly absorbs you?"

"I used to be fond of history and geography," I said. "My father helped me to cultivate an interest in foreign lands and antiquity."

I fancied a flicker of attention and surprise in his face, but his next question had nothing to do with my education.

"You had a brother, did you not?"

I didn't want to talk about Richard. He had been so young to die—just before his twelfth birthday. And yet, although I missed him with all my heart and had not yet been able to face the task of putting away his toys and small possessions, I knew death had been a release from a burden too heavy for one so young to bear.

With more self-possession than I had shown before, I managed to return Mr. Reid's measuring look.

"My brother died in the same accident that took my mother," I told him quietly.

Perhaps his manner toward me softened a little, but his words remained remote, objective. "I can understand your pain in this recent bereavement, Miss Kincaid. A mutual

8

friend has told me of how good you were with your brother, of how he improved to the fullest of his capacities because of your interest and care."

"My brother was injured at birth. Mentally he would never have been more than a child," I said with dignity and then was silent, not understanding what this interrogation signified.

The man behind the desk set down the paperweight, and I followed the movement, noting his long, thin hands and strong, flexible fingers. He rose abruptly and stepped to the windows behind the desk, staring through them, not looking at me now. With the removal of his gaze, I stirred in my chair, feeling as though I had been released from a spell.

"Why are you asking me these things?" I inquired.

His gaze was fixed upon the street and the square, and he spoke over his shoulder without turning.

"It was at my suggestion that my wife wrote asking you to come here today. Neither of us is interested in your dressmaking skill. She has a son—the son of my brother who is dead. He is a difficult, unbalanced boy. Neither his mother nor I, neither his tutor nor governess, has been able to handle him. He responds to no one. We have reached a point of desperation with him. Would you, Miss Kincaid, consider coming here to devote yourself to this boy?"

The suggestion was so startling that I could only stare at him. My reply when it came was faltering.

"But I have no training as a teacher. Caring for my brother was a simple matter. A matter of loving him dearly. I doubt that it would be wise for me to let my mother's business go while I attempted something for which I am unprepared."

"I've taken that into consideration," Mr. Reid said, and mentioned a monthly salary that made me gasp inwardly. It was more than I could hope to gain in months of dressmaking. Yet something held me back and I could not give my assent readily.

9

"I cannot see that what I have to offer is sufficient to justify this experiment," I told him.

He swung away from the window. "It may be that you will make a frock or two for my wife while you are under this roof. If you wish at any time to withdraw from this . . . arrangement, Mrs. Reid will see to it that you do not want for dressmaking orders from her friends. Is that not enough of a guarantee?"

It was more than enough, yet still I hesitated, unprepared to the core of my being for this sudden turn of events. There was an air about this house, about the somber, handsome man before me that set up an uneasiness in my spirit. There was more here, I sensed, than was to be easily fathomed or quickly explained, and however much I might need employment, I must now move with caution.

"This boy is unbalanced in his mind, like my brother?" I asked.

"Unbalanced, yes. Not in the same way as your brother, however. We believe that his mental growth is not impaired. But he is unpredictable, moody, with a violent, dangerous temper. There is nothing easy, I warn you, about this assignment, Miss Kincaid."

I did not want him to think I was afraid of the difficult. "May I see the boy?"

Brandon Reid seemed to hesitate for a moment. Then he gave a flick of his fingers that indicated decision. With a long stride he crossed the room to a braided rope of dark red silk and jerked it. A bell sounded in the depths of the house.

"I will send you up," he said. "It will be better if I do not go with you. Perhaps a little dissembling is necessary for the moment. There is another child—Jeremy's younger sister, Selina. The boy is nine, the girl eight. They are together in the nursery at the moment with their governess, Miss Garth. Let us say you are here in the role of dressmaker—to make a

10

frock for Selina. It is she you wish to meet. Perhaps you can take her measurements—something of the sort?"

I had brought with me the equipment of my trade in a small basket and I nodded. When the maid appeared, Mr. Reid gave her directions and I was led into the hall and up a second flight of stairs to the top of the house.

On this floor the somber gloom of dark wood and wallpaper continued to prevail, and again the hall area was lit by a single gas globe. There were closed doors all around and from beyond one at the front of the house I could hear voices raised as if in anger or excitement. The pert young maid gave me a sidelong glance and rolled her eyes skyward as she tapped on the panel. From her look I gathered that this sort of thing was not uncommon in the nursery.

A feminine voice bade us enter, and the door was opened upon a room of moderate size in which a roaring fire blazed and the atmosphere was stifling for the bright, mild weather outside. I was to learn that Thora Garth was always cold to her very marrow and no room could be too warm for her.

The maid bobbed a curtsy, murmured that the master had sent me to measure Miss Selina for a dress, and fled as if she could not wait to get away. With the door closed, facing the angry scene in that hot room, I did not blame her. The turkey-red carpet on the floor seemed to add its own burning heat to a room busily crowded with furniture—sofas, chairs, tables, cabinets, all set in an array that made them seem as quarrelsome as the persons in the room.

The governess, a tall, full-figured woman in a severe dress of brown merino, must have been in her late forties. She wore her thick, ungrayed brown hair in fashionable waves and puffs that revealed a certain vanity in its arrangement. Her face, with dark, deep-set eyes beneath the forehead puff, was handsome if forbidding. She wasted hardly a glance on me. All her attention was for the slight, brown-haired boy who sat at a

11

round table near the fire, his head bent intently over the pages of a book.

About them danced a sprite of a little girl with long fair hair floating about her shoulders, her face screwed up in a mischievous grimace.

"He took it, Garthy, he took it!" the little girl shrilled. "Make him give it back to me at once!"

Miss Garth held out her hand to the boy. "Whatever you have taken of your sister's, give it to me immediately."

The boy might have existed in a world of his own. Indifferently he turned a page and continued to read, ignoring her. While the girl was probably pretty when she wasn't grimacing, I found the boy had about him the look of an angel—a dark and sullen angel.

I stepped hastily to the table to present myself to the governess and interrupt this unpleasant scene. "You are Miss Garth, I believe? I am Megan Kincaid. I'm to make a frock for this young lady and I would like to take her measurements if I may."

The little girl whirled across the room to me, petticoats flying beneath her pink pinafore, offering herself readily to my tape measure.

"There!" she cried in triumph. "Mama is going to let me have a length of the new China silk after all. I knew she would if I cried for it hard enough."

For all Selina's effort to capture the center of the stage, it was the boy I watched as I unrolled my tape measure. For the first time he raised wide dark eyes from the page to stare at me, and a strange interest came alive in his face.

"Someone has died in your family," he said. It was a statement, not a question.

I realized that he was staring at my black dress and I answered him quietly. "You're very observant. It's quite true that I'm wearing mourning."

"Don't make impertinent remarks, Jeremy," Miss Garth

chided. "You are a wicked boy for taking your sister's things. Pay attention to me and give whatever you have back, or I shall have to smack you."

The long, deadly look he gave her before returning his attention to the book was not reassuring. Her words echoed through my mind. *Wicked boy,* I thought, and something stirred, tugging at my memory. I gave my attention to Selina, measuring and jotting down figures, turning her about.

"Tell me what sort of dress it is to be," Selina beseeched. "Is it really the green China silk?"

It was hard to resist her coaxing ways, and I smiled. "I won't know until I've had a chance to talk to your mother. Then I'll tell you all about it and we can plan it together."

She started to clap her hands and fumbled because of one closed fist. Suddenly suspicious, I took her delicate wrist between my fingers and turned her hand over. The child did not resist me, but only laughed as I opened the fingers to reveal a small red emery strawberry. I held it up for the boy to see.

"Your sister was teasing you, I think. See—here's what she thought she had lost. You didn't have it after all."

"Of course I didn't have it," the boy said scornfully and went on with his reading.

Miss Garth glanced at him impatiently and then turned a fond look upon the little girl. "You mustn't tease us like that, dear," she said and came to watch my measuring with a critical air. There was an aura of violet scent about her that I found a little oppressive in the stuffy room.

Everything I observed here increased my feeling that what Mr. Reid had asked of me was impossible. No matter what the boy's need might be, he would welcome no further supervision, and Miss Garth would clearly resent any filching away of her authority. I would make this dress for Selina and end the matter there, I told myself firmly.

"Who was it in your family that died?" the boy asked, fixing me again with his queerly avid gaze.

I made no attempt to evade his question, but answered him simply before the governess could interfere. "My mother and my brother were killed in an accident a few months ago. By a runaway horse."

The child's eyes were dark and fixed, the iris almost as black as the pupils, and I sensed in him a thirst for horror that troubled me. In a moment he would ask for details, and I changed the subject quickly.

"Your face seems familiar to me, Jeremy. Perhaps I've seen you playing when I've walked through Washington Square."

The dark eyes flickered and excitement came into them. "I never play in the square," he said. "But my picture was in all the papers a couple of years ago—drawings of me. That's where you must have seen me."

"That is quite enough, Jeremy," Miss Garth snapped. "If you are through, Miss Kincaid, you had better go. The boy is becoming unduly excited. I can't think why you were brought to this room in the first place. Selina could have come to you in the schoolroom."

I put my things away in silence. There was nothing to be said to this woman, but my heart went out to the sullen, morbidly excited boy. His trouble was very different from Richard's, and I felt myself untutored for so disturbing an assignment. In spite of my pity, it was impossible for me to accept this post.

As I went into the gloomy hall, closing behind me the door to that overheated, tension-filled room, I had a sense of escape and at the same time the feeling that I was abandoning someone in dire need. If I did not try to help that boy, who would?

At the top of the stairway leading down to the second floor, where Mr. Reid awaited my decision in the library, I hesitated, torn and uncertain. The words Miss Garth had spoken flashed through my mind again—that phrase no one should use to a child, no matter what the provocation— "wicked boy." And suddenly I remembered. Jeremy had been

14

right. The papers, spilling sensation across their pages, had first shown me his face. I recalled his father's name and identity now. Dwight Reid, the younger brother, had enjoyed a brief and brilliant career as District Attorney in New York, a career ended by a tragic accident with a gun—at the hands of this very boy. Yet, remembering, I found my sorrow mainly for the child, who must carry so terrible a guilt through the rest of his life.

Further indignation against Miss Garth for terming him wicked stirred in me. She would be a formidable woman to oppose, and I had no desire to enter a life of tumult and emotional conflict. Jeremy Reid had no suspicion that he had sent my way a plea for help. Indeed, if I offered him the slightest assistance, he would undoubtedly reject me at once. And yet . . . I had no choice. I'd had none since my first glance fell upon that face of a very young angel, dark and lost.

Resolutely I put doubt and reason behind me and followed my heart down the stairs to the library where Mr. Reid sat behind his desk, looking as though he had not stirred since I had left him there.

He rose when I entered the room, waiting in silence as I came toward him.

"I don't know whether there is anything I can do," I told him, "but I see the need. I would like to try—for a time at least. I will not stay if I find myself failing."

He came round from behind the desk and held out his hand. His smile did not light his eyes. "Thank you, Miss Kincaid. All I have learned about you indicates courage. This acceptance most of all."

It was disconcerting to realize that I must have been covertly observed, that questions must have been asked about me, and all the small details of my life looked into.

I put my hand into the one he proffered, and his fingers closed over mine. There was a strange instant in which I sensed through his clasp something of the stormy force of this man, and it alarmed me. I drew my hand away too hurriedly and was aware that he noted the fact.

"I must tell you," I said, "that I have remembered the story the papers printed—though I don't know how much of it was true. I believe it was through an accident that your nephew shot and killed his father two years ago when he was seven."

A stiffening seemed to run through Brandon Reid. "Very little of what was printed during that unfortunate time was true," he assured me, his tone bitter.

I asked no questions then. Eventually I would have to know the full story. I would need to learn all I could about Jeremy Reid. If his uncle imagined that I would respect a natural reticence regarding the past, he would have to discard that notion. But this, I knew, was not the moment to press for information. There would be time later on.

"When would you like me to come, Mr. Reid?" I asked.

"As soon as possible. When may we expect you?"

There was nothing to keep me longer in the two rooms my young brother, my mother, and I had occupied in a boarding-house. It would be possible, I said, to come by the middle of next week. But if I were to approach the boy gradually and win his trust, I would prefer to come as a resident seamstress and appear to be working on frocks for Selina.

Mr. Reid thought this an excellent plan. There was a room I might have on the third floor next to Jeremy's. He would see that it was made ready. And he would send a carriage for me whenever I wished.

There was one point about which I felt uneasy. "I wonder," I began, "would it be wise to return for an interview with Mrs. Reid before . . ."

He broke in upon my words decisively. "The matter is settled, Miss Kincaid. We will expect you next Wednesday in the afternoon, if you can be ready by then."

He saw me to the door himself and added a last word before

I left. "Would you mind very much if I request that you give up your mourning dress before you come here? The women in this house avoid black. It is better for Jeremy not to be reminded of death."

"Of course," I said. "I understand."

I did not mind. Black was something one wore in order to conform to custom. Grief for those who had gone was not based on the color of a dress, or the wearing of a black veil.

He opened the door for me and said a polite "Good day," but he did not offer his hand again. I went down the steep flight of marble steps and walked toward Broadway, where I could find transportation home. With every step away from the house, I could feel his eyes upon me and it was an effort not to look back.

2.

THERE WAS pain for me in the next few days. Once the dress order was completed I could give myself to packing my few possessions and to disposing of what it would not be wise to keep. My brother Richard's things were the hardest for me to touch. I gave away his toys except for a small music box carrousel he had loved. This I packed along with a few pieces of my mother's jewelry and my own trinkets and clothing.

By Wednesday afternoon, when Fuller, the Reid coachman, came to carry a portmanteau and small trunk to the carriage, I was ready. It was pleasant to travel in a victoria instead of by horsecar, and I tried not to look back, or to think of the ties with the past I was breaking.

This time the haughty butler was busy elsewhere and the little maid, who said her name was Kate, came cheerfully to let me in. She would not allow me to carry my portmanteau upstairs but took it herself. Mr. Reid was not in evidence, and I was led at once to the small room that had been prepared for me at the third-floor rear.

Kate set down my bag, murmured doubtfully that she hoped I would be comfortable, and hurried away. As before, she seemed eager to escape the third floor.

The small room had a bare, unwelcoming look, as though it had been prepared hastily with necessities rather than comforts. There was a narrow brass bedstead, with one of its brass head knobs missing, and a worn rag rug on the floor beside it. A plain, square table, its surface scarred and without covering, had been set before the window at the rear, a single straight chair drawn up to it. The bureau was tall and severe, topped by a somewhat watery mirror. The washstand needed varnishing, but the basin and pitcher upon its marble top were flowered and not unattractive. At least the room had a fireplace and a narrow mantel, and there was a good drop-front secretary, though paper had been folded under one leg to prevent its wobbling.

I told myself resolutely that the plain little room could be made attractive and I did not mind being given what came to hand. Nevertheless, the lack of tempering touches to indicate that someone thought kindly of my coming, left me, in my present mood, a little depressed. I took off my hat and hung my cloak on one of the bare hooks provided for my clothes. Today I wore a dress of gray-blue, serviceable, but not by any means the color of mourning.

I was about to approach the window and look out when a tap on the open door behind me made me turn. Miss Garth stood there, impressive in dark green, with an elaborate, bow-trimmed bustle, her heavy hair as fancifully combed as I had seen it before. She greeted me formally and without a smile. As I had sensed, I would find no welcome here.

"Mrs. Reid wishes to see you," she said curtly. "If you will come at once, please, since she is going out."

I nodded agreeably and followed her to the floor below. It had disturbed me that I had not seen Jeremy's mother on my previous visit and I was glad to have this matter remedied without delay.

As she walked ahead of me, I could not help but observe Miss Garth's high, proud carriage of shoulders and head.

20

Again I would have found her handsome had she been less formidable.

She opened a door off the middle of the hall and showed me into a small, very feminine boudoir in which a lamp burned on a table and a fire was dying to red coals. A cushioned chaise longue of brocade and gilt, brocaded chairs, and a small marble-topped table, bearing a vase of flowers, made up its attractive furnishings. The single window looked out upon an air shaft shared with the next house and introducing gray-filtered daylight into the room. On my left hung long draperies of light-green velvet, perhaps hiding a door. On the right were similar draperies, half parted to reveal the adjoining bedroom.

Miss Garth stepped to this opening to announce my presence, and a woman came through to greet me. I could see at once that she was a great beauty, and she looked amazingly young to be the mother of two children. She was dressed for the street and her high-piled red hair gleamed beneath iridescent brown feathers on her hat. Her skin was pale and clear —the fair skin that went so delicately with that shade of hair. Her eyes, wide beneath dark lashes, had an amber tinge. Her gown was of a rich, deep violet, and over one arm she carried a sealskin cape. A muff of the same fur dangled from one slender hand. A knot of hothouse violets had been pinned to the fur, and there was a faint, delicious scent of violets about her. The odor made me wonder if Miss Garth had borrowed her perfume the other day when she had worn it so copiously.

In spite of the governess' urgent summons and the fact that Mrs. Reid was about to go out, there was no haste in her movements. She seemed rather languid and lacking in vitality. Her amber eyes were indifferent as she turned them upon me, and she brushed a hand across her forehead, as if troubled by pain. Nevertheless, when she spoke, her words recalled the imperious handwriting of the note she had sent me and I

21

realized that this woman was not likely to condescend to friendliness.

"I must tell you, Miss Kincaid, that I do not approve of this experiment of my husband's. If Miss Garth is unable to help Jeremy, it is unlikely that a stranger can do any better. Naturally I will not oppose my husband's wishes, but I think it wise for you to understand my own feelings in the matter."

I was dazzled by her beauty and would have liked to win her respect and liking. I repeated what I had told Mr. Reid —that I would not stay if I found there was nothing I could do for the boy. But first I would like to try. Miss Garth sniffed audibly, and her mistress' eyes flicked her way, then back to my face.

"I am late for tea at Sherry's," Mrs. Reid said. "If you will excuse me . . ."

But I would not let her go as quickly as that. "Will you tell me when I may see you?" I said hurriedly. "There are matters I would like to consult you about as soon as possible."

She seemed surprised and reluctant, but she set the time of ten o'clock the following morning. Then she went gracefully past me to the door and Miss Garth and I stood looking after her.

The governess spoke aloud, though more to herself than to me. "A good thing it is for Miss Leslie to get out of this house and see her friends now and then. These days she stays too close to home."

"Isn't she well?" I asked.

Miss Garth remembered my presence with an impatient glance, but before she could answer there was a sound on the stairs and I turned to watch the encounter that took place. Mr. Reid was mounting from the lower floor, momentarily blocking his wife's descent.

My first glimpse of Brandon and Leslie Reid together was a picture I was to carry in my mind for a long while. How handsomely they were matched, those two! How right that his sort of man should have so beautiful a wife. Mr. Reid took his wife's hand affectionately, and the look he turned upon her was hardly less than ardent.

"You're off for tea, aren't you? Have a pleasant afternoon, darling," he said.

She turned her head languidly so that his kiss just grazed her cheek, and drew her slim, ringed hand from his touch. She did not answer him and a moment later she had moved out of sight down the stairs. Mr. Reid glanced at Miss Garth and me standing in the doorway of his wife's boudoir. He nodded to us casually and went by before I could so much as say, "Good afternoon." His look in my direction carried with it no recognition, and I must confess to a certain annoyance. After all, I had come here at his request. Yet apparently he had forgotten my face, or was now indifferent to my presence in this house.

Miss Garth flicked her handkerchief beneath her nose as if in disdain, and I caught a scent of lavender that was less lavish than the violet she had used the other day.

"Come," she said to me. "I'll show you where you can do your sewing on our floor upstairs. This is not a large house, you understand. It will be necessary to arrange some sharing."

Again we climbed the stairs, and she led me into a room at the back that was being used for lessons. A tutor came in to instruct the children five days a week, she explained. Naturally, she taught them French, deportment, and other graces. Since lessons were held only in the morning, the room was empty now. It could be used for my sewing as well as lessons, Miss Garth said, and pointed out the long table suitable for spreading materials, and the sewing machine that had been placed in a corner. It was a bare room, with an odor of books and chalk about it that was not unpleasant. To me it seemed a more comfortable place than the hot, crowded nursery at the front of the house. Nevertheless, there was a bleakness here that I regretted. It had always seemed to me that children respond best to cheerful surroundings and work better in them. At least it was so with my young brother Richard.

Well, we should see. I would have to move slowly, I knew. My mere presence was apparently a revolution in this house, and if Mr. Reid had not even recognized me at our second meeting, I might find myself with less backing than I had hoped for.

Miss Garth left me, and I returned to my own small room. This time I went at once to see what view I might have from the window. Its curtains were fresh and crisply white, and I looked out between their folds upon the mews behind our row of buildings. Across an alleyway were the stables and coach houses that serviced this block. There was brick paving and little in the way of vegetation, except for a hardy ailanthus tree that reached its branches toward my window. The long leaves were turning brown, and clusters of them had drifted on the bare ground beneath. Looking through the branches I could see Fuller the coachman rubbing down one of the horses. Beyond were nearby rooftops, but no great expanse of view. At least there would be human activity within sight, and the coming and going of domestics. The thought made me feel less alone.

Now I must unpack and begin to make something of this desolate little room. There was an insistent voice in my mind all too ready to ask how I had dared to give up a life that was at least familiar for the uncertain task that faced me in this house. My meeting with Mrs. Reid, her admission that she did not want me here, the indifference Mr. Reid had shown on our second encounter were far from reassuring. But I thrust these thoughts aside and went to work.

I could almost hear my mother's voice after the news of Father's death had reached us. "We must work, dearest—keep busy. It's the only way to lessen pain."

My first move was to light the coal fire, ready laid in the grate. The kindling caught at once, and lizard tongues of

24

flame licked upward through the coals. No room could remain completely cheerless with a fire burning. Now that I had its gentle humming for company, I opened my portmanteau and began to hang up my clothes, set out a few of my possessions.

I found an embroidered table scarf and brought out my mother's blue Lowestoft tea set. I could never touch the pieces of that set without remembering her hands moving graciously from teapot to cups, without remembering how much she had enjoyed a pause in her afternoon's work for tea with Richard and me. The pang of loneliness was there again, and I fought it down.

There was no reason to feel sorry for myself. In a week I would have made this room my own, and I had an absorbing challenge ahead of me in the person of Jeremy Reid. How to approach him was my first concern, how to win his trust and then his liking. These were the things I must think about. I took out Richard's little music-box carrousel that had cost me more than I should have spent one Christmas. Though I was glad now, for it had given him much pleasure. I wound the key and set it upon the mantel, where it made a gay touch of bright color. Small red and green and yellow figures on horses, a little sleigh with miniature children, turned merrily about and the old nursery favorite, "Frère Jacques," tinkled through the room.

A somewhat demanding knock summoned me to the door. I blinked away a stray tear and went to open it. On my threshold stood Selina Reid, her eyes dancing and soft folds of green China silk spilling through her hands.

"I have it!" she cried in triumph, holding up the material. "So when will you make my dress?"

Here, I thought, was my first approach to Jeremy, to learning all I could know about him. I stepped aside and invited her into my room. The carrousel still turned and the music played.

She walked directly to the mantel. "I like this," she said. "May I have it to play with?"

I shook my head gently. "It belonged to my brother, who is dead. Sometimes when you visit me, I will wind it for you, but I don't let anyone else touch it."

She looked at me in no little surprise, and I gathered that few requests of Miss Selina's were refused in this house. All the more reason it was wise to have an understanding between us at once. She seemed to think better of sulking as I took the silk from her hands and examined it in admiration. What thin, soft stuff it was—like gossamer, yet strong and finely woven. The color was pale—the new green of leaves in the springtime. It would suit her coloring beautifully.

"We'll start your dress tomorrow," I assured her. "This is lovely silk. It will make up beautifully, though it's more suited to spring and summer than to chilly fall. I have some fashion books to help us. Perhaps we can design it together."

That pleased her, and she gave me a charming, sunny smile. "What am I to call you?" she asked. "I don't remember the name Garthy said when you came here before."

"Would you like to call me Miss Megan?" I suggested. "It seems more friendly than to use Kincaid."

She tried the name over softly to herself and then spoke it out loud as though she had decided to favor it. The music-box tune came to an end, and Selina suddenly remembered that she had been sent here with a message.

"Oh dear, I forgot! I'm to ask you to come downstairs at once for high tea. That's what we have at five-thirty in the dining room. It's an early supper really, but Miss Garth has been to England and she likes English ways. You are to eat your meals with us, Miss Megan."

Though it was early for supper, I could accommodate my habits, and I was happy to have this opportunity to join the others. This would enable me to see more of Jeremy.

We folded the China silk carefully and put it in a drawer

of my bureau. Then, while Selina waited for me, I washed my hands in the blue-flowered basin. The Reids' house was extremely up-to-date in having a bathroom, but it was downstairs on the second floor. When I had poured the water into the slop jar hidden below and dried my hands, we went downstairs together.

For this dark and somber house, the dining room on the first floor was surprisingly bright. The dark paneling of the wall reached only halfway up, and above it a light wallpaper sprigged in delicate green gave the room a bright and airy appearance. The furnishings were elegant, as they were throughout the house, and a handsome chandelier hung from the center of a plaster medallion in the high ceiling. Through the glass doors of an enormous cabinet I could see an array of fine china and crystal.

At the front of the house French doors opened upon a small iron balcony overlooking the square. Though they were closed, the light of late afternoon poured in from the street.

Miss Garth and Jeremy were already seated at the long table, with a coal fire murmuring cheerfully beside them. Miss Garth's chair was, as always, closest to the blaze, but this was a large room and not easily made stuffy. Somewhat curtly she indicated my place at the table and remarked that promptness at mealtime was a virtue.

I found myself opposite Jeremy, who did not look at me at all. Through most of the meal he remained silent and remote, indifferent to those about him. He ate listlessly and without appetite, and more than once Miss Garth chided him, criticized his table manners, or urged him to finish what was on his plate.

Selina went her own charmingly impertinent way, often addressing her remarks to her brother, whether he paid any attention or not. She told him delightedly about the carrousel music box in my room and warned him not to touch

27

it. She boasted about the new clothes she was to have, speaking as though "Miss Megan" were her private acquisition.

I remarked casually that when I had time I would perhaps make a new suit for Jeremy. Still he did not look at me, but he spoke in a rough, ill-mannered way.

"I don't want any new clothes. And I won't be measured or fitted."

"As you like," I told him. "I'll be quite busy as it is."

"You will have new clothes if your uncle wishes it," Miss Garth insisted.

For once the boy raised his eyes and threw her a quick, resentful look. "Why should my Uncle Brandon wish it? You know he hates me. You know he wishes I were dead."

I though this a terrible and shocking thing for a little boy to say with such conviction and I wondered if Mr. Reid knew of this notion. But for the moment there was no way in which I could contradict it. I was still feeling my way toward an understanding of the relationships in this house. Until I knew the meaning behind the emotional undercurrents I sensed, I could not tread with safety on what might well be unstable ground.

When the long, wearing meal was over, I returned to my room and sat down in the single straight chair to think about the problems which rose like a series of mountain ranges ahead of me. It was clear that Jeremy wore a prickly armor all about him—armor without a visible chink. Yet he was a child and he had needs of which he could not be wholly aware. Needs perhaps that he had suppressed after the tragic accident in which his father had died. Somewhere there would be a way through his defenses, and I must find it. I must have the patience to wait and the wisdom to recognize the way when it presented itself. This seemed a very large order, and I did not dare allow myself to be frightened by it.

The evening, after so early a supper, stretched endlessly ahead, and I found myself restless. I knew that ladies did not

28

walk alone after dark in New York streets. The assaults of footpads and thugs, the accosting of lone women, and even unarmed men, were commonplace in these dreadful times. But to sit here for hours when I did not feel like reading or sewing seemed a greater danger to my spirits than was possible outward danger to my person.

I put on the gray dolman mantle with its capelike top that my mother had made me in a new and fashionable style, and tied gray bonnet ribbons under my chin. When I left my room I found the upper floor quiet and I heard and saw no one on my way downstairs. But as I descended the lower flight, I came upon a scene so magical, so warmly felicitous, that I paused with my hand on the rail and stared without conscience.

The double doors to the dining room had been left open, and I could look down upon the long table where the children and I had so recently sat through that unhappy meal with Miss Garth. Now the table was bright with fine linen and silver. Lavish chrysanthemums made a centerpiece, and candles burned in branched candelabra. At each end of the table sat the master and mistress of this strange household.

Again Leslie Reid's beauty caught at my breath. What is it a woman feels when she beholds such perfection in another woman? There is envy perhaps—but I think curiosity as well. We look and marvel and try to see this vision as a man must see her, and thus gain some knowledge of what it is we ourselves should emulate.

Mrs. Reid had dressed for dinner in a yellow brocade gown that set off her red hair—more beautiful than ever now that she wore no hat. Diamonds shone at her ear lobes and on her fingers. Candlelight enhanced and softened the amber of her eyes.

When I had studied his wife, seeking an answer to a tantalizing enigma, I looked at Mr. Reid to observe his response. Henry, the haughty butler, was serving, and as

29

Henry helped him from a silver dish, Brandon Reid bent the same ardent attention upon his wife that I had noted earlier in the day. He was asking her about her afternoon, as a husband might, and she was answering him, seemingly less remote and cool now, telling him of someone she had seen at Sherry's. There was a vivacity in her manner that had been lacking before.

I believe I am not more envious than others. Yet in that moment I ached with loneliness and—let us call it longing, rather than envy, since that is a kinder word. How fortunate Leslie Reid was—there at her own attractive table, with a husband so attentive, so loving and admiring.

Mrs. Reid remarked on a draft just then, and the butler came toward the doors to close them. I blinked the vision from my eyes and fled down the stairs and out through the heavy front door to Washington Square. I would walk until I was weary and drink in great draughts of fresh air and forget those who dined graciously by candlelight.

Only a few years before, the old Washington Parade Grounds had undergone a transformation, turning the square into one of the most beautiful parks in the city. Flower beds had been set out and shade trees planted. The sidewalks were of concrete, the roadways of new wood paving—all centering about a huge fountain basin and converging into Fifth Avenue.

I had read in the papers that some political chicanery had resulted in the building of more lamp posts than was necessary in the square. At least it was the best lighted park in the city. The lamplighter had already gone his rounds and in such a brilliance of gaslight there seemed little danger that any of the city's criminal element would be abroad. I walked along the paths and around the broad basin of the fountain, my feet scattering crisp leaves at every step.

The scene at the dining table still haunted me. I hoped that Mrs. Reid was kind to so obviously loving a husband, and

30

that he was gentle and loving with her. From my observation he had not seemed a particularly gentle person, but perhaps he reserved this quality for his beautiful wife.

Her coolness earlier had perhaps been due to some small marital spat. My mind skipped and speculated. What had Dwight Reid been like? Had the younger brother been as fascinating as the older? Fascinating? Now where had I come upon such a word for a man who repelled me no little?

I could recall only a smattering of information about Dwight Reid. He had been something of a Galahad in city politics, fighting crime, helping those in need, and doing a great deal of good during his time in office. The papers had seemed to attack him less than they did other men in our venal public life, and his death had been a blow to the honest element of the entire city. Since Leslie had married him first, he must have been the better man. How dreadfully the whole household must have suffered over his death. Yet in a year's time she had married the older brother. Now how had that come about?

So my thoughts ran in the manner of a mind which lacks sufficient life of its own to feed upon.

I walked briskly around the square, glad to see others out on this pleasant autumn evening. I put my speculations aside and by the time I returned to the house, I had cleared my head of cobwebby doubts and foolish envy. Tomorrow I must be up early, ready to approach my new duties.

As I reached the steps I glanced up and saw that the dining room was still radiantly lighted and that Mr. Reid had come to stand in one long window, open now upon the square. I lowered my eyes and hurried across the sidewalk, thinking he would not observe me, or would ignore me if he did.

But he called out to me suddenly. "Catch!" he cried, and I looked up in surprise to see him toss out something that resembled a yellow ball. I moved instinctively, without

31

thinking. Often I had played ball with young neighbors, and even a bit with Richard, who could not throw or catch very well. I reached up with both hands and caught the sphere f yellow as it fell toward me. The man in the window above la ghed out loud as he closed the shutters. I stood there foolishly, holding in my hands the orange I had caught in so unexpected a manner.

I couldn't help smiling as I let myself into the house with the latchkey Kate had given me. Mr. Reid was nowhere in sight as I went upstairs, but now I knew something I had not known before. It seemed that the dark and somber Brandon Reid could also be a man of light impulse. He knew perfectly well who I was, and though this was an odd way of showing it, I felt somehow reassured.

My steps were soft on the carpeted stairs. The second floor was as usual dimly lighted by its single globe-encased gas jet. The small figure bending before a closed door next to Mrs. Reid's boudoir did not hear me until I was directly behind him. Then he whipped around to face me with one hand hidden behind his back. But not quickly enough, for I had glimpsed the key in Jeremy's fingers. We stared at each other, equally surprised, and it was the boy who spoke first.

"You'd better not tell Garth," he whispered, and there was a threatening note in the words.

I answered him calmly. "I really don't know anything to tell."

He gave me a long look, guarded and enigmatic, before he dashed ahead of me up the stairs. By the time I reached the floor above, all doors were closed and I went to my own room, feeling more pity for the child than anything else. What secretive life went on behind that darkly handsome young face? To what room had he a hidden key, and why?

32

Before I went to bed I peeled and ate the orange Mr. Reid had tossed me. Its tangy aroma scented the air and clung to my fingers. Somehow, in spite of the strange happenings of the day I felt more determined than ever to help Jeremy Re. And I did not feel nearly so discouraged.

3.

THE NEXT morning I was up early. As Kate had explained to me, all of us on the third floor—myself, Miss Garth, and the two children—were expected to breakfast in the nursery and stay out of the dining room mornings. In the crowded nursery I found a pot of hot coffee on the table and a covered dish of scrambled eggs, cold toast, butter, and marmalade. It was pleasant to eat alone and then get to work in the schoolroom, setting my things out at one end of the long table. Perhaps I could make a start before the tutor came for lessons.

I was deep in fashion books, searching for a style that would become the flyaway sprite that was Selina, when Miss Garth came to summon me to Mrs. Reid's room. Jeremy's mother would see me now instead of later. She had slept badly and was having an early breakfast in bed. I was to come downstairs at once. Again the summons seemed imperious, though perhaps that was due to Miss Garth's delivery.

This time I was taken directly into the front bedroom adjoining the green and gold boudoir. It was a room of satin and lace, of furbelows and mirrors. But in spite of the fact that bright morning pressed at the windows, the gold brocade draperies were drawn and the light that lay upon the room was cast wholly by flickering candles. Set upon the highboy was a branched candelabrum of silver, its six candles burning tall. Small candleholders of painted china lighted each side of the dressing-table mirror, and beside the hearth stood a giant brass candlestick awash with golden light. There was no denying that this soft illumination flattered and enhanced the beauty of the woman in the bed.

She sat up with lacy pillows behind her, a small lap table across her knees. Her red hair, tied youthfully with a green ribbon at the top of her head, fell about her shoulders, and its warmth held my eyes. Once more I caught the whisper of a light violet scent pervading the room.

Miss Garth left me there, and I was glad to see her go. I might accomplish more with Mrs. Reid without the presence of the governess.

This morning I was prepared with specific questions and a few suggestions, but Mrs. Reid, sipping coffee, and playing delicately with a bowl of fruit, took the interview from my hands. She invited me to draw a chair beside the bed and began to speak of my duties and hours with the somewhat haughty air of mistress to servant.

"Perhaps," she said, "it will be possible for you to help with the children on Sundays when Garthy goes to visit her father. Perhaps you can also free her on an occasional evening when I need her, or when she wishes an hour or so away from the house. She is more than a governess, you know. Much of the management of this house rests in her hands, since I am not strong enough to cope with it. I am not always well, and, as a result, Miss Garth has been overworked."

I would be happy to comply, I agreed, but I did not mean to have this interview entirely one-sided and when she had paused and turned to her tray as if she were done with me, I began my questions.

"I've been wondering about the children's activities," I said. "What sort of things do they like to do? What are

36

Jeremy's main interests? When I understand these matters I will be in a better position to make friends. Not that this will be difficult with Selina. We already have a bond between us because of the dress I'm making for her."

Leslie Reid looked slightly bored. "Oh, yes—the China silk. I had planned to use it myself, but my husband believes this is more important."

She yawned, tapping her fingers to her mouth, and seemed to forget me and my questions.

"You were going to tell me about the children's interests, Mrs. Reid," I prodded gently.

"Was I? But what is there to tell? I suppose they like the usual things. Dolls, toys, games—what else?"

"A boy of nine often has some special fancy that absorbs him," I pointed out.

The woman in the bed gave me her sudden, full attention, and there was a note of distress in her voice as she spoke. "He has become such a difficult child—not at all like other boys. He seems to enjoy destructive things. Miss Garth and I, and even his tutor, Mr. Beach, are at our wits' end to deal with him. My husband feels that you may have something new to offer the boy. We will be more than grateful if you can turn him from his present course of moody wildness, but as I've told you, I have little hope of this, Miss Kincaid."

"Perhaps that's the one thing we must never let him sense," I said. "That we have lost hope would be too discouraging. Perhaps he needs a belief in his ability to grow. Has he no special pastimes? No hobbies?"

Leslie Reid's long lashes fluttered for an instant upon pale cheeks, and a shiver seemed to run through her.

"My son is fond of guns," she said. Dwight—his father— had a collection of fine pistols with which Jeremy was obsessed. I warned my husband long ago that such an interest was not wise for a child. But no one would heed me."

This, I sensed, was dangerous ground, and it would not

37

help me in my search for Jeremy's interests. I spoke again of the dress I would make for Selina, asking whether Mrs. Reid wished to instruct me as to the style. Again she seemed listless and ready to leave the matter in my hands, eager only to have our interview come to an end. I asked if there were any particular hours she liked to spend with the children, any time that should be saved for her visits with them.

She pushed the tray from her with a small gesture of distaste and tugged at a bell rope beside her bed.

"Selina comes to see me here whenever she likes. Often I take her with me when I go for a drive. But when it comes to Jeremy, I can find no pleasure in his company. This is not an easy matter for me, Miss Kincaid."

She reached toward the table beside her bed and picked up a double miniature in twin silver frames. Wordlessly she handed it to me, and I saw that it contained the portraits of two men. From one side Brandon Reid's dark countenance looked out at me, his mouth unsmiling, his eyes upon faraway things. The other man was totally different in appearance, though I knew this must be Dwight Reid. The younger brother had a bright, sunny look about him. Except for his fair coloring he resembled his son amazingly. He was younger and far handsomer in a boyish way than was Brandon Reid. I returned the miniature, wondering why she had shown it to me.

"You may have heard of my first husband," she said. "There were many who blessed his name. Since his death, New York citizens have been building a memorial to honor him—the Dwight Reid Memorial Home, which will be opened before long and will care for homeless children. Dwight had a great future ahead of him. It's possible that he might have been governor, or gone on to the national legislature."

I waited, troubled by the sudden flash of feeling I saw in her face. The amber eyes were no longer cold, but misted with tears when she turned them upon me.

38

"It was all destroyed—everything! Do you understand? Do you see why it may be painful for me to have Jeremy in my company?"

For the first time my sympathy went out to her, and yet I could not accept her attitude. Jeremy was a child, whatever he might have done.

"I can understand," I told her. "Yet even something so dreadful must be forgiven when the boy's life and sanity hang in the balance. Perhaps your son blames himself more than anyone else can possibly blame him. Perhaps he is in desperate need of love and help."

Diamonds flashed on Leslie Reid's hand as she brushed it across her face. Listlessness had fallen upon her again.

"Do as you wish," she said. "I am not an unnatural mother, but he is an unnatural son."

Kate tapped on the door and came in to remove the lap table and tray. The interview was over, and I followed the maid soberly from the room. At least I knew now that there was little I could hope for from Jeremy's mother. Undoubtedly her wounds had been as deep and as shocking as the boy's. In spite of her marriage to Dwight's brother, it was clear that she had not entirely recovered from the experience. It was not for me to judge her, but my sympathy still lay with her son.

In the hall I spoke to Kate as we passed the door in front of which I had found Jeremy the night before.

"What room is this?" I asked.

Kate gave the door a quick, fearful look and paused at the head of the back-stairs flight. "It's no one's room now, miss. But it used to belong to him that—that died. Cook says it was right in there it happened. They keep it locked now. And a good thing it is I'm no believer in haunting."

She hurried downstairs, and I returned thoughtfully to the third floor. How strange that Jeremy should have a key to his father's locked room.

When I reached the schoolroom, I found that someone was there ahead of me. A man stood before the table where I had left the folds of China silk, and he seemed to be surveying the room with an air of wry dismay. This, of course, was the tutor, and I could not blame him for regarding my intrusion with something less than enthusiasm.

"Good morning," I said. "I'm Megan Kincaid. They've put me here to work on a frock for Selina. I hope I won't be too much in your way."

He turned his attention from the table to me, and I faced Andrew Beach for the first time. I could not know then the role he was to play in my life and I saw before me only a young man of rather nondescript appearance. He was of medium height, stocky, and rugged of feature. Like Mr. Reid he was clean-shaven in this day when mustaches were the fashion. His brown hair fell over a high forehead and his eyes, regarding me from beneath sandy lashes, were a bright blue and sharply perceptive. There was a twist to his smile as he returned my greeting and introduced himself. I suspected that he might be as ready to laugh at Andrew Beach as at the rest of the world.

"I'll admit," he said, "that I was prepared to object strongly to having my schoolroom invaded by your pins-and-needles brigade. But now that I've met the dressmaker, I withdraw my opposition." He made me a mocking bow, his look impertinently flattering.

Somehow I could not take offense or resent his words. Even when the day came that he became critical of me and outspoken in his disapproval, I could never be angry for long with Andrew Beach. There was a quality in him that disarmed one at the very moment when his words cut deepest.

"I know my presence will make it difficult for you with the children," I told him, "but I'll do my best to distract them as little as possible. My work at the sewing machine can be postponed till afternoon and—"

40

"Don't worry," he said. "If I can't make my lessons interesting enough to hold my pupils in spite of your competition, then I'm not much of a teacher, am I?"

Relieved, I began to clear everything to the far end of the school table. And as Mr. Beach set out his books and papers, I studied him covertly. Here, I suspected, was my road to the understanding of Jeremy's interests and problems that Mrs. Reid had not given me. But I did not want to launch outright into questions. For all this young man knew, I was merely the hired seamstress with nothing more on my mind than the making of frocks for Selina.

It was he who disabused me of this notion and opened a door between us before the children came in for their lessons.

"You might as well know," he said over his shoulder as he wrote something on a small blackboard, "that I've been told why you are here. And I might as well add that I don't envy you the task you've taken on."

"You mean—Jeremy?" I said. "But isn't he your task too?"

"Not in the same way, I'm relieved to say."

I asked my questions hurriedly then, no longer dissembling. "Perhaps you can help me more than anyone else. There are surely subjects which interest Jeremy. If I am to make friends with him, I must find an approach. His mother would tell me nothing."

For all his wry mockery, there could be a gentleness in Andrew Beach, as I saw for the first time.

"How could she?" he asked. "Mrs. Reid has her own suffering to live through. I can only tell you that the boy has withdrawn inside himself. Those of us who are with him constantly know this. His uncle won't face it. Perhaps Mr. Reid's conscience troubles him. Who knows?"

I did not understand what Brandon Reid's conscience had to do with the matter, but I had another question to put to this young man while I had the opportunity.

41

"How long have you been tutoring the Reid children?" I inquired.

He put down the chalk and dusted his fingers. "Nearly two years. A very long time, it seems to me, when I consider it."

Two years? It had been two years ago that Dwight Reid had died. Had Andrew Beach been here during that time? I wondered.

He seemed to guess my thoughts. "I was not here when the tragedy occurred," he told me. "Though I had occasion to come to the house very soon after. Later it was decided that Jeremy needed a man to take him in hand, and I was offered the task. To little good effect, I'm afraid. But if you don't mind, Miss Kincaid, there are some things I don't particularly want to talk about."

I flushed at his implication. "I've no intention of prying and I am not a gossip," I said with spirit.

His good nature returned, and he grinned at me in impudent mockery as if he did not believe my words.

I returned to my main quest, caring little what he thought. "If you've held this position for so long, Mr. Beach, then you must know something of Jeremy. You must have learned what interested him before the accident. I don't mean his father's pistol collection. Mrs. Reid has already mentioned that."

Andrew Beach seemed to muse over my question. "I believe the seeds of trouble have always been evident in the boy. His nature is high-strung, even violent at times. It's likely that he would have been in serious difficulty sooner or later. And it's likely that he will be again. Do you understand that, Miss Kincaid?"

I nodded impatiently. Jeremy was a child and in grave need of help. "I want to know everything about him I can learn," I persisted.

"There's little I can tell you," he said. "I believe he was devoted to his uncle in the past and fascinated by Mr. Bran-

42

don Reid's travels to distant places. Miss Garth has mentioned that he used to enjoy stories about Egypt and the work his uncle has conducted in expeditions there."

Egypt? Expeditions? I recalled a certain strangeness about Brandon Reid. Perhaps there was a quality in those who had beheld far horizons that set them apart from the rest of us, who merely dreamed. My interest quickened.

"I didn't know that Mr. Reid had worked in such expeditions," I said.

"It was the Reid money that worked," Andrew Beach assured me sardonically. "Brandon's mother died when he was young, and she left him wealthy in his own right. For all that his father wished him to join the firm of attorneys headed by his name, Master Brandon chose another course. It's probable that he lacked his younger brother's flare and brilliance. His taste was for adventure, and he had an interest in Egyptology. He had the money as well to call in experts to take charge of the actual work. So he has been off in Egypt and India and other distant places much of the time for a good many years. That is, until his brother died and he settled down in this house to become a tamely married man."

There was a scornful undercurrent here telling me clearly that Andrew Beach did not like his employer. None of which mattered to me.

"If the boy was interested in Egypt once, then perhaps he can be interested again," I said. "My father was a history teacher, and I've always been fascinated by the subject."

The tutor regarded me in quiet appraisal. "You are very young, Miss Kincaid. You have a good deal to learn. But don't say I haven't warned you."

I did not care to be weighed and dismissed as if I were a child. "Warned me of what? Will you tell me clearly what you mean?"

"The boy is not interested in Egypt or anything else. He has gone outside our reach. Do you think I haven't tried? Do

43

you think I've not seen the road he was taking and attempted to bring him back? His uncle is too much occupied elsewhere to see what has happened. Or he's afraid to see it. I'm not certain which. You've been given a thankless task, Miss Kincaid. An older, wiser woman would have refused it. I can only hope that you've given up nothing else of consequence to come here."

This young man was probably not yet thirty, and I found his patronizing attitude toward my youth ridiculous and infuriating.

"I have given up nothing of consequence," I said stiffly. "If experience means the facing of difficult problems, then I'm not so young as you think."

With that I turned to my sewing materials, ignoring the faintly pitying amusement with which he regarded me. I had no intention of accepting his word as final, no matter how well he thought he knew Jeremy. If I gave up, the boy's future might be dark indeed. So far I had yet to take my first steps in his direction and I did not discourage easily. If no one in this house would help me, then I must manage to help myself.

4.

IN THE days that followed, the children grew accustomed to my presence in the schoolroom, in the house. Selina, at least, accepted me in a friendly, though slightly superior, manner. Since Jeremy seemed to move in some remote world of his own with little recognition of those about him, I could not tell, much of the time, whether he knew I was there.

As I sat sewing during lessons, I had considerable opportunity to observe him. He did not seem to dislike Andrew Beach as he did Miss Garth, but so neutral an attitude could hardly be called liking. He did what he was told, and I found his obvious skill in mathematics and in answering questions on paper an encouraging sign. Mr. Beach let me look at his written work, and while it now and again indicated a mind that followed tortuous routes, there was obvious intelligence revealed. Yet he would not recite aloud at all. While Selina chattered away, giving wrong answers blithely, Jeremy froze into sullen resistance whenever he was asked to recite. Only by an occasional scornful glance was it possible to see that he thought his sister foolish and could easily have corrected her answers.

Nevertheless, for all her teasing and her spoiled ways, he

did not seem to dislike his sister. She could approach him as no one else dared, and I noted more than once that both Miss Garth and Mr. Beach reached him through her when they could get his attention in no other way.

Mealtime was always an unhappy period, though more bearable at midday because it was the custom for Andrew Beach to be with us then. He stood in no awe of Miss Garth and often teased her mercilessly, paying her exaggerated compliments, pretending to flirt with her. That she had no love for him was evident, and there were times when she would plead a headache and retire, merely to avoid him.

During this period I came to know a little more about the children's tutor. I discovered that he had a talent for sketching and a flare for caricature. Occasionally his lampoons on city officials appeared in James Gordon Bennett's *New York Herald,* and in his spare time he often visited courtrooms and drew sketches of those on trial. Tutoring had given him this steady position in the Reid household and provided him with a living. From some of his drawings I had cause to think that he might do well if he applied himself seriously to his talent.

Of the Reids I saw little in those early days. Now and then I passed Mrs. Reid in the halls and she nodded absently, offering me no opportunity to speak to her. As Miss Garth had intimated that first day, she seldom left the house, seldom entertained, and seemed content to nurse her precarious health in the candlelit twilight of her green and gold rooms. For all her imperious ways, she seemed a strangely shadowy figure in the house.

Mr. Reid was often away at one museum or another during this time, delving into matters concerning the excavation of historic ruins, in which he was still interested. Sometimes, I learned, he visited his invalid father, who lived with a sister in a New Jersey seacoast town. These visits seemed to give

46

him both pleasure and concern, and he often came home from them in a saddened mood.

Kate was my cheerful informant on all these affairs, volunteering information without being questioned. I was eager to know all I could, for only through knowledge could I help Jeremy, and I made no effort to still her chatter.

I soon came to note how quiet the house seemed without my employer's vigorous and somewhat disquieting presence. He too, now that he had installed me here, showed no further interest in what I might or might not be accomplishing. I told myself that I did not care. The only thing that mattered was how I moved ahead in my relationship with Jeremy.

As far as the boy was concerned, I still bided my time, allowing him to accustom himself to my presence, learning perhaps that he could trust me a little. After all, he must realize that I had not betrayed my knowledge of the key in his possession.

During this time I became increasingly aware of the favoritism shown to Selina. Miss Garth clearly doted on her, and the child even wound Andrew Beach around her small fingers. When things went wrong with Selina's studies—a common enough matter—the tutor was summoned at once to confer with Mrs. Reid. But no one bothered to consult about Jeremy and I found myself growing jealous for the boy, indifferent though he was to my presence.

All too quickly October's mild days slipped away and it was mid-November. The green silk dress was finished to my lady Selina's pleasure, though not to that of Miss Garth, who remarked that she could have done better herself. While I did not admit it, I felt she was probably right, and the next frock I began to work on was of a less ambitious pattern.

One morning I put my work aside and slipped out of the schoolroom for a walk through the neighborhood. It was time, I felt, for a definite move in Jeremy's direction. On my wanderings through Greenwich Village I had noted a basement bookshop and it was to this I went that morning. I had seen maps in the window, and it was a map I wanted.

"Of Egypt," I told the bespectacled bookseller. "And I'd also like a book about recent expeditions and excavations in that country."

Fortunately he had both a large map and a recent book by a well-known authority on Egyptology. Pleased with my finds, I started home, my parcels under my arm. The first step had been made in purchasing the bait. Now it must be tactfully placed in the hope of attracting a nibble.

As I walked toward the square I passed a billboard advertising a lighthearted comedy in which Cicely Mansfield had recently opened. I paused to read every word while a new idea came into my mind. I had always loved the theater and with my present fine salary I should be able to attend an occasional performance. But this notice appealed to me because it was the sort of play children might enjoy. I would consult Mr. Reid about taking them both to a matinee. What child could reject or resist the magic of the theater? It was the sort of thing Jeremy needed.

While Selina had friends whom she visited, and who came to play with her, Jeremy seemed to have no one. There was no gaiety in his life, no playtime. Sometimes he read the novels of Dickens, of the French author Victor Hugo, the romances of Sir Walter Scott, or other such light reading. But often when he was not at lessons he would sit staring at nothing with a blind, vacant look that I felt was a mask for some frightening tumult that went on within. A matinee would be good for him, if Mr. Reid approved. It did not occur to me to ask his mother.

I returned to the schoolroom during the recess that Andrew wisely ordained in mid-morning. The young should frequently stretch their legs, he said, and have their stomachs filled. So he would send them off to the nursery for milk or hot chocolate, and do some very wide stretching and yawning himself, oblivious of my presence.

Miss Garth was with him when I stepped into the room, stiffly consulting over some problem of Selina's unsatisfactory lessons. I paid no attention to either of them, but unrolled my map upon the table to admire the brightly colored area where fabled Cairo, the Pyramids, and the Nile had their being. I could not read these names without a tingle of excitement running through me. Surely they would bring a response from Jeremy.

"What have we here?" Andrew asked and came to stand beside me.

Miss Garth glanced at the map and sniffed in disdain.

I was not discouraged. "It's time for action," I said. "Perhaps the map will interest the boy. And if it doesn't, I have a book—" I patted my brown paper package. "Furthermore, I mean to ask Mr. Reid if he will permit me to take Selina and Jeremy to see Cicely Mansfield in her new play. A Saturday matinee, of course, so there'll be no interfering with lessons, or staying up too late at night."

I was so pleased with myself that I did not at once note the silence that greeted this announcement. When I looked up from the map I saw incredulity in Miss Garth's eyes. She was struggling for speech, while Andrew clearly stifled an impulse to laugh out loud.

"What is it?" I asked in bewilderment. "What have I said?"

Miss Garth answered me coldly. "Miss Mansfield is a person of low reputation. Mrs. Reid will certainly not approve of your taking the children to see her. The idea is outrageous."

As if she could scarcely contain her indignation, Miss Garth flicked a lavender-scented handkerchief to her nose and swept regally from the room. I could only turn to Andrew in bewilderment.

"You've shocked the lady to her very toes," he told me, chuckling. "You're going too fast for her, I'm afraid. But I'm

49

with you on this, Megan. Go ahead and beard Reid in his den. Tell him to get you those tickets. A little excitement will be good for this mausoleum of a house."

It was odd how easily Andrew and I had fallen into the use of first names. There was an informality about him that dispensed with anything stuffy. I did not feel that I knew him well—indeed, I kept glimpsing facets to his character that surprised and puzzled me—yet I felt quite comfortable in calling him Andrew. It was good to have him behind me on this, and I told him so. A little to my surprise his amusement vanished.

"Don't count on me," he said. "Never count on anything when it comes to a man, Megan. Stay safe and doubt us all."

This sudden shift puzzled me. "Then you don't think this matinee—"

He slapped one square hand down on the map of Egypt. "Put this away for now. And listen to me, Megan. No one in this house has been fair to you—including myself. But Mr. Reid is to blame most of all. There is a conspiracy to keep the truth from you. However, no one has asked me to be silent and I think you must know."

His words alarmed me. "What must I know?"

Once more an odd, rare gentleness of tone wiped away the mockery. "It was no accident in which Dwight Reid was killed. His son shot him to death deliberately, monstrously. The boy planned exactly what he meant to do and he carried out the plan. All this was kept from the papers. Brandon Reid would do almost anything to keep the family name unsullied—mainly for his father's sake, I think. There was scandal, of course, but not as bad as it might have been. Between them, he and Leslie convinced the police that it was an accident. Those who knew better were silent. I can sympathize with the purpose behind this action. The truth would have been far worse for everyone, and particularly for the unfortunate boy."

50

I heard him through in growing dismay, but I was not yet ready to accept his words as fact.

"How do you know these things?" I asked. "If you came here afterwards . . . ?"

He answered me almost curtly. "Jeremy was taken into court. I was there for my paper to do sketches of those concerned. I couldn't help feeling sorry for the boy, and the drawing I did of him was kinder than others that appeared in the papers. Because of that drawing, I came to Brandon Reid's attention and he learned that I did odd tutoring work when I had the chance. He called me in for an interview, since Mrs. Reid was leaning heavily on him for assistance at that time. I seemed to suit them, and they gave me the task of coming here mornings to instruct the children."

"They told you the truth when you were employed?" I asked.

Andrew shook his head. "Not immediately. They couldn't be sure of my discretion at first. When they were convinced that I wouldn't run to my paper with the story, Mrs. Reid told me exactly what had happened. She felt that I must know that Jeremy was capable of dangerous, deliberate violence. Just as I feel you must know now, Megan. They've let it go too long."

My sense of horror and shock were not because of any fear for myself, but because I could now realize the weight that lay on Jeremy's shoulders. How could a young, unformed mind deal with so dark a crime? The problem seemed larger now, more appalling, but this new knowledge did not deter me.

"You are not afraid of the boy," I said to Andrew. "Why should I be?"

"I am a man. And I don't live in this house. Did you know that Miss Garth sleeps with her door locked at night? She has said so."

"I would expect that of her in any case," I said. I felt

disturbed and angry without recognizing as yet the true direction of my anger.

We could hear the children leaving the nursery down the hall, and Andrew spoke to me hurriedly. "You are a generous person, Megan. Don't let your generosity be given in so wasteful an effort."

I did not answer. There was no time, for the children were in the room. Besides, I already knew that Andrew considered Jeremy beyond recall. He considered my hiring a foolish last effort on the part of Brandon Reid to save his brother's son. But I have always been of an independent frame of mind. Too much so at times, as my father used to tell me. At any rate, I was far from ready to give up without trying. My campaign with the boy had only just begun.

I found myself looking at him compassionately, wondering what torturing, confused thoughts went on behind that handsome young brow. He sensed my regard and for once he looked at me uneasily as if he could not altogether dismiss me as he dismissed Miss Garth. That was fine, I thought. Let him come out of his apathy and puzzle about me a little.

Selina had begun to babble about the return of her Uncle Brandon from his latest trip. He had brought her a new doll, and she could not wait to go and play with it. How dull to do sums on such a morning!

"He brought Jeremy a game," she added. "But Jeremy will only break it up or throw it away. I don't know why Uncle Brandon bothers."

"The games he brings me are childish," Jeremy said.

But you are a child, I thought to myself. You are not an elderly, world-weary criminal, poor little boy.

The news that Mr. Reid was home gave a sudden focus to my rising indignation. Now I had an object for my anger. Andrew was perfectly right. I should have been told the truth when I was brought into this house. How did they think I could be useful when my whole conception of what had happened was incorrect?

Gathering up my rolled map and the book on Egypt, I took them to my room and summoned Kate. When she came upstairs I requested her to ask Mr. Reid if he would grant me some time at his earliest convenience. She was back in a few moments to say that if I would wait for him in the library Mr. Reid would see me in ten minutes.

I wasted not a second but flew downstairs to await his coming. A fire had been newly started, but the day was dark and the common gloom of the house penetrated to the library this morning. A jet globe burned high on one wall, and an oil lamp had been lighted on the great mahogany desk. I did not sit down, but stood looking about me. It was the first time I had really studied the room. When I had been here before, my employer's presence had held my full attention and I had scarcely noted my surroundings.

Now I observed the portrait of a distinguished, bewhiskered gentleman over the mantel. He had Mr. Reid's strong nose and firm jaw line, and he was extremely sober of expression. Mr. Reid's father, undoubtedly—Rufus Reid, whose reputation had once been without peer in the courts of law.

I noted too the indications of wide travel on every hand. An elephant tusk rose in an ivory column at one end of the mantel, and dwarfed beside it was a little jade Buddha. In a nearby glass case were amulets, seals, and tiny figurines that I learned later were made of diorite, quartzite, and the fragile blue faïence that dated back to the Eighteenth Dynasty in Egypt.

Then as I turned, I saw the object that dominated the entire room. Once the eyes rested upon it, it was difficult to look away. The life-sized head and shoulders of a man had been sculptured in some whitish stone and polished to a cool sheen. The head stood on a pedestal before a tier of bookshelves and it was recognizable at once as Egyptian. The tall

53

headdress, almost like a bishop's miter, but decorated with the rippling body of a snake, its head raised above the human forehead, was clearly Egyptian. The stylized beard, the elongated eyes, were those I had seen in drawings of Egyptian art.

So strongly did the stone face hold my attention that it made me forget for a moment why I had come to this room. It seemed a narrower face than that of most Egyptian statues and ageless in its expression, with maturity of wisdom in the brow and in the all-seeing eyes. The nose was proudly aristocratic, while the mouth betrayed a trace of tolerant humor in its curves. This man had been a king, I was sure, and no mere princeling or nobleman. Yet, for all the stylization, a living man had surely been its model. One sensed in the eyes, the brow, the mouth, those same tribulations and emotions which burden men who walk the earth today, and who in turn must belong to antiquity.

I didn't hear Brandon Reid's step on the soft carpet, did not know he stood behind me till he spoke.

"I see you've made the acquaintance of Osiris. You know who he is, I presume?"

I knew of the cult of Osiris. "Lord of the dead and judge of all souls in the hereafter," I said softly. "Yet I think he must have been a man first. A man who learned wisdom through suffering."

My employer's eyes, so cool and gray, regarded me with a certain surprise, as though he had not expected my comment on the statue.

"This came from a tomb in Egypt," he said. "I couldn't resist keeping it for the time being, though eventually it must go to a museum."

"You found it yourself?" I asked.

His smile was disparaging. "I was permitted to brush the earth away from the surface when the discovery was made. I am not regarded as a trained archaeologist. But I'm sure, Miss Kincaid, that you didn't come here to talk about Egypt."

"Oh, but I did!" I told him and almost smiled at his increasing surprise.

He waved me toward a chair beside the fire, but today he did not retreat behind the great expanse of the desk. Instead, he seated himself on a corner of it, with one leg swinging, and regarded me intently.

"You have a report for me about Jeremy?" he prompted, since I did not at once follow up my remark about Egypt.

I was marshaling both my thoughts and my indignation and I straightened in my chair. "I have no report as yet. I've been giving the boy time to grow accustomed to my presence. Now I'm ready to make certain moves in his direction. But I've just been told the truth about his father's death, Mr. Reid, and I find myself astonished that this information was not given me when you first interviewed me for this position."

Absently, he fingered the carving of the ivory paperweight on his desk. His gaze, however, did not waver from my face. Behind him lamplight etched the outline of his fine, vigorous head, touched to a gleam the thick dark hair. I turned my eyes upon the fire.

"And if I had told you, would you have taken this assignment?" he asked.

I was not sure. Truthfully, I did not know. I could see his reason for silence, and yet it was a silence that should have been broken before this.

"Now that you have been—informed—are you afraid?" he persisted.

I shook my head vehemently. "No matter what he has done, Jeremy is a child. He needs help, not condemnation."

"And you think you have found some way to help him?"

I waved my hand at the head of Osiris. "Perhaps that is the way. I've been told he once had a great interest in Egypt and in your travels. I've bought a map of Egypt and a recent book about discoveries there. If I could touch off a spark of attention, perhaps I can fan it to life."

55

I hesitated, wondering if I dared go farther. Then I steadied my resolve and looked directly into those remote, chill eyes.

"I would like your help in this," I told him.

There was an almost visible withdrawing about him. "Whatever you please, Miss Kincaid. Help yourself to my books as you choose. Or if you have specific questions, I will try to answer them."

"That isn't what I meant," I said. "The boy has almost no contact in this house with his mother or with you. Surely this isn't wise?"

For once his gaze shifted and did not meet mine. He stared across the room at the proud, calm face of Osiris as if he would gain wisdom from it. Then he shrugged and turned back to me.

"I'll make you no promises. It may be that you will ask more of me than I can give. The boy must have his chance. After that—there are human limits to patience and fore-bearing."

He flicked the air with strong fingers, and I sensed that if he made a final decision against Jeremy it would be immutable. I would have to move as cautiously with the uncle as I did with the child.

"Have you anything else to tell me?" he inquired.

I was not ready to conclude. This man was busy and difficult to see. I would say what I had come to say while the opportunity offered.

"The boy shows an unusual interest in the room that used to be his father's," I said, and related my experience the night I had come upon Jeremy outside the door of the locked room. I did not, however, betray the fact that Jeremy possessed a key to that room.

Brandon Reid's dark, winged brows drew down in a scowl. "I've been told about this obsession of his. So morbid a preoccupation with the room in which his father died must be stopped. We can't allow it to continue."

"And how," I asked, "do you propose to stop it?"

He threw me a quick, impatient look. "You have some plan?"

My heart was thumping at my own audacity. I did not like to admit that I found my employer a little overwhelming in his force and somber vitality. I did not know what would happen if I openly opposed him in his wishes. Yet I had to follow my aim no matter how angry I might make him.

Deliberately I kept my voice low and even. "I would like to take Jeremy openly into his father's room and let him tell me about what happened there—if he wants to talk about it."

The anger I feared exploded about my hapless head. Mr. Reid took a quick turn around the room as if he sought to control himself, and then came back to face me.

"The idea is ridiculous and probably dangerous," he said. "I forbid you to do this. The boy is not to go near that room again. He is not to be encouraged in this morbidity. I would have expected greater wisdom from you, Miss Kincaid."

I was not accustomed to being spoken to in so arrogant a manner and I could feel the blood flame into my cheeks. I reminded myself that I must not be so foolish as to lose my temper with this man. Yet I was not entirely in control of myself as I rose from my chair to confront him.

"You won't help your nephew yourself, but bring a stranger into the house to do what you are unable to do. Yet now you want to tie my hands, revoke my plans, tell me what I may or may not do. If that is the way I am to work I might as well leave now, Mr. Reid."

If he had told me to pack my bag and go at once, I would not have been surprised. I had said more than I intended and now I could only stand there with my eyes snapping and my cheeks flaming, waiting for my dismissal.

Strangely, it did not come. Mr. Reid returned from another wheeling about the room and stood staring at me as if I were some doubtful object he had just unearthed on one of his expeditions. Something he might properly throw back. We eyed each other, bristling with antagonism. Then he threw up his hands.

"Have the matter your own way!" he flung at me. "But don't come weeping to me if you make the boy worse."

"I will not come weeping to you under any circumstances," I told him evenly. "And now there is another matter about which I must consult you."

His exasperation was clear, but before he could protest, I hurried on. "Jeremy goes nowhere, has no friends, no pleasures. I would like to take both children to a Saturday matinee performance of Cicely Mansfield's new play."

He gaped at me in blank astonishment, and dark blood flushed into his own cheekbones. What an angry-looking, red-faced pair we must have seemed to anyone passing the door.

"You would do *what?*" he demanded.

I could not understand why so mild a request should result in this reaction but I repeated my words. By this time my voice was no longer steady and it broke into a squeak that annoyed me no little. His manner changed with startling suddenness. Without warning he put his head back and allowed hearty laughter to ring through the room. He laughed as he had laughed the time he had flung the orange out a window at me. I waited in amazement until he recovered himself enough to speak.

"A capital idea, Miss Kincaid," he said. "You shall have your wish. I'll get the tickets for you myself as soon as possible."

Before I could thank him there was a sound at the door and I turned to see Leslie Reid coming into the room. Clearly she had heard him laughing and there was a question in her eyes.

"May I see you for a moment?" she asked.

I said, "Good morning, Mrs. Reid," and would have gone

58

past her from the room in order to leave them alone, but Mr. Reid touched my elbow, holding me there.

"Wait—we must tell my wife your plans. Leslie my love, Miss Kincaid feels that it will have an excellent effect on Jeremy and Selina to take them to a Cicely Mansfield matinee. Can I persuade you, my dear, to make one of the party?"

Mrs. Reid gazed into her husband's face for a long cool moment. Then she turned without a word and went from the room, not stopping to tell him whatever it was she had intended.

The smile he turned upon me as she swept away was not altogether mirthful. "You are small to be such a hurricane," he said. "You have all the devastating results a storm carries with it. Perhaps like a storm you'll sweep away dry brush, sweep the air clear in this house. Or perhaps you will simply bring the whole structure down about our ears. Which, remains to be seen."

I did not know what he was talking about and I asked no questions. I had achieved my aims and was ready to leave. But he spoke to me again, his voice as casual as though he had never raised it toward me.

"I've observed that you sometimes walk alone in the square of an evening. May I advise you not to, Miss Kincaid. The streets of New York are far from safe for an unescorted woman after dark. Even I never go abroad at night without a loaded pistol in my pocket."

I could afford not to oppose him on this. "Thank you for the warning," I said meekly. "I'll try to heed it."

As I went away, I carried with me a picture of Brandon Reid staring again at the Osiris head as if he sought to gain from it some answer that eluded him.

5.

THE NEXT morning, when I saw Jeremy at breakfast, I asked him to come and help me in the schoolroom before lessons started. He obeyed indifferently and informed me without interest where I could get a hammer and tacks when I asked for them.

In the schoolroom I had him help me hold the map in place above the mantel and keep it steady while I stood on a chair and tapped in the first tacks. When I glanced at him carelessly, I saw that he was reading some of the names on the map. However, he remained indifferent when I turned hammer and tacks over to him and he worked with them so awkwardly that I had to take them back and finish the task myself. It had been my hope that he might ask questions, or show some curiosity, as any other child would have done. But he did not, and I had to make my own opening.

"I've seen that wonderful head of Osiris in your uncle's library," I said, "and it has renewed an interest I've always had in Egypt. This room is too plain anyway, and I thought it might be ornamental to put this map on the wall. While I'm working I can look at it occasionally and learn more about its cities and rivers."

My speech sounded unconvincing in my own ears and I

was not surprised by Jeremy's continued apathy. At least I had placed Egypt in view. If there was any latent interest in the boy, the map might renew it. If there was not, then I must try some other course.

During the morning Mrs. Reid made one of her rare visits to the schoolroom. She excused herself pleasantly to Andrew and asked if she might have a word with me. I put down my work and went to the door. She was going out this afternoon, she told me, and Miss Garth was coming with her. It was her wish to take Selina as well, and she wondered if I would look after Jeremy for two or three hours while they were gone.

Her manner was less that of mistress to servant than it had been and she seemed truly grateful when I agreed to take charge of the boy. Nothing could have pleased me more. For the first time Jeremy and I would be left alone and I would have an opportunity to talk to him without interruption.

In the beginning, however, the chance seemed to promise little. When Selina, gay in her new green frock, had gone off with her mother and governess, we had the upper floors of the house to ourselves. Mr. Reid was out, Andrew had finished with his lessons and gone, and the servants were in their own quarters below stairs. Jeremy settled down to read in the nursery, ignoring me.

From my room I had brought the book on Egypt and in what I tried to make a cheerful, companionable atmosphere, I too settled down to read. Once I laughed out loud over an amusing paragraph and then read on without explanation. Jeremy gave no sign that he had heard me. At another point I said, "Listen to this!" and read aloud a passage that mentioned the splendid discoveries of an expedition a few years ago, made possible by Mr. Brandon Reid of New York City.

Jeremy looked up from his book, and I suspected a normal curiosity. But he suppressed it at once and returned to his own reading. Now, however, his book did not seem to hold him as it had. He seemed to be attending to something outside this room. It was as if he listened for some special sound. The house was still and though I listened too, I heard not even a footfall from the floors below.

Finally he put his book aside and went softly to the door, opened it, and looked out into the hall, his slight body tensed with listening. Still he heard nothing and he came back to his chair without looking at me. I began to feel uneasy and Andrew Beach's warning about the boy returned to my mind. My uneasiness, however, was not fear. It was more like the feeling one might have with an unsettled companion who listened for—ghosts. Was that what he listened for?

His restlessness was growing, and he began to roam the room. He poked among Selina's dolls and dishes, grunting scornfully to himself. He picked up tin soldiers and tops and jacks; he went to a shelf and pulled out a large thin geography from beneath a stack of books. This he brought to the table, placing it before me. Without explanation he flipped open the pages as though he knew exactly where to look and drew out a square of drawing paper. He gave the paper a quick, intent look and then held it out to me, still without speaking.

As I took it from his hand, I saw that it bore a pen-and-ink sketch of Jeremy's face. The likeness was excellent, though this was a younger Jeremy. The artist had caught shock and tragedy in the eyes and a mouth that was clenched to suppress emotion. Yet there was nothing here of viciousness or violence. I remembered my own first impression of a dark young angel and found that the artist had seen the resemblance too. In a corner of the paper were the initials, "A.B."

"This is very good," I said. "Mr. Beach drew it, didn't he?"

Jeremy nodded. "Uncle Brandon liked it, so he kept it. I took it out of his desk after he married my mother and came here to live. He has forgotten about it by now. It's not a good picture though. It's a lie, and Mr. Beach knows it is a lie. He's painting a portrait of Selina and my mother now, but he doesn't want me to be in it."

I felt my way warily. "I don't understand what you mean. This seems a wonderful likeness to me. Though of course you're older than you were then."

The boy took the picture abruptly and replaced it in the geography. I had a feeling that I had disappointed him in some way. Had he wanted me to deny the likeness, to tell him he did not look like that?

When the book had been returned to its shelf, he went to the door and opened it once more upon the hall. The air of listening was upon him again, and I knew he was deliberately challenging my attention. This was the opportunity I had waited for. I spoke to him quietly, almost carelessly.

"Jeremy, would you like to show me your father's room downstairs?"

This time I had his full attention as I had never had it before. He turned from peering into the hall and faced me, dark-browed as his uncle, but with a child's startled fear in his eyes.

"What are you up to?" he asked rudely.

"You have a key to the room," I reminded him. "Though I've never told anyone that you have. The other night you wanted to go into your father's room and you ran away when I surprised you in the hall. Who is to stop you now if you show the room to me?"

Distrust was visible in every line of his body. When I rose and touched his shoulder I found him as stiff as one of his own tin soldiers.

"Get the key and come along," I said as lightly as though I had suggested a stroll in the park.

His shoulder rejected my fingers. Stirred to sudden action, he darted down the hall to his room and returned a moment later with the key in his hand. When he held it out to me, I reached for it, but he snatched it back at once.

64

"You'll be afraid," he said. "Everyone's afraid of that room. Everyone but me."

He, I suspected, was the most frightened of all, but I did not say so.

"Try me," I told him, and started ahead down the stairs.

He slipped past me, and in the lower hall we both stopped in mute accord and listened for sounds from the floor below. All was quiet. Yet now irresolution seized him and he stared at the key in his hand as though he did not know where it had come from, or how to use it.

I spoke to him gently. "I've heard what a fine person your father was, and of how generously he gave his help to those who were in trouble or in need. I would like to see the room where he lived. I think it must be a pleasant, friendly place. If you can't manage the key, I'll do it for you."

"Miss Garth will give you the very dickens," he said, as though he half hoped I would draw back. "My mother will cry if she knows, and my uncle will be in a rage."

I smiled at him. "Your uncle has said I may take you into the room any time you like."

He grimaced like a street urchin. "You're lying to me. Everyone lies to me. But I don't care. I'm not afraid of my uncle."

Gathering up his resolve he attacked the door with the key. That was the very word for the rough, angry way he went about inserting it in the lock and turning it. Then he pushed the door ajar upon the cold stuffiness of a place long unused and unaired.

Shutters had been closed and draperies drawn so that a thick darkness lay upon the room, scarcely penetrated by thin light from the hall. I will confess to a faint prickling at the back of my neck as if the supernatural had touched me. But I would have none of that.

"I'll open the shutters," I said and started resolutely across the room.

Jeremy flew after me and caught me by the arm. "No!" he cried. "No!" and there was terror in the syllable.

I wanted to force nothing upon him that he did not wish. "Would you rather we went back upstairs?"

That was not what he wanted either. It seemed that it was bright daylight he feared. He went to the place where matches lay upon a bureau and held one out to me in silence. As silently I struck a light and reached upward to a gas jet, turning the cock. With a puff the gas caught and the illumination of evening lay upon the room.

While Dwight Reid's personal effects had been put away, it appeared that nothing else had been touched in the room and I looked about it, seeking to know what manner of man Jeremy's father—Brandon Reid's brother—had been. There was no austerity here. Two or three small, bright rugs, figured in a mixture of brown, yellow, and green, lay upon the over-all gray carpet. A four-poster bed of walnut boasted a valance of dark gold and a spread of gold-green. The fine old highboy had brass handles to every drawer. A painting hung above the mantel—a hunting scene that picked up the gold and greens of the room, and added a warm splash of red. While Leslie Reid's room had seemed to indicate a love of ornate luxury, Dwight's room showed true elegance of taste without severity.

But it was the boy who interested me more than the room. He was moving almost systematically, opening a drawer here, the doors of a commode there, touching, searching. What it was he looked for I could not guess and I did not ask. I waited quietly for this fever of reacquaintance with the room to wear off. There seemed some purpose behind his actions and if this search gave him ease, I did not mean to obstruct it.

There was a long carved box on the bureau, and he removed the cover, looked into it, found emptiness, and went on. He even touched the pillows on the bed and groped beneath them. I half expected him to get down on his hands and knees and look under the bed, but he did not. When he had searched beneath the coverlet along one length, he rounded the foot of the bed to the side nearest the door to the adjoining boudoir. Dark draperies of heavy green brocade hid the door, and he thrust them apart and examined the bolt that locked the door from inside the room.

"They always keep it locked now," he said over his shoulder. "But my father used to leave it open. I had only to come through the curtains that day. He was standing right there by the bed."

He turned and gave me a long, searching look.

"I can show you something," he said. There was a gleam of excitement in his eyes, and his usual apathy had vanished. He seemed a different boy—a more frightening one.

I knew he was measuring me in some way, testing me, perhaps, and I steeled myself against any betrayal of emotion.

"Very well," I said. "Show me whatever you like."

He bent swiftly and caught up a corner of the small rug on the floor beside the bed. With the air of a magician producing something sure to confound me, he jerked it away. I stared at the faint brownish stain on the gray carpet and felt the finger of horror touch the back of my neck again.

"I'll bet you don't know what that is!" Jeremy cried, his voice chill with an eerie triumph. "You'll be afraid when I tell you. You'll be sick!"

It took all the self-control I could summon to keep from running off to the safety of my small room upstairs. Away from this place of tragedy, from the stain on the carpet, and the suddenly evil child. For the sake of Jeremy's sanity I fought for control.

"Of course I know what it is," I said as calmly as I was able. "It's a bloodstain, obviously."

A little of his wild elation subsided. More than anything else he seemed puzzled by my response. I went on quickly before he could speak again.

"When a person is shot there is always blood," I told him in matter-of-fact tones. "It was in this room that your father died, wasn't it? So this must be a bloodstain."

"So much blood," Jeremy whispered. Then he spoke more loudly, defiantly. "Now you see why it is that you can't like me. You needn't try to fool me by pretending to be friends. No one likes me. Mr. Beach knows that picture he drew was a lie, and Uncle Brandon hates me. So does my mother and Garth. And you will too. Only Selina doesn't because she's too young and silly to understand what I did."

I thought of the bloodstain no longer, but only of the desolation I saw in the eyes of the child before me. I too needed the wisdom of Osiris to deal with this matter, and I possessed so little sagacity. I could only follow my instinct and hope it was sound.

"How can I know so soon whether I like you or not?" I asked him. "I never make up my mind about people that quickly. When I do decide, it's because of how a person is with me and not because of what may have happened long ago. Or because of what other people say about him."

Jeremy looked at me without trust, but as though I continued to puzzle him. His next words surprised me.

"Would you like to see the pistol collection? It's downstairs in the drawing room. I'll show it to you if you like."

Was I wrong? I wondered. Was I letting him excite himself unwisely? Should I put a stop to this as I knew anyone else in the house would have done? Against reason, I once more gave him the lead. I turned out the gas and he relocked the room, pocketing the key. Together we started downstairs. There was no one about, and he opened the door of the drawing room softly.

Again there was gilt and damask elegance, and underfoot the rich soft colors of Persia. Though the room was reserved for special occasions and the shutters closed, the shadows here were not so dense. Enough light to see by seeped in. Jeremy

68

went directly to the rear of the room, where a tall glass cabinet stood on spindly carved legs. Upon its shelves lay spread an array of small arms from all over the world.

Now Jeremy seemed more like a small boy showing off his knowledge. For the moment the horror of the room upstairs had faded into the background. This was a dueling pistol, he pointed out, and there was its mate. That one with the silver fittings had been carried in Napoleon's army, while this plain one with the bone handle came from our own West. Here was a revolver, there a clumsy, old-fashioned double-barreled pistol. He had learned his father's hobby well and forgotten nothing. But he could not touch the pistols or take them out, for the cabinet was securely locked.

"They always keep it locked now and the key hidden," he said. And added with a meaning that turned my mouth dry, "That's because of me."

As I watched, he counted the guns carefully, then counted them again, and yet a third time.

"It's always the same," he assured me. "They never put it back. I keep looking and looking for it, but I don't know where they've hidden it."

I knew what he meant. The missing gun must be the pistol he had used that terrible day.

"Why do you want it?" I asked him.

He held out his hand, the forefinger curling as though he pulled a trigger. "I like guns," he said. "I like to feel them in my hand. But I can't get these out without breaking the glass. Maybe I will break it someday. When I want to shoot someone."

The entire eerie experience was beginning to wear on my nerves, and something of what I felt must have revealed itself in my face. Jeremy pounced upon my reaction with malice.

"You're afraid of me, aren't you?" he demanded, looking pleased with himself. "You know what I'm like now, and you're afraid!"

69

I rallied my last resources against him. "Yes, I know what you are like," I said, sounding cross. "You are a little boy showing off, and people who show off rather bore me. I believe I will go upstairs and read my book about Egypt."

I did not wait to see what he made of that, but went briskly to the door of the drawing room. I heard him follow me and I turned toward the stairs. Just behind me he paused.

"I'd like to go outside for a while," he said. "I'm tired of the house."

So normal a suggestion pleased me. "That's a fine idea. Let's get into our coats and go out for a walk."

For the first time I heard him laugh, but the sound was far from reassuring.

"I'll race you upstairs!" he shouted and tore past me.

I lifted my skirts and went after him, but he had a head start and beat me soundly. I was out of breath, but laughing when I joined him at the head of the stairs.

"I can beat a girl any day!" he announced, triumphant again and overly excited. "You can't catch me going down either."

He turned and ran down again before I could move to stop him, and as I watched he opened the front door and disappeared outside, slamming it shut behind him.

That alarmed me, and I hurried down and stepped out into the cold brisk air. He was already out of sight. Perhaps he was hiding nearby, playing a trick as any boy might. It was too cold to be out without a coat, so he wouldn't stay long. I called him, but had no answer. When I turned shivering to the door I found the latch had caught and I had to disturb the butler in order to get in.

With little effort Henry managed to imply that he did not regard me as gentry. He stared in disapproval at my disheveled and uncloaked appearance. I did not stand on ceremony, but told him at once that Jeremy had run outside and I didn't know where he had gone. Undoubtedly he would

70

return as soon as he got cold, but perhaps someone should look for him.

"If you've let him get out, he's off and gone by now," the man said, his disapproval of me increasing. "He has run away in his nightshirt—that one. We didn't find him till morning one time."

I was truly frightened now. I sent Fuller and Kate to search for him, put on my wraps, and stood outside for a while, calling. Kate went to the nearest police station, but there had been no sign of Jeremy. At last I returned indoors to pace the hall. It was there Brandon Reid found me when he came home. I could only tell him at once that the boy was gone.

His cold look let me know that he placed the blame upon me—where, after all, it belonged. But I wanted no time wasted on reproach or questions.

"What can we do?" I cried. "Where can he have gone? He will be cold without his coat!"

"Don't chatter," Mr. Reid said. "Or if you must, go upstairs. I dislike excitable females."

He strode toward the rear of the hall, and I heard him giving orders for the carriage to be made ready at once. For all that his words angered me, they steadied me as well. At least the problem was now in sure hands and I could hold my anxiety for the child in abeyance. I stood where I was until my employer returned to the front hall.

"I have an idea where he may have gone," he said curtly. "I'll drive out in search of him as soon as the carriage is ready."

"Let me come with you," I pleaded. I could not bear the thought of waiting here, inactive. And besides, if the boy were found I wanted to be there to take some of the blame from him. I did not trust the bright anger that had replaced the chill in Brandon Reid's eyes.

71

He stared as if he found everything about me distasteful, and I could see refusal coming.

"I'll promise not to chatter," I said meekly. "I know what has happened is my fault. But please let me come and help you, Mr. Reid."

"Help me?" The dark brows drew down in a scowl.

I faced him with increasing determination. "It may be better if I am there. I think the boy doesn't altogether dislike me."

"This is a fine way of showing his liking," Mr. Reid said. Then to my relief, he said, "Come if you like. This is not a life-or-death matter, I fancy. We're not unaccustomed to dealing with such crises. Though they disturb his mother. Is she home as yet?"

I told her she was not. We waited in silence until the carriage was brought around and Mr. Reid and I went down the steps together.

6.

IN THE carriage I sat stiffly beside my employer, sensing his continued anger, though I did not know whether it was directed against the boy or against me.

Without looking at me, he spoke. "Please tell me exactly what happened that led up to this running away."

I told him all that we had done, keeping nothing back. He listened in chill silence to my account of the visit to Dwight's room and of how Jeremy had revealed the stain upon the carpet, of how he had shown me the pistol collection downstairs. When I was through he made a single, devastating comment.

"You are very young, Miss Kincaid, to have been given so difficult a charge. The fault may be more mine than yours."

It distressed me to realize that he thought my judgment immature, my actions lacking in wisdom. For all I knew, he might be right, yet a spark of stubborn conviction within me insisted that I would behave again in just the way I had, and that in spite of Jeremy's running away, I was not yet proved wrong. The most important thing now was to have my chance. I could sense the promise of dismissal in the very stiffness of Mr. Reid's posture and in the tone of his voice when he spoke. Somehow I must find the way to forestall him.

The carriage had turned off Fifth Avenue and was moving

among the heavier, less elegant traffic of the West Side. Drays and carts shouldered us wheel to wheel, there were single riders on horseback, and the citizenry on the sidewalks seemed a rougher lot, both in clothing and manner.

"I'd better tell you where we're going," my employer said abruptly. "Jeremy has had some sort of compulsion about this place ever since its conception, and he has run away to it twice. You've heard, perhaps, of the Dwight Reid Memorial Home that has been built through donations given by admirers of my brother?"

His tone had hardened, almost as if he resented such honor being paid to the name of his dead brother. I glanced at him in surprise.

"I've heard of it," I said. "Its purpose is to serve homeless children in New York, I believe? But why should Jeremy go there?"

"You ask me riddles I've no answer for," he said. "I suppose it's the same sort of thing as going to his father's room—a wallowing in horror."

Fuller pulled the horses over to the curb, and I saw that we had stopped before a large building of brownstone, still marked by scaffolding across its face. The arched doorway stood open, and workmen were tramping in and out. My companion called one of them to the carriage and asked if he had see a small boy, but the man shook his head and went back to his work.

When Mr. Reid got out of the carriage, I followed him before he could tell me to stay where I was. We started up the wide steps and just as we reached the door someone called his name from the sidewalk. We turned, and I saw a police captain dismounting from his horse. He secured the reins to a hitching post and ran up the steps to join us.

"Good morning, Captain Mathews," Mr. Reid said. "This is Miss Kincaid, Jeremy's—history instructor."

The captain touched his cap and smiled at me. "Good morning, miss. Kate came over to the station a while ago to learn if we'd seen anything of the boy. Said you were frantic with worry. So I thought I'd ride over here and see if he was up to his old tricks. But you've made it ahead of me."

He seemed a kindly man, with a smile nearly as wide as his shoulders. But as the three of us went into the building, I noted a jaw line that might well have been cast in metal. This, I suspected, was a man who could hold his own in the rough and dangerous life of a policeman in New York.

Painters and wallpaperers were still at work on the interior of the building, and bare floors echoed to our steps. Captain Mathews took over the task of inquiring for Jeremy, but no one had seen him. We went through a long hall with tall windows down one side—a dining hall, in all probability— and then across to other rooms, and at length upstairs to a large dormitory.

Here the work had been finished, and iron bed frames were already installed. Here our search ended. In a far, shadowy corner of the room Jeremy sat on the floor, still and huddled, with his knees drawn up and his forehead against them. I saw him first—a small, touching figure in the long dim room— and I put a hand on Mr. Reid's arm.

"Let me, please," I whispered, but neither man paid any attention to my plea.

"Ho there, boy!" Captain Mathews called out cheerfully while Jeremy's uncle started down the room toward him with long strides I could scarcely keep up with.

At the first shout, Jeremy uncurled and jumped to his feet. I saw terror in his face and a frantic desire to run. But he was cornered, and there could be no escaping the two who bore down upon him.

"It's all right, Jeremy," I said and ran past them to hold out my hand to him.

Jeremy seemed not to see me. He stared at Captain Mathews, and the same horror looked out of his eyes that I had seen in evidence in his father's room earlier that day. He said nothing, but stood as if frozen, watching the police officer in a strange agony.

"Come now, boy, don't look like that," Captain Mathews said. "We're old friends, aren't we? I'm here just like your uncle is, to see you safely home again. You're a big boy now; you oughtn't to go frightening your family with this running away."

"He knows that," Mr. Reid said quietly. He took Jeremy by the arm, not unmindful of the boy's upset state, and led him out of the room and down the stairs. Once outside, he assisted him into the carriage seat. Then he turned and held out a hand to the officer.

"Thank you, Captain. We're sorry to have troubled you. We shouldn't be taking up your time like this."

The look Captain Mathews turned upon Jeremy in the carriage was both stern and kindly.

"I remember him from that bad time you had at the house, sir," he told Brandon Reid. "I've taken what you might call a personal interest in him ever since."

"You understand that, Jeremy?" Mr. Reid asked. "If you don't want to be in wrong with the police, you'll have to stop running away."

With that he handed me into the carriage. Captain Mathew mounted his horse and rode away.

Jeremy said darkly, "If he knew—if he really knew—he'd arrest me, wouldn't he, Uncle Brandon?"

His uncle did not answer, but gave Fuller the signal to drive us home.

I felt Jeremy's shivering as he huddled between us, and pulled the lap robe over him.

"How cold you are," I said. "Here, tuck your hands under

76

this. It was foolish to go off without your coat. We could have come outside comfortably, if you'd waited."

He stared straight ahead without answering. Only when the carriage turned back into the brisk stream of Fifth Avenue, did he speak again.

"Are you going to punish me, Uncle Brandon?" he asked in a voice that was far from steady.

"You've done what you know is forbidden and you deserve punishment," his uncle said. "I'll think about the matter and decide upon a proper course."

Beside me Jeremy still shivered, and I rebelled inwardly against his uncle. When we reached home Mr. Reid did not release his hold on the culprit, but took him up the steps and into the house, leaving me to follow as I pleased.

Miss Garth was home, though Leslie Reid was not, and Mr. Reid turned the boy over to her at once.

"Give him some hot milk and put him to bed," he ordered. "Get him warm, if you can."

I longed to offer Jeremy some comforting word as he was led upstairs in Miss Garth's undisputed grasp, but there was nothing I could say, no assurance I could offer. I too was a culprit and I went despondently upstairs and into the deserted schoolroom. The fire had gone out, and there is little more dispiriting than a cold hearth, gray with the ashes of a dead fire. I was cold now and shivering like Jeremy. Cold and not a little despairing.

Had I taken on a task that was too big for me? It was quite likely. The future did not look bright at that moment. I was not likely to get a recommendation from Brandon Reid that would serve me in finding another position as either seamstress or governess. Yet it was not my own probable predicament that troubled me most. I could recall Jeremy's white face as he sat so stiffly between his uncle and me in the carriage, hear the quiver in his voice as he asked about punishment. With all my heart I longed to help him, to be allowed

77

to help him. Yet by tomorrow I might very likely be sent packing.

"May I come in?" It was Mr. Reid at the door behind me.

I whirled to face him, and my chin came up. I would not have him guess my discouragement.

"I'd like to apologize for any unconsidered words I may have spoken," he said stiffly.

I was too astonished to do anything but stare at him.

"The fault was not entirely yours," he went on. "If you were to be left in full charge of the boy, you should have been warned about his propensity for running away."

I sensed that apology did not come easily to Brandon Reid and knew I should accept his words with gratitude and humility. But while I was trying to don the proper manner, he spoke again.

"I'd hoped, Miss Kincaid, from what I'd learned about the excellent results with your young brother, that you would be able to exert a gentling influence upon Jeremy. I realize that it's too soon for definite results, but I must admit that I'm disappointed in your choice of action this afternoon."

How quickly I forgot to be grateful and humble! My temper began to rise at once.

"Why do you think the boy behaves in this way?" I demanded. "Why shouldn't he run away from the unloving atmosphere of this house? He told me this afternoon that no one can ever like him, and that is a horrifying belief for a child to hold. He even believes that you wish him dead."

A somewhat exasperated sigh escaped my employer, but at least he did not accuse me now of "chattering." When he spoke his impatience was well contained, his tone even.

"Love, Miss Kincaid, is not easily simulated."

"I know that," I said. "I know how hard it must be for you, considering what happened. But your brother is dead, and his son's very life is at stake."

Mr. Reid closed the door upon the hall so that our voices

would not carry and motioned me to a chair near the cold hearth. He seemed in that moment a sadder man than I had seen before. He did not sit down but went to stand at a rear window, looking out upon the ailanthus tree.

Quietly, without emotion, he began to tell me of his brother. Their mother had died when the two sons were young, and he, being the elder, had taken to looking after Dwight a good part of the time. Their father had been older than his wife—a severe, proud, brilliant man, with a deep love for his sons, but often preoccupied with his work in the firm of attorneys he headed.

"He hasn't been well for some years," Brandon Reid said heavily. "Dwight's death was a crushing blow, and the full truth of what happened was kept from him. He lives in southern New Jersey now with a younger sister. My aunt is devoted to him, though he is still strong-willed enough to give her trouble at times. We all feel it best that he live away from New York. He forgets his triumphs when he comes here and remembers only the disappointments and hurt the city has held for him."

As he spoke, I sensed the affection in which Brandon Reid held his father, and I sensed something more—perhaps a lacing of deep regret or pain.

"To lose his favorite son and have left only the one who disappointed him . . ." He moved his hands in an expressive gesture and smiled at me wryly. "The least I can do is see that his last years are peaceful."

"What was so remarkable about your brother Dwight?" I found myself asking.

"He had the flashing brilliance of a comet," Brandon said. "And sometimes as little forethought. I pulled him out of more than one scrape in his younger years. Jeremy resembles him a great deal. Looking at him, I can almost see Dwight again. Believe me, for Dwight's sake, for the boy's own sake,

I want to give him every possible chance. But don't ask me to love him, Miss Kincaid. Love is not something I give easily. Unfortunately that is my nature and there is nothing I can do about it."

I thought of Leslie Reid and the ardent attention he seemed to pay her. There, at least, he had given his love, and I wondered irrelevantly what it must be like to be loved by such a man. Nevertheless, though I was reassured by the fact that he had wanted me to understand, I could not be merciful.

"You could at least pretend," I told him. "Even a pretense of affection and interest would help. How do you think the boy feels when he senses revulsion in all those about him?"

Brandon Reid shook his head. "He would not be fooled by pretense. He is not stupid."

I gathered my courage and put the question this conversation gave me a chance to ask.

"How did it happen? Would you mind telling me?"

He paid me the compliment of answering without hesitation, though his telling was brief. In swift, sure words he made me see what had occurred that night when Dwight Reid had been killed by his own son. Earlier on the day of the tragedy the boy had misbehaved in some way. All the Reids, it seemed, had quick tempers, even the gentler Dwight. That afternoon Dwight Reid had lost patience with his son and had shaken him soundly. Jeremy's own temper had flared. He had always resented physical chastisement and he struck his father's hand away, uttering threatening words. His father recovered at once and laughed at him. No one took the boy seriously.

But that night while Dwight Reid was getting ready for bed, the boy got a pistol from the collection downstairs. He knew where bullets were to be found and he knew all about the loading and shooting of guns. On trips to the country, Dwight had indulged him in his own hobby, believing that every boy should be trained to handle guns safely and shoot like a gentleman.

"By odd chance I was in the house that night," Brandon Reid said. "I had been abroad for more than a year on my last trip to Egypt and had returned only that morning. Late in the evening I went to Dwight's room to talk with him. I had just stepped to the hall door when Jeremy came through the curtains from what was then his father's dressing room and is now Leslie's boudoir. Before I could realize what he was about, he pointed the gun at his father and fired. I dashed the pistol from the boy's hand and rushed to my brother. There was nothing to be done. At that range Jeremy could hardly have missed."

His voice had grown hard in the telling, and I listened unhappily.

After a moment's silence, he went on. "Perhaps now you'll better understand what you refer to as the unloving atmosphere of this house. Afterwards the boy showed a bold, unrepentant attitude. Captain Mathews, as you may have gathered today, worked on the investigation. He never learned the whole truth and he gave the boy every consideration and kindness within reason. But it was as though Jeremy was proud of what he had done. We can't trust him or rest easily with him in the same house. Yet no school would take him under such circumstances, and in any case it would not be fair to submit other children to his company and influence. The only person he seems to like is Selina, and my wife is afraid he may harm her in some violent rage."

My eyes were swimming with tears, yet it was still the child my heart ached for. I could not rid myself of the conviction that, in spite of everything, it was he who suffered now, concealing his suffering as no child should have to conceal so terrible a self-blame. Concealing it behind a guard of pretense and antagonistic behavior.

My employer was regarding me almost kindly, and it

81

seemed strange to see those gray eyes warm a little and lose something of their condemnation.

"Truly," he said, "I'm grateful for your interest and your sincerity in dealing with Jeremy. What I fear is that your youth and your own feminine instinct to forgive a child will blind you to sensible action. I don't dismiss the possibility that you may still help the boy. But too much softness will not be good for him either."

"What softness has he had?" I asked quickly. "Must you punish him for running away today?"

"The boy wants to be punished," he told me. "He is constantly asking for punishment."

"That in itself should be a warning to you," I said. But I didn't want to oppose him further. Events had moved in my direction, and I was to have my chance to help the boy if I could.

For the first time Mr. Reid glanced about the room and noted the map of Egypt I had tacked up over the mantel.

He nodded toward it. "What, exactly, do you hope to gain by that?"

"All I ask for is a show of interest," I said. "The boy isn't as indifferent as he pretends. I'm sure of that. For one thing —he admires you tremendously."

Mr. Reid looked shocked. "It's possible that he did in the past. His imagination was caught by my adventures in distant places, as any child's might have been. But now he looks at me sometimes with hatred in his eyes. Don't count too heavily on his devotion to me or you'll only delude yourself. At least you've brought a quality of mercy into this house, Miss Kincaid, and I'll grant you that has been lacking. Perhaps it will reach the boy. I hope you'll continue to forgive what isn't always to your pleasure and do your best."

I rose and held out my hand in frank acceptance of so fair a request. He took my fingers in his and held them for a moment. Again I felt the vigor and strength of this man as it

82

flowed to his very fingertips, but this time I did not flinch away as I had before.

"I haven't forgotten about the matinee tickets," he told me. "I hope to have them for you early in December. I want a box, not the lesser seats. Perhaps the children would enjoy a box."

I assured him that they would, hoping it was true, and he went away, leaving me more reassured than at any time since I had come to this house.

When I returned to the hall, I met Miss Garth coming out of Jeremy's room.

"He's warm at last, and asleep," she told me. "What did you do this afternoon to excite him into running away?"

I had no intention of giving Miss Garth fuel for her already smoldering resentment, and I countered with a question of my own.

"Why didn't you warn me that he was given to running away? Then I could have been on guard against what happened."

She drew herself up, regarding me out of those dark, deeply set eyes—a handsome and redoubtable woman. "We expect you to exert extreme caution with this boy at all times, Miss Kincaid. Specific instruction hardly seemed necessary." She swept off down the hall, her full brown skirts rustling, wafting behind her a strange mixture of scents—lavender blended today with just a whiff of violet.

I went gladly to my own room. My nerves had been strained more than once today, and I wanted to rest and speak to no one. Beneath my door I found a folded sheet of paper of the sort on which Jeremy did his sums. Spreading it out, I discovered that Andrew Beach had written me a note.

Would I, he requested, have a modest supper with him tonight? He had returned to the house to leave some books this afternoon and had learned of Jeremy's running away. He hoped all was well by now, but I undoubtedly needed a change from gloom and the company of a half-mad little boy. He would call for me at six.

I read the note through with pleasure. Andrew's astringent company would be good for me tonight. I did indeed need a change from the depressing atmosphere of this house.

7.

KATE, MY one friend among the Reid servants, came at six to tell me that Mr. Beach awaited me in the sitting room downstairs. I had already let Miss Garth know that I would be dining out and I went down to greet him.

It had been fun to dress up for once. My wardrobe was not extensive, but my mother had insisted that I own at least two good dresses and she had put hours of loving work into making them. Tonight I had chosen a long-sleeved gown of garnet satin with a loose-falling skirt draped up at the back in a slight bustle. It was not overtrimmed, but had a touch of black lace running from my throat down the front of the tight-fitting bodice. I had fluffed my bangs and pinned my hair in loose curls at the nape of my neck, finding in such frivolous gestures the sort of release only a woman understands.

I went downstairs rather slowly, not wholly admitting to myself that I wished Brandon Reid would appear in the hallway, not wholly admitting that I would like him to see me in my finery, instead of as the gray dove of a seamstress I had become. Mr. Reid did not appear, however, and when I went into the sitting room I found it empty. This time I did not resist the pull of the mirror and I was standing before it studying myself when Andrew entered behind me.

"I'm sorry to keep you waiting, Megan. Mrs. Reid summoned me upstairs to reprove me for disciplining Selina this morning. They're a difficult pair to please at times—both master and mistress. But let's forget all that. Turn around and let me see your fine feathers."

I turned and saw the half-amused lighting of his eyes.

"You're a bit elegant for the little place where I'm taking you. But I'm flattered and I'll make the best of looking at you. You're a very pretty girl, Megan."

He helped me into my mantle and we walked the few blocks to the Italian restaurant he had chosen.

"As a matter of fact," he explained as we strolled along, "I have my lodgings upstairs at Mama Santini's, so I know her fare is hearty and good, if not as fancy as Delmonico's."

The November night was growing sharp after the cold day, and there was almost a feeling of snow in the air. I have a liking for the winter months and find them enlivening, invigorating. My earlier nervous shivering had vanished, and this entire change was already doing me good.

The small restaurant seemed a cheerful, unpretentious place, with bare table tops scrubbed to the bone, and an appetizing odor of tomatoes and onions and peppers perfuming the air. There were no soft lights here, but bright gas globes everywhere and a cheery clatter of voices and laughter from diners already eating.

Mama Santini came to greet me herself and eyed my garnet gown with approval. I did her place honor, she stated, implying cheerfully that the place deserved it. Did she not, after all, serve the best Italian cooking in New York?

Because Andrew was clearly a favorite, a corner table had been saved for us, and we were shown to it with as much flourish as any headwaiter could have managed. Mama Santini clearly enjoyed her own cooking and she shook with good-natured laughter that seemed to start with her cheeks and ripple downward over generous bosom and a stomach no whaleboning could restrict.

I took my chair in the corner and pulled off my gloves, smiling at Andrew. "What a lovely place! Thank you for thinking of this."

His faint cynicism did not disturb me tonight. Andrew might entertain a mocking attitude toward the world and the people about him, but even when he stated unflattering truths, he never cut me to the quick as Brandon Reid could do.

By now a desire to talk was bubbling up in me, and, while we ate the delectable antipasto and sipped red wine, I began to tell him of all that had happened that day. He stopped me short almost at once.

"None of that!" he ordered. "Your unhappy adventures will keep for another time. We'll not spoil good food with them. Tell me about yourself instead, Megan. Where do you come from, where are you going?"

The first was easy to answer, and I told him of Princeton, New Jersey, the town in which I had grown up and where my father had taught. I didn't mind that a certain nostalgia crept into my words, although I knew that Andrew was wholly city-bred and would regard a small university town with amusement. I told him briefly of my father's death during the war and of my mother's struggle to earn us a livelihood here in New York.

"Unfortunately," I confessed, "I lack her skill with a needle. Indeed, I was doing so badly that I was at my wit's end when Mr. Reid offered me this position."

"And what will happen," Andrew asked, "when your position ends?"

"It's not necessary to worry about that now," I objected. "Indeed, Mr. Reid gave me a reprieve this afternoon. I'm to have more time to work with Jeremy and try to help him. After all, I've scarcely begun."

Andrew broke off a thick crust of Italian bread. He did not look at me, but I heard again the bitter note that sometimes came into his voice when he spoke of Brandon Reid.

"If I were you, I would not count on staying too long in Reid's good graces. When he's through using you, he'll make short shrift of letting you go. And he'll trouble himself not at all as to what happens to you once you are out of the house. Take care of yourself first, Megan. A bit more self-interest would serve you well."

I had no answer for him and I did not attempt one. Our steaming plates of spaghetti came and I found myself eating more hungrily than I had in days. Andrew watched me knowingly.

"Even your eating improves when you're out of that house. Don't think I haven't seen you pick at your food with Garth presiding. Not that she wouldn't ruin anyone's appetite if you let her. I turn the tables and interfere with hers. Have you noticed how fond she is of me?"

I laughed, glad to get away from the subject of Brandon Reid and my position in his house.

"It's your turn now," I said. "Tell me about your own ambitions. I know what skill you have in capturing likenesses on paper. Jeremy showed me the drawing you did of him during the investigation of his father's death. I thought it sensitive and penetrating. You saw past the ugliness of what had happened to a shocked and frightened child."

"I doubt that," Andrew said dryly. "I merely gave the public the sentimentality it wanted. Most adults would rather weep over a child than believe him a monster."

I hated to see Andrew so harsh when it came to Jeremy, but when I would have protested, he changed the subject.

"I'm more interested now in the oil portrait I'm doing of Selina and her mother. The child is an ideal model, the mother more difficult to catch. Unfortunately, sittings aren't as regular as I'd like."

88

I knew Andrew sometimes stayed after lessons, or returned in the afternoon to work on the portrait Mrs. Reid had commissioned, but so far he had not shown it to me.

"I'd like to see what you're doing," I told him.

"I'm not sure you'll approve," he said cryptically, and went on to speak of his free-lance work for the newspapers.

Often, it seemed, he was called in on assignment and had developed a faculty for doing quick sketches of those in the public eye. I had seen some of his fearsome drawings of convicted criminals and could realize by comparison how gentle he had been with Jeremy.

He spoke now with matter-of-fact good cheer of pickpockets and thugs, of political spoils and sanctioned law-breaking as if they were everyday matters to the newspaper world. As indeed, they must have been.

I brought up the subject of Dwight Reid and his work in fighting crime and mentioned that we had pursued Jeremy that afternoon to the Memorial Home being built in Dwight's honor.

Andrew seemed unimpressed. "Dwight tried hard enough, I suppose. But Sir Galahad himself would have been lost in New York City today, what with our corrupt judiciary and the selling of justice."

"Even with Jim Fisk behind bars?" I asked.

"Only a start has been made. Dwight Reid made scarcely a dent. More's the pity, since he had captured the public eye." He changed the subject abruptly. "Are you still planning to take the children to the matinee of Cecily Mansfield's play?"

I told him that Mr. Reid had mentioned getting us a box only that afternoon, and Andrew whistled softly.

"A box! The man must be out of his mind. Doesn't he know that Selina and the boy are likely to be recognized, even if you are not?"

"What of it?" I asked in exasperation. "Must everyone go

on behaving as though a tragedy that happened in the past must blight these children's lives forever?"

Andrew pushed a lock of hair back from his forehead as if he puzzled over something.

"What is it?" I asked. "What is the matter with this play that everyone behaves in an odd way the moment I mention it?"

"You might as well be told," he said. "Though I don't know why I must always be your informant. At least I have no sense of delicacy about Reid's reputation. It's not a savory reputation, you know. His name has been coupled with the Mansfield woman's for some time. His infatuation with her is public knowledge."

My silence was filled with dismay. I disliked gossip and never cared for such columns in the papers. Yet if what Andrew had just told me was true, it explained much that had puzzled me. It gave me the answer to Mr. Reid's own re-action—first of anger, then of amusement when I had made the suggestion. He had decided easily enough to play this outrageous joke upon me. It explained Miss Garth's dismay, too, and the way Leslie Reid had walked out of the library that day when her husband had suggested that she join the party.

Andrew was watching me, aware of my groping bewilder-ment, even a little amused by it. "Now you are in difficulties, aren't you? What is a genteel young woman to do under such circumstances? Are you going to tell Master Brandon off and refuse to go?"

"Stop looking at me as if I were someone you meant to sketch for your paper," I said indignantly, still struggling with my confusion.

"Perhaps that's just what you are," he said, laughing out loud. "You'd make a charming heroine for a news story, though perhaps you're full of more contradictions than most of the ladies I sketch. Perhaps that's part of your attraction, Megan. You don't always do exactly what I would expect of a young woman in your proper position. It's entertaining to watch you. But you haven't answered my question, you know."

I made up my mind abruptly, dismissing his nonsense. "If what you've told me is true, then Mr. Reid is playing an inexcusable trick on me, amusing himself at my expense and the expense of his wife. But how am I to know what the truth is? You've repeated gossip, and gossip is not my affair. I'll take the children to the performance when the time comes. Their enjoyment is more important than what people think."

With that, I hoped I had settled Andrew, Brandon Reid, and my own conscience in one swoop.

"Bravo!" Andrew cried and reached across the table to cover my hand with his own. A mustachioed Italian gentleman at the next table smiled in approval and toasted us gallantly with his glass of wine.

"To be perfectly fair," Andrew said, "Brandon Reid is not wholly to blame. What else is a man to do when he's married to a woman who loves only his dead brother?"

So that was it? No wonder Mr. Reid so often seemed chill and remote and unhappy. I remembered the warm looks I had seen him turn upon the beautiful Leslie and the cool way in which she seemed to slip away from him. That felicitous scene at the dinner table my first night in the house must have been make-believe after all. And that was sad to contemplate.

"Come now," Andrew said. "Don't feel too sorry for him. He's not the man to suffer long from unrequited love. He has an appeal for silly women. Don't let it touch you, Megan."

I could feel myself flushing. "Touch me? You're being ridiculous. The boy is my only concern."

"You're an obstinate girl," he said. "And you're also rather a darling. I wish I could believe in a favorable outcome for your hopes. But I don't. I continue to feel lucky to be out of that house when darkness falls."

Like the silly sort of woman Andrew deplored, I fastened

my attention on the word "darling" and forgot the rest. While Andrew was not, I told myself, the type of man who appealed to me romantically, I liked him and I could not help feeling pleased to have him call me a darling. Even though I knew he used the word lightly. I gave him a smile and he blew me a mocking kiss. We were friends again.

It was past nine by the time Andrew squired me back to Washington Square. I'd had a pleasantly gay evening and I told him so. He held my hand a moment longer and more warmly than he should have.

"Be careful, Megan," he warned me again. "Do take care."

The words meant little to me. Already I had forgotten my uneasiness in Jeremy's company that afternoon. I let myself in with my latchkey and went upstairs, humming softly to myself because for once I felt young and irresponsible and not unattractive. There would be time enough tomorrow to become again my workaday self.

When I had taken off my outdoor things, I went to the door of Jeremy's room next to mine and asked if I might come in.

He was sitting up in bed reading a book and he stared at me in bright defiance. I noted the title with surprise. It was the book on Egypt that I had left in the schoolroom.

"I see you've been out of bed," I said.

His manner dared me to scold him. "I'm reading about Osiris."

I was more than pleased, but I did not betray that fact. "A most interesting subject."

"My father is an Osiris now," he announced, the defiance still in evidence.

"What do you mean?" I asked.

He seemed to sense that I was not going to scold him for getting out of bed, and he seemed to relax a little. Most intelligently he explained what he had read in the book. The Egyptians had believed during the period of the Osiris cult

92

that when a man died he became "an Osiris," accountable to the god for his sins on earth.

"Some day," Jeremy said, "I will stand in the Judgment Hall of Osiris and be punished for everything I've done on earth."

My heart went out to him in pity. I sat in a chair beside his bed and spoke quietly of the sort of God in whom I believed. A forgiving, understanding God.

"Not even the modern Egyptians believe in Osiris any more," I said.

"But I've *seen* Osiris," Jeremy insisted. "He's there in Uncle Brandon's library, wearing the White Crown with the plumes. And I'm not afraid of him. He's beautiful and stern and wise. If he wants to punish me, it will be right."

His words distressed me. It didn't seem wise to identify the head in his uncle's library with some supernatural force, and I tried to persuade him from the notion.

"Perhaps all the old gods add up to one God in the end," I said. "Osiris is part of a very big pattern."

He looked at me with something strangely like hope in his eyes, but I lacked the wisdom to know exactly what I had said or done that had helped him. Before I could tell him good night and leave him, Miss Garth came to the door and saw him sitting up in bed with the book on his knees.

"You should be asleep," she said and took the volume from him so quickly that he had no time to hold it from her. When she saw the title she frowned her disapproval.

"What sort of heathenish trash are you reading?" she demanded, and then looked at me. "I believe this belongs to you, Miss Kincaid?"

Even as I nodded, I found myself wondering how this handsome woman, with her fine carriage and beautiful dark hair, could be so invariably unpleasant. For the dozenth time she was making me feel myself a culprit who could do nothing but harm to Jeremy. I supposed that was her purpose—to be so unpleasant that I would eventually leave this house in defeat and her jealously guarded prerogatives would be again unchallenged. I would not play into her hands. I took the book from her and set it on the table next to Jeremy's bed.

"Mr. Reid approves of our interest in Egypt," I told her. "It's perfectly all right for Jeremy to borrow my book if he likes."

I glanced at the boy and found him watching me in a curiously intent way. He ignored Miss Garth and spoke directly to me.

"Sometime will you let me play with your carrousel?" he asked. "Selina talks about it all the time. She says you won't let her touch it."

"Perhaps I'll let you play with it sometime," I said and smiled at him.

8.

BACK IN my own room I found myself restless and disturbed. The words Jeremy had spoken about the Osiris head had touched me with a now familiar chill. His identifying the head with his own destiny was somehow frightening. When he said, "My father is an Osiris now," he touched on something deeper and more menacing.

It was too late to light my fire anew, and I got ready for bed quickly. Yet when I had bound my hair in plaits and put on my warm flannel nightgown with the feather-stitched collar that spoke of my mother's patient fingers, I sat absently on the edge of the bed, lost in thought.

It was encouraging, I told myself, that Jeremy had shown interest in the book about Egypt and in the carrousel. Perhaps both these things could be used to draw him into further interest, even if his notions about Osiris followed a strange road. If only I could prevail upon his uncle to talk to him as he used to about Egypt and his experience there, his own interest might help to counteract Jeremy's apathy.

The thought of Jeremy's uncle led me down another road. If Leslie Reid was still in love with her first husband, as Andrew said, who could blame Brandon for finding solace elsewhere? How must he feel when his brother had won Leslie as he had not been able to do? A pattern had begun to reveal itself concerning Brandon's relationship with his brother. Dwight had been the gifted, handsome, successful younger son. Or so everyone seemed to claim, though it was hard for me to imagine Brandon in a lesser light when it came to comparison with any man. Yet it seemed that Dwight had stood in his older brother's way at almost every point. He had been favored by a father Brandon loved devotedly. He had carved out a successful political career, and his star had been brightly on the rise at the time of his death. He had married the beautiful Leslie, who had loved him and still did.

All this was clear. Yet still I could not understand how it happened that a year after Dwight's death his grieving, loving widow had married the brother she could not love. The more I puzzled, the more confusing the maze became. Somewhere there must lie a key, but so far I had not found it. It was even possible that an effort was being made to keep it out of my hands. Even, perhaps, by Brandon himself?

The room's chill penetrated my preoccupation at last and I turned out the gas and got under the covers, pulling the quilts over me to my very nose. Now that I lay in bed and tried to sleep I began to hear the wind. It had risen without my noticing and it rattled the branches of the ailanthus against my window pane, and set a distant shutter banging. What a wild dance it must be enjoying through Washington Square with all those trees to play among and all that space in which to wheel about.

I fancied the wind as a dark, hooded figure, stormy-browed and bitter, stripping the last dead leaves from the trees, hurling winter upon us before it was time. In this fanciful state it was easy to confuse the dark and hooded figure of my imaginings with Brandon Reid. He too was stormy and bitter, strewing bleakness about him, offering little of warmth or reassurance. And yet . . . and yet . . .

96

I suppose I dozed, for I know that time passed and I occasionally waked from some uneasy dream. Then the wind held its breath and the very lull wakened me so that I lay listening to the sudden quiet. In the hush it seemed that the stairs creaked with the weight of feet upon them. Was Garth up? I wondered. It was unlikely that either Mr. Reid or Jeremy's mother would come to the third floor at this hour. There was another creak, and, thinking of Jeremy, I knew I must investigate.

Slipping out of bed, I threw my blue flannel wrapper over my gown and lighted a candle. Then I opened my door and stepped into the hall. The gas was always turned off at night and shadows stirred and wavered as chill drafts touched my candle flame. The dark wind capered over the rooftops and pressed at every cranny, puffing its breath the length of the hallway. Jeremy's door stood open and when I stepped into his room I found that he was indeed gone from his bed.

I had no doubt as to his goal and I ran down the stairs, shielding my candle from drafts, hoping its feeble flicker would not forsake me on this windy night. Beneath the library door there was an edging of light which told me that Brandon Reid was working late.

Dwight Reid's door stood closed, but the knob turned beneath my fingers and I went softly into the room. Here heavy draperies drawn across shuttered windows muffled the wild sounds outdoors, and only the sobbing of the boy on the bed filled the room. Here my candle flame burned straight, and the shadows were quiet. Jeremy lay face down upon his father's bed, weeping his heart out. I did not touch him, but stood close by.

"I'm here, Jeremy," I whispered. "Cry all you like. I'll wait for you until you feel better."

After one startled instant when he turned his head to look at me, he paid no further attention, but gave full vent to a grief so terrible that it wrenched my heart. I put the candle upon the high bureau and sat in a chair to wait. The boy's sobs grew stormier, and I wondered if I had better try to calm him.

In the distance the library door opened, and I knew that Brandon Reid had heard. His footsteps sounded firmly as he strode down the hall. I rose to face the door and was sharply aware of the picture he made, impressively, darkly handsome in the deep burgundy of his dressing gown, his thick hair touched to brightness by candlelight.

I put a finger to my lips and went swiftly to him. He blocked my path in the doorway as he had done once before when I had first met him. But this time I stood upon no ceremony. I put a hand to the smooth satin facing across the chest of his gown and pushed him back into the hall in no uncertain manner.

He was clearly displeased, and his dark brows drew into a frown. "What is wrong?" he demanded. "How did Jeremy get into that room?"

"Don't let him hear you," I pleaded. "He needs to cry, as he needed to run away today. Perhaps when he has released all this pent-up emotion he'll be quieter, happier."

I could sense a stirring of high impatience in Brandon Reid, as though he too had borne more than enough for one day and was moving toward some explosion.

"There has been too much of coddling," he said angrily. "The boy must be stopped at once."

He moved again toward Dwight's room, but at that moment Leslie's door opened and she came into the hall, her red hair in soft disarray about her shoulders, a lacy, silken gown caught half-revealing over the full curves of her bosom, her amber eyes wide with alarm. In both hands she held the tall brass candlestick I had noted beside the hearth in her room, and its flame dipped and bowed in the drafty hall.

"What is it?" she cried. "What has happened?"

For once her husband seemed to look in cold distaste upon

her tremulous beauty. "Your son is in Dwight's room," he told her curtly.

Leslie's gaze flew toward the source of those wrenching sobs and then back to her husband's face. "But that's dreadful! He must be brought out at once!" She put the great candle-stick down upon the hall table and flung out her hands in entreaty to her husband.

"Go in and comfort him, then," Brandon Reid challenged. "Go in yourself and bring him out."

She shrank before the whiplash of his tone, and I saw tears in her eyes, saw the wide searching look she turned upon him, as if she beseeched him for something without speaking a word.

He looked into the white face, lifted so pleadingly to his own, and a derisive smile touched his mouth. "Always so beautiful," he said. "There's no disarray that doesn't become you, my dear. Dwight was a fortunate man."

What his words meant to her I did not know, but she turned from him and fled back to her room, leaving her candle to add to the guttering shadows. From the open door-way Jeremy's sobs had lessened a little, though they still wracked his small body. His uncle wasted no further time on me. He strode to the door and went into the room. At least his encounter with Leslie had taken the edge from his anger, for now his tone was more restrained.

"Listen to me, Jeremy," he said. "I have decided on your punishment. Sit up and take it like a soldier."

To my surprise, Jeremy gave a long, strangling gulp and then sat up on the bed, his face puffy and streaked with weeping. Brandon Reid took a large white handkerchief from the breast pocket of his gown and gave it to the boy, waiting sternly until Jeremy had wiped his face and blown his nose. Then he spoke with the air of a judge pronouncing sentence.

"Because you willfully disobeyed my rules this afternoon and ran away, causing much grief to Miss Kincaid and worry to me, I have decided that you will not be permitted to attend the matinee for which I now have tickets."

Jeremy, of course, had known about the planned outing, but he had never given any sign as to whether it pleased him or not. Now his eyes widened and I saw his lips quiver.

"Yes, sir," he said, swallowing hard, and I knew he had been stricken with a dreadful disappointment.

His uncle gave him a curt good night and went out of the room. But while he was done with the boy, he was not done with me. I flew into the hall after him.

"How could you be so cruel?" I demanded, forgetting that I was hardly more than a servant in this house. "Your punishment is too severe; it's the wrong one. He needs the pleasure of that matinee. I won't have him cheated of it!"

He looked at me impatiently and without liking, and the chill in his gray eyes cut through my every defense. Clearly he did not like importunate women.

"Have it your own way," he said coldly, "but get the boy back to his own room."

As he turned from me his look fell on the oversized candlestick. He gestured toward it as carelessly as though there had been no clash between us.

"My wife has forgotten her favorite illumination," he said. He picked up the huge ornamental stick and held it high, smiling without amusement. "It is not inappropriate that this once graced a seraglio in the days of the Ottoman Empire. If you'll excuse me, Miss Kincaid, I'll put this where it belongs." He carried it toward Leslie's door, and from the tail of my eye I saw the door open, as though she had been watching.

I had no interest in candlesticks, seraglios, or the Reids' marriage and I returned to Jeremy at once. He still sat on the edge of the bed, with his uncle's large white handkerchief clutched in his fingers.

"Come," I said, and held out my hand to him gently.

He let me take his hand as if he were a very small child, and came with me docilely. Back in his own room I tucked him into bed. With all my heart I longed to put my arms about him, to offer the unspoken comfort of a caress, but I did not dare more than a light pat on his shoulder.

"Don't worry," I said. "Everything's going to be fine. You'll sleep well now. And you needn't worry about the matinee. I've spoken to your uncle, and he has relented. The punishment is withdrawn and you'll have a lovely time at the play."

I waited for some sign of pleasure, but he lay back quietly on his pillow, staring at me as though I had offered him a gift of ashes. With a flash of understanding I knew that Brandon Reid had been right and I wrong. Jeremy had *wanted* to be punished and he had wanted a punishment that was real and would deprive him of pleasure. In the same flash I knew that I must undo the harm I might have wrought in canceling his uncle's edict.

Conversationally, as though I had noticed nothing, I began to talk to him. "I've never liked the word 'punishment.' It's true that when we do wrong things, we must pay for them. That goes for grownups as well as children. So I'm going to choose a payment for you to make. You've asked me to let you play with my brother's carrousel. But now I will not, after all, allow you to touch it. And that is final."

For a moment longer he stared at me. Then he closed his eyes heavily as though he could stay awake no longer. I knew he had accepted my authority and was not dissatisfied. He was still a little boy who wanted very much to go to a play.

I stood looking down at him, so quickly and peacefully asleep, and wondered how I had ever felt a moment's fear of Jeremy Reid.

9.

THE FOLLOWING days were surprisingly quiet. As I had hoped, Jeremy had spent himself completely and it had done him good. He was not markedly different in his general attitude or behavior, but he was not so wound up with tension within himself. As a result, I felt more secure in my position. My employer would have to admit, if he troubled to observe Jeremy at all, that I had not been wholly wrong.

One December morning when Miss Garth and I were having breakfast with the childen in the nursery, Selina brought up the subject of Christmas and the presents she wanted to make for her mother and her Uncle Brandon. She bubbled with her usual enthusiasm, and I saw Jeremy watching her with something like speculation in his eyes.

"What are you going to make for your uncle?" I asked the boy.

Selina, always swift as a hummingbird, answered before he could find words in his more thoughtful way.

"Last year he never made a thing for anyone!" she cried. "He was a very selfish boy."

Jeremy retreated into his shell of indifference and would

not be coaxed out. I could have spanked Selina for quenching the look I had seen in his eyes.

However, after breakfast, when I went into the schoolroom to start my work on a set of pinafores I was making for his sister, Jeremy followed me there, a thoughtful expression on his face. I did not press him and paid no attention as he roamed about the room, poking into things as he liked to do. He paused before a basket of assorted trimmings I had stored on a shelf, and after a moment's searching he brought out a small box of tubular, cut-steel beads and held them up to me.

"What do you do with these?" he asked.

I told him they were used for embroidering a pattern on a lady's gown.

He rolled a few of the shiny beads out upon the table and studied them for some time in silence. This way and that he pushed them, as if he were attempting some design. I waited for him to tell me what he was about.

"Have you any wire?" he asked me finally.

I shook my head. "I can let you have some strong thread, but I have no wire."

"Mr. Beach will get me some if I ask him," Jeremy said. "Miss Megan, may I have these beads?"

"Of course you may have them, Jeremy. Take them all, if you like. And if you want more, I can get them easily."

"Thank you," he said with unwonted courtesy. "I have an idea for a Christmas gift I may make for Uncle Brandon."

"That's fine," I approved. "Let me know if there's any way in which I can help you."

He nodded absently and did not explain. He took the box of beads away to his room and later I heard him asking Andrew to bring him a few lengths of fine wire.

Curious and interested though I was, I asked no questions. It was enough that Jeremy seemed more cheerful, that he had some private absorption. Several times he asked me about the play we were going to see and appeared to be looking forward to the occasion.

On the Saturday morning of the matinee, Mr. Reid appeared in the nursery—there were no lessons that day—to astonish us with an announcement. He had decided, he said, to come with us to the play. It was a fine day, and he expected that we would all enjoy ourselves. He mentioned the time when the carriage would be ready, warned us not to be late, and went out of the room. I could have sworn that he gave me a swift look in which amusement was evident, but he was gone so quickly that I could not be sure.

The news had a varied effect upon us. Selina clapped her hands in delight and said she would wear her new green dress. Jeremy said nothing, yet there was a glow of pleasure in his eyes that touched me. I only hoped that his uncle would not disappoint him and that this unusual good cheer on the part of Brandon Reid would last through the afternoon.

My own reaction was curiously mixed. I did not in the least like the quickening of my spirits at the thought of being in his company under more pleasurable circumstances than were usually the case. I told myself several times that morning that his was a violent nature and that this light mood would not last. Surely the man repelled me far more than he attracted me. Besides, in spite of my determination to ignore gossip, Andrew's words about Cicely Mansfield returned to prick me further with distaste for the children's uncle. Must he sit with us and dote upon this actress as she coquetted with him from the stage? No—having Brandon Reid with us was an altogether unfortunate turn of events, and his presence would undoubtedly set a blight upon the occasion, regardless of the children's pleasure.

So I guided my thoughts and warned myself. At the same time I took great pains when I dressed in my garnet satin, even to the final touch of fastening on my mother's garnet earrings and sunburst brooch. After all, this was a more suitable occasion for dressing up than the evening of the dinner I'd enjoyed with Andrew Beach. Andrew, I knew very well, would not approve of Mr. Reid's accompanying presence and I was just as glad he was not about on Saturday to scowl at me and make biting remarks.

Miss Garth's reaction was one of outraged indignation. At the moment of Mr. Reid's announcement she merely smoldered, then looked her disapproval when he had gone out of the room. She released her feelings by telling Selina she had spotted her green dress and could not wear it and she lectured Jeremy on all that his uncle would expect of him by way of good conduct. She did not, however, speak her mind openly until a few moments before we were ready to leave.

There was a long mirror at the head of the third-floor stairs and I had gone out to examine myself from head to toe. By this time I had thrust back all doubts, shut Andrew out of my mind, and felt as ridiculously gay as though I had been Selina's age. Or as though a man were taking me alone to the theater. Miss Garth caught me before I could pretend I was only passing the mirror, and she took time to speak her mind in a low, deadly voice.

"What a little fool you are," she said. "Don't think it isn't clear for whom you're preening. Do you think he'll really look at you? It's hardly likely, when all his attention will be for his inamorata there on the stage."

Her words left me shocked and nearly speechless with fury. Before I could manage an indignant retort, or she could continue in this outrageous vein, Selina popped out of her room in a whirl of green silk, spots and all, and hurled herself upon me.

"Do let's go downstairs, Miss Megan! It would be dreadful to be late." Then she saw my dress and circled me in delight. Mischievous and teasing, she might be, but there was a warmth in Selina as well. "Why, you look beautiful!" she

106

cried. "That's a lovely, lovely red. And you've combed your hair in such a pretty way, so it shows under your hat. Uncle Brandon will approve of you . . . he likes pretty things."

Miss Garth fairly snorted, but she said no more. She went off to rout Jeremy from his room, and I tried to put out of my mind the sharp things she had said. I would not listen to gossip. If she thought I was primping for Brandon Reid, then the rest of what she had said was as likely to be untrue. I gave Selina a hug for her compliments and tied her sash a little higher to hide the more prominent spottiness. The frock, quite aside from spots, was not as great a success as it should have been, but I was glad it gave Selina pleasure.

Miss Garth returned in a moment with Jeremy and now she was doing her best to make him uncomfortable.

"This is altogether too much excitement," she said. "The boy will be sick at his stomach, you'll see. Probably disgrace you all right there in the box. And that will teach his uncle to take him out in public."

She made me so angry that if the children hadn't been present I would have given her a piece of my mind. The sooner I persuaded Mr. Reid to put the boy wholly into my hands, the better. There was at least a quiet acceptance between Jeremy and me by now, and the pretense of being a seamstress alone need not be continued.

Having given us the worst possible send-off, Miss Garth flounced away to her room and I held out a hand to each child so that we could walk downstairs together in a gay and friendly fashion.

"Don't you worry," I told Jeremy. "You've eaten nothing to make you ill. And besides, happiness never upsets anyone. This is going to be a lovely day."

Brandon Reid was waiting for us at the foot of the stairs. He had an approving word because we were a good two minutes ahead of time, and he admired our dressed-up state collectively, with no special compliments for anyone. As he

107

helped me into my dolman, I noted how very fine he looked. Though that was not unusual. Under the black Inverness cape that he wore with such aplomb, his suit was a fine weave of broadcloth in pearl gray, and when he had settled us in the carriage he put on his pearl-gray topper. We could not, I thought, have found a more distinguished-looking, more striking escort in all New York.

As Fuller flapped the reins and the carriage drew away from the curb, something made me glance up at the front of the house we were leaving. A woman stood at a window on the second floor, and, with a start, I saw that it was Leslie Reid. Until now she had not appeared to say good-by to either her husband or the children, and the glimpse of her at the window disturbed me. So often Mrs. Reid seemed hardly more than a shadowy background figure in the house. Her frequent headaches, the spells of illness that made her languid and given to remaining in bed for days at a time, removed her from the rest of us so that we almost forgot her presence. Now it was as though I had glimpsed a melancholy ghost watching us from an unreal world of candlelight and violets.

No one else saw her, and, as we drove away, I did not look back. Yet the memory of her standing there was not something I could easily shake off.

The children's uncle was in an extraordinarily light mood, and I suspected that he had made a pact with himself to give Selina, and particularly Jeremy, a pleasant afternoon.

The theater was just off Union Square, and carriages were already drawing up before the doors when we arrived. By the time Mr. Reid had handed us into the blue, white, and gold auditorium, and had settled us in the best seats of our box, we were all atingle with excitement. Jeremy was quiet, but there was a shine in his eyes that delighted me and he missed nothing as the house filled up. From the vantage point of our lower box, we could look out over the entire sweep of the theater. I could not help but note, however, that Brandon

Reid remained in the shadows at the rear of the box and made no attempt to join us in our scrutiny of the house.

Once he leaned forward to speak to me. "Do you like the seats?"

I could only nod raptly. I had never sat in so fine a place before and I didn't dare try to tell him how I felt, lest I sound as young and enraptured as Selina. At last the house lights went down, the rustling of programs quieted, and the gas-jet footlights came on in all their brilliance against the lowered curtain.

Cicely Mansfield did not appear until near the end of the first scene, and the play moved with an amusing sparkle toward the moment of her entrance. Then she whirled on-stage with the gaiety that was so essentially hers and from that moment on took possession of the audience.

I edged a little forward in my seat because I wanted to see exactly what sort of woman she was. Certainly she was not beautiful—not in the sense that Leslie Reid was a beauty. Pretty—yes, and with a warmth about her that reached across the footlights to embrace the audience. "Of course you love me," she seemed to be saying. "You love me because I love you!"

The play was light froth. The children loved it, and I laughed aloud with them. Once, when I glanced back at Mr. Reid, seated in the shadowy rear, I saw that he was not even watching the stage. Indeed, he looked as though he might be dozing. Of course he must have seen the play before—perhaps several times. Yet I would have expected him to feast his eyes upon Miss Mansfield at every opportunity and this display of indifference gave me a sudden hope that the gossip, after all, was untrue. Or, if there had ever been any truth in it, perhaps the affair was well in the past. Even as the thought came to mind, my own readiness to be pleased, to hope that the gossip was untrue, dismayed me as something shameful. There in the darkened theater I could feel the burning of my

109

cheeks, the unwelcome quickening of my heartbeat. Why should I care? Why should I be concerned one way or another with Brandon Reid's past or present infidelities?

When the curtain came down on the first act, I tried to applaud with as much eagerness as the children. Perhaps they had not understood every line, but the pace was fast and I felt I had chosen well for their pleasure.

During the interval I watched the rustling theater with interest. In the box directly across from us several women had gathered for this matinee, and I realized that opera glasses were being turned upon us and that the ladies were whispering to each other. Did this mean that Selina and Jeremy had been recognized?

Mr. Reid spoke from the shadows. "The twittering has begun. The ladies in the opposite box are puzzled about your identity."

"Why should they be puzzled?" I asked, not turning my head. "I'm obviously here with the children."

His voice went on softly, mockingly. "Since you scarcely look like a governess, they're wondering who it can be who is so new and fashionable in town and has escaped their attention."

For the first time I realized the impropriety of my dress. As the children had dressed up for theatergoing, so had I, and my gown was quite suitable for a matinee had I been here in a social position. As it was, I should have clung to my dove gray or wren brown.

"We might as well give them something to twitter about," Mr. Reid went on, and before I knew what he was about, he left the dark recesses of the box and stepped to the rail beside me, holding out a program, bending over my shoulder as though he pointed something out.

"Please don't," I said. "You're quite right that I shouldn't have dressed like this. I'm sorry, Mr. Reid."

"Don't be ridiculous," he told me, impatient again. "You're

110

more bearable to look at the way you are this afternoon than in those drab things you wear at home."

A retort was rising indignantly to my lips when the curtains at the rear of the box parted and an usher appeared with a note for Mr. Reid. He took it, frowning, and read it through.

"It appears," he said, "that I will have to go backstage for a moment."

He bowed to us and was gone so quickly that I could only stare at the blue velvet curtains swaying gently from the briskness of his passing. He had gone backstage to see Miss Mansfield—that was evident. He had not even troubled to dissemble. And he had not minded in the least if I knew what he was about. I began to fume inwardly, though I kept my feelings from the children.

So I was more "bearable" to look at today and he did not care for the way I dressed at home! He behaved as though I had no feelings, no pride. Andrew was right, and Brandon Reid was an insufferable person. He had the arrogance and lack of consideration that was sometimes typical of the wealthy—particularly when wealth was inherited instead of earned. I bit my lips and kept my gaze from the interest of that opposite box. By the time the curtain rose on the second act, I had studied its slightly rippling scene until I knew every painted line by heart.

Mr. Reid was late in returning and he uttered no apology as he slipped into his chair. I did not look at him, but kept my attention fixed upon the play. Though the second act was even more lively than the first, my pleasure in the production had faded. Once or twice it seemed to me that Cicely Mansfield glanced directly at our box and that her famous smile was flung rather challengingly in our direction.

During the second-act intermission Mr. Reid seemed restless and increasingly bored. Once or twice he pulled out his handsome gold watch and studied the time, toying with the long chain that looped across his waistcoat. He had dropped all pretense of playing the role of benevolent uncle and he made no further effort to keep the children happy. It was at this worst possible moment that Selina asked the question she had been saving up for hours.

"Uncle Brandon," she said, "what is an inamorata? At home Garthy and Miss Megan were talking about your having one."

In spite of the voices and rustling all through the theater, there seemed an area of deadly quiet about our box. I felt cold perspiration dampen the palms of my hands, but my mind was blank of any possible response. There was, after all, nothing I could say, no defense I could offer.

After a moment of endless silence, Mr. Reid addressed Selina coldly. "I suggest, my dear, that you ask Miss Kincaid for the answer to that question. I suspect that by now she is an authority on the subject."

His words shocked and angered me, yet still I could not answer him. My position was one I could not readily defend, however indignant I might be, however unfair his attack.

He rose and made us an elaborate bow that must have been quite visible to anyone in the theater who happened to be looking.

"I hope you will excuse me from remaining for the rest of the play. I confess that it bores me and I am never willingly bored for long. I'm sure you can get the children home, Miss Kincaid. I will not need the carriage."

I said nothing at all, and in a moment he was gone, completely spoiling our afternoon.

I knew it was spoiled even before Selina's wail of protest. I saw the withdrawal in Jeremy's eyes and knew that he was blaming himself, however mistakenly, for this sudden departure. He had been quietly enjoying both the play and his uncle's company. I had sensed this in the way he hung on Brandon Reid's every word and gave him all his attention. I

112

tried to find some lame excuse for his uncle's going, but I think not even Selina believed me. Both knew that he had lost interest in our company and taken himself away because he did not care to be with us any longer.

Through the final act any last trace of embarrassment I might have felt died away as my anger increased. Neither the children nor I had deserved such treatment. His lack of consideration, his indifference to the feelings of others was insufferable. When the opportunity arose I would tell him so —and let him dismiss me if he liked.

Andrew was right, and I should have listened to him!

We were far from gay on the drive home down Fifth Avenue. When we should have been full of talk about the play and still under the spell of the theater, no one had any desire to talk.

Just before we reached Washington Square, the first snow of the winter began to fall, drifting down lightly, thickly, with every promise of going on forever.

At least Jeremy waited until he was home before fulfilling Miss Garth's prophecy and being dreadfully ill. We were busy with him all evening long.

When it was that my employer came home that night, or if he came home at all, I did not know. And I certainly did not care. What I had to say to him would not lose its strength by waiting.

10.

CHURCH BELLS wakened me the next morning, and I heard the whisper of snow against the pane. I left my bed with the eagerness one feels to view the unsullied beauty of winter's first snowfall.

White fringe clung to the branches of the ailanthus, and a quilting lay thick upon my window sill. Drab rooftops were padded with white coverlets, and the chimneys wore little caps of snow. Even the dreary alley of the mews had been touched with beauty. Fuller was already up and busily shoveling a path from carriage house to back door. The hush of a snowstorm lay upon the city.

I pulled on my wrapper and went to light the fire. Usually on Sundays I traveled some distance by horsecar to the church my mother and I had attended, but I did not want to battle snowdrifts and slowed traffic this morning. I had noticed a church nearby on Fifth Avenue that I might attend. The Reids—Mrs. Reid, at least—went farther uptown to one more fashionable, and the children often accompanied her. What Mr. Reid did I had no idea. One hardly saw him of a Sunday.

Remembering my anger, I fed it anew to make sure the coals remained hot until my opportunity came to confront him and speak my mind. Yet even as I stirred my indignation with reminding, I was troubled by a contrary yearning for peace and quieter thoughts.

Sunday had one rather pleasant aspect, for it was the day when Miss Garth went home to visit her elderly father. She waited till after churchtime and midday Sunday dinner, then took herself off, and was gone for the afternoon and most of the evening. Thus for part of the day I had both children to myself unless Mrs. Reid went calling and took Selina with her.

That morning Jeremy did not rise for breakfast, and when I looked in on him, I found him listless and interested in nothing. There was no more to look forward to now, and the reality of the matinee had disappointed him. Not even my inquiry as to how the gift for his uncle progressed roused him from apathy. He had kept the secret of what he was making, working on it only when he was alone. This morning that interest too had forsaken him.

I needed my escape to church. Apparently the snow had changed Mrs. Reid's plans and Selina was not going out with her, so both children were left in Miss Garth's charge until I returned.

Our front steps had been swept of one layer of snow, but already they had filmed over as the thick fall continued. At least the fall lacked the biting sting of a blizzard. The flakes fell, slow and thick, without wind to set them whirling. Washington Square was a great white field, its dull browns hidden and every bush and tree wearing puffs of white. Snow lay thick upon the fountain, and a few sparrows hopped about its rim, seeking the crumbs some kindly citizen had sprinkled there.

My skirts brushed the snow, and I lifted them high so that I would not sit indoors with their wet hems against me. The effort of tramping through snow that had not yet crusted to offer solid footing, set my blood tingling by the time I

116

reached my destination three blocks away. There was the usual traffic on the Avenue, with a few sleighs adding their melodic jingling of bells to the sounds of this snowy Sunday.

The church was small and built of the same brownstone that was quarried across the Hudson at Weehawken, furnishing a favored building material for so many New York homes and buildings. In contrast the steeple wore a frosting of white and the doors and windows were bright with welcome. I entered the enclosure of a little iron fence and went up the steps along with others who had not been kept home by the storm.

The organist was playing, and the deep full tones sounded through the quiet place and added to the feeling of light and warmth and peace that met me as I stepped inside. I sought a long bench near the rear and took a seat near the wall aisle where I might be alone and quiet with my thoughts. This moment before the service began was always one I prized. I could make my own prayers best and did not need a minister to tell me how to pray.

Quietly, avoiding the banked fires of my anger, I went over in my mind the disturbing problem of Jeremy Reid. More than anything else I needed strength and guidance to help him. A beginning had been made. He must not be allowed to slip back into the old way that was so filled with darkness for him. It was for these things I asked in my heart that quiet Sunday morning.

The little church was filling up, and before long the choir began to sing. The congregation rose to join in a hymn, and at length the minister took the pulpit to give his sermon. By now my disquiet was stilled and I felt hushed and strengthened. I knew that when the time came I would fight for Jeremy with renewed courage and vigor.

I will confess that I did not at first follow every word the minister spoke. I prefer a quiet preacher, and this man was breathing fire. Nevertheless, when he launched into an attack

117

upon the wave of crime which held New York in a fearsome grip, I began to listen. Vice and corruption were the sins of man, the minister admonished us, but with the help of men of good will, they could be opposed and stamped out.

Not long ago there had been a man in New York, he reminded the congregation, who had fought against these things with courage and selflessness. This good fight had been led to a great extent by Dwight Reid, and the good he had begun was now being carried on by others. We must remember that early in January the Dwight Reid Memorial Home for children was to be opened with a ceremony which he hoped many of us would attend, and he advised us to contribute to the cause. The building itself was virtually completed, but its running must be assured for years to come.

A collection was taken for this cause, and, as I made my contribution, I thought of the day when Jeremy had run away to this very building of which the minister spoke. In the boy's mind the place must seem to offer refuge to the son of the man it honored.

When the service was over and the congregation began to file out, I sat on for a few moments, waiting for the church to empty. Then I left my seat and stepped into the uncrowded wall aisle, turning toward the back of the church. Two rows behind me another woman had waited for the crowd to thin before leaving her seat. She sat with her head bent, her furs drawn closely about her, as though she were cold in this stove-heated interior. With a start I recognized the brown feathered hat with glossy wings of red hair showing beneath, and in the moment of my recognition, Leslie Reid looked up and met my eyes. For an instant I thought she would look away purposely, not choosing to see me. Then she seemed to reconsider and nodded in my direction. She rose, edging along the row. I waited, and, when she reached me, she indicated a side door that offered an easy exit.

Outside the snow was deep in the churchyard, and we

clasped hands in order to help each other through it to a side gate. We did not speak until we were on the sidewalk, moving toward the Avenue. Then Mrs. Reid threw me a quick melancholy look.

"I did not want to be recognized," she explained softly. "There would have been a great to-do if someone had seen me there. But I knew this sermon was to be preached and I wanted to hear it."

She appeared gently sad this morning and not so far removed as she had sometimes seemed before. As always, I beheld her beauty with wonder that a woman could be so lovely. Her skin at close range seemed flawless, the lashes that shadowed her eyes were thick and upward-curling, her brows neatly drawn in a line of perfection. This was the woman Brandon Reid had married. How could he look at Cicely Mansfield?

I was surprised when she began to speak to me, not as if I were a semi-servant in her house, but a woman in whom she could confide. The imperious manner had vanished.

"Nothing must happen to keep the Memorial Home from opening," she said, speaking from behind the shelter of the muff she held to her cheek. "The good my husband began must live on. It must not be wasted."

"Is there any danger that it won't open?" I asked, a little startled by her outburst.

"There must not be!" she cried vehemently. "Though from the first my husband has set himself against the entire project."

It seemed strange that Brandon Reid should oppose what was done to honor his brother, and I said as much, with something less than tact.

Mrs. Reid threw me a quick, tragic look. "Brandon has always been envious of Dwight. From the time they were children, it was Dwight who did everything well, Brandon whose aims were futile. The older brother has never forgiven the younger for being all he was not."

119

It did not seem that such a word as "futile" could be used in regard to Brandon Reid, but it was not for me to defend him to his wife. I offered no comment, and for nearly a block she was silent. When she spoke again it was in a lost, sad tone.

"Dwight died in January and my father in March. Within two months of each other. This time of the year, as we move toward January, always seems unhappy to me."

I felt a little impatient with her. I could sympathize with suffering such as she had endured. I had known suffering too, and great loss. But it seemed to me that she had every resource within her grasp for renewed happiness.

"Most of my family is gone now," she went on. "My father, Hobart Rolfe, built a house on the Hudson River to please my mother. When the financial crash ruined him, that was all that remained. Our home on Bleecker Street was merely loaned us by a friend. Now my mother lives alone up the Hudson. Perhaps I'll visit her soon, If I can persuade my husband to take me up there. Perhaps it would do me good to get away from New York for a little while."

There was a plaintive note in her voice, as though she had been dwelling too long in solitude on old grievances.

"I'm sure you'll enjoy a trip up the Hudson," I said cheerfully.

She sighed. "How wonderful to have such robust good health as you enjoy, Miss Kincaid. You seem not to know what it is like to have a day's illness."

I suppressed a desire to tell her that I was too busy to afford time for illness. It was clear, I think, to everyone in the house that Leslie Reid's poor health had its basis more in her mind than in her body. Doctors kept her plied with nostrums but seemed unable to do anything for her.

"What of the children while you are away?" I asked.

"We plan to take Selina with us," Mrs. Reid said. "Miss

Garth will remain here with Jeremy. The boy doesn't travel well, and it's wiser not to take him."

Besides, you can't endure him, I thought rebelliously. Perhaps she sensed my unspoken criticism, for she gave me a wistful smile.

"I know you think I am ungrateful, Miss Kincaid, and that isn't wholly true. I believe you are trying very hard to help Jeremy and I hope with all my heart that something can be done for him. In the meantime the thing that concerns me most is his continued association with Selina."

"He likes his sister," I said in quick defense. "He never minds her teasing, and I think he has a real affection for her." Then, since I had gone this far, I decided to go farther. "I feel, however, that Miss Garth is often too severe with the boy. He's still recovering from a serious shock and should be dealt with more gently."

"I'll speak to her," Mrs. Reid promised. "I know she believes in bringing up children very strictly. After all, she was my governess when I was a young girl. Undoubtedly she feels privileged in my family. I trust her judgment completely, but I'll try to persuade her to be more lenient with Jeremy, if you think that is wise."

Such a concession surprised and pleased me, though I doubted that it would have much effect on Thora Garth. At least Mrs. Reid seemed more human this Sunday morning, less remote, less chilly and superior. I wondered if she were perhaps a rather shy person, since shyness can often make one seem unfriendly.

As we neared Washington Square we found the sidewalks fairly well shoveled and the walking became easier. Mrs. Reid, however, did not quicken her pace. Indeed, she seemed to slow her steps even more.

"You enjoyed the play yesterday?" she asked suddenly, and I saw the rising color in her pale cheeks.

121

"It was quite amusing," I answered carefully. "The children enjoyed it very much."

"And this actress—this Cicely Mansfield? I've never seen her. What is she like?"

I could not meet the entreaty in her eyes. "She seems a gifted comedienne," I admitted.

"Is she—is she very beautiful?"

Mrs. Reid had forgotten to shield her cheeks with her muff and white flakes fell upon her uplifted face unheeded, or were caught and held for an instant in those breathlessly long lashes. I warmed toward her more than I ever had before, and my resentment against Brandon Reid deepened.

"Miss Mansfield isn't beautiful at all," I assured her quickly. "She's rather pretty and she has a certain charm and good humor. Nothing more."

Mrs. Reid seemed to take a pitiful comfort from my words, and I felt both touched and distressed by this revelation. It seemed likely that Andrew was wrong about her love for the younger brother and that Leslie Reid had far more of an interest in the husband she treated so coolly than he suspected.

Yet even as I considered this, she spoke of Dwight again, repeating without self-consciousness some compliment he had paid her. Perhaps she wanted to show me that she had once been placed very high in the estimation of a man she had loved.

My feelings were a mingling of embarrassment and pity, so that it was a relief when we reached the house. I was no little disturbed by this glimpse behind the mask of Leslie Reid's cool, untouchable beauty. There was an indication of hidden fire here, and it troubled me. Jeremy's mother was not indifferent after all, but driven in contrary directions by her own unhappy memories.

When we entered the house, I went at once to the third floor. I could hear voices in the nursery, and knew Miss Garth was there with the children. As I turned toward the rear, the door of the schoolroom opened and to my surprise Andrew Beach looked out at me. Ordinarily he did not come to the house during the weekend.

"How did the matinee go?" he asked without preliminary greeting.

I was deliberately casual. "Well enough. The children seemed to enjoy the play."

"And the master?" Andrew persisted, quirking a disbelieving eyebrow.

"Perhaps you'd better ask him," I said firmly. "Why are you here today?"

"I'm to be given an extra sitting for the portrait." He gestured toward the room behind him. "Come and see what I'm doing."

It was the first time he had offered to show me the portrait, and I followed him into the schoolroom, where an easel stood near a window. On it rested a small canvas—the unfinished portrait of a woman and a child. I studied it with interest.

Andrew had captured the sauciness of Selina's expression, the flyaway quality of her fair hair, the suggestion of ready laughter around her mouth. Work on the child's face was well along toward completion. The mother was still no more than a hazy suggestion—the oval of a face with an ethereal beauty about it and more than a hint of sadness. So it was the ghostly Leslie he meant to paint—though apparently without the plaintive, self-pitying quality so often evident.

"She's very hard to catch," he said. "I'm still groping for the right approach."

I thought of the several Leslie Reids I had seen—the imperious mistress, the all-but-forgotten sick woman in a candle-lit room, and in contrast the emotion-torn wife I had met just now in the church.

"I'm not sure you've found it," I said thoughtfully. "First you will have to decide which Mrs. Reid you will paint."

Andrew smiled. "I suspected that you'd not approve. Don't underestimate her, Megan. There may be more there than meets the indifferent eye. But at least our little seamstress has got the master out of the way long enough to notice the mistress."

The anger that flared in me was out of proportion to the cause, and it was as well that I was saved an answer by Kate's sudden appearance in the doorway.

"Mrs. Reid is ready if you'll come for the sitting now," she said to Andrew, and then spoke breathlessly to me. "Mr. Reid has been asking for you all morning, miss. Will you please go to the library at once."

I nodded to her and went to my room without another look at Andrew or his portrait. Once there, I did not hurry. As I took off my mantle and bonnet and combed the black bangs over my forehead, my reflection in the glass startled me. With the mere mention of Brandon Reid's name an angry light had come into my eyes. I might be dressed as a brown wren, but an indignation, further aroused by Andrew, had given me life. It was not displeasing to find that I looked ready for battle.

When I went down, I found the library door open and my employer standing before the pedestal on which rested the Osiris head. He seemed to be studying it in complete concentration, though he sensed my presence and spoke to me without looking around.

"Come in, Miss Kincaid, and close the door behind you, please."

My movements were decisive, my step firm. There was no banking of angry fires now. I walked straight toward him, meaning to speak my mind quickly and have it over with. Unfortunately this determination went unnoted and he spoke first.

"I never tire of the artistry of such sculpture," he said and drew an admiring finger along the proud Egyptian nose. "How well it reveals the man behind the god. Look at those elongated eyes. They aren't wholly the eyes of a stylized pattern. There's thought and intelligence there. But what I like best is the humor of the mouth."

His finger moved, touching the wide, full lips that were strangely like his own—though it seemed to me that the mouth of the man lacked the humor he admired in the statue. However, I had not come here to discuss an Egyptian head. I braced my shoulders and spoke before he could stop me again.

"I don't wish to remain in this house under a false pretense, Mr. Reid. I must express myself concerning your conduct yesterday."

This opening remark, stiff-sounding to my own ears, at least arrested his attention. He gave me a quick, startled look and pulled a chair toward the comfortable fire.

"You needn't stand up like a schoolmistress while you lecture me. Come and sit here. You can be just as indignant with me sitting as standing."

I did not mean to be disarmed and made fun of. I stayed where I was.

"In the first place," I continued, "it was not necessary for you to accompany the children to the play. But since you chose to do so, it was your obligation to carry the afternoon off cheerfully. Since you started out with a pose of good humor, you should have continued it, whatever the effort cost you. You had no right to vent your own displeasures and private resentments upon two children. Particularly upon Jeremy. He was ill last night. This morning he didn't want to get up and he has lost the progress he has been making in the last few weeks. I feel that the blame is yours."

I paused, a little astonished at my own outburst, but not in the least regretting it. His face was expressionless, guarded.

He stood at ease before me, listening—and I could not tell at all what my words meant to him, or what their effect might be. When he stepped toward me suddenly and put his thin, strong hands upon my shoulders, I gasped. I could feel their warmth and strength through the goods of my dress.

"Whether you like it or not, you will sit down," he commanded. "I'm quite sure that you enjoy making me uncomfortable, but I don't enjoy it myself and I don't propose to endure it. You will sit here by the fire and relax a little."

Without an unladylike struggle I could not move except in the direction he wished. Into the seat before the fire he plumped me in a far from gentle manner. Then he took the opposite chair and gave me his brilliant, startling smile.

"What else have you to scold me about, Miss Megan?" he said.

How very cunning he was! How clever. His smile, even his use of the children's name for me was intended to dispell my anger, to dispose me more gently toward him. And I did not mean to be so disposed. I sat upright in the cushioned chair and stared at him even more angrily than before.

"I do have something else to say. I would like to tell you that while I have heard gossip, I have not indulged in gossip. I have no knowledge as to whether any of the things I've heard are true or untrue, and it's not for me to judge you. However, your behavior in the theater box yesterday was indecorous and without consideration for the children or for me."

There—I had said all that I had come to say. The words were out, and I sat stiffly on the edge of my chair, waiting for the skies to fall.

Mr. Reid was no longer smiling. He did not look at me now, but away from my face into the fire.

"I asked you here to offer you an apology," he told me after what seemed a struggle for composure. "As you say, I behaved badly yesterday. And even before—when I used your suggestion to take the children to this play as an instrument

126

for humiliating others. Since it's quite true that Miss Mansfield's name and mine have been coupled in the newspapers, I had no business encouraging you to attend that particular play, or to take the children to it. I didn't know I would feel so deeply ashamed of my action, Miss Megan. This has been a chastening revelation."

I did not altogether trust him, and I could not tell whether he was wholly serious. Prepared as I was to meet anything but this, I could not immediately retreat from high indignation and respond with grace.

"I accept your apology," I said stiffly. "But the damage has been done, and it cannot be easily remedied."

There seemed no trace of mockery in him now, but an acceptance of my words in almost sorrowful regret. How strange a man he was. How filled with contradictions and driven by who could know what inner demons. Often he seemed misplaced in his present role. With him I had always an awareness of a man who had lived in far places, whose eyes had beheld incredible sights, whose thoughts were concerned with worlds far removed from my own.

"I've wanted to tell you how much I appreciate the effect you are having on Jeremy," he said when the silence grew too long between us. "His improvement has been visible even to me, though I see him so seldom. Let's hope this setback won't be permanent."

This was a subject I could warm to. "He's making you something for Christmas," I told him. "I don't know what it is, but I know he wants to please you and gain your approval. Whatever the gift my be, I hope you'll accept it warmly when the time comes."

The somber look touched his eyes again. "I'll accept it with a proper expression of appreciation, I hope. But warmly— no. That's too much to ask of me."

"But it's not!" I cried. "So much has already been withheld

127

from the boy. It must be made up for. You are an adult. You have the strength he lacks."

I could sense that I had touched him on the raw. He gazed up at the portrait of his father over the mantel, and I was once more aware of the affection in his look. Had it pained him as a young man, I wondered, to disappoint his father, to be less in his father's eyes than his brother Dwight had been?

"Jeremy destroyed a great deal," he said quietly. "There is a point past which you cannot push me."

I did not speak, and he changed the subject.

"Mrs. Reid has been pressing me to take her up the Hudson to visit her mother. She feels such a trip will improve her health. While I'm not convinced this will be the case, I intend to do as she wishes. Selina will come with us, but I want to leave Jeremy in your charge while we are gone."

"What of Miss Garth?" I asked.

"Miss Garth may be free to visit her father, or attend lectures, or do whatever she pleases. I'm not sure how long we'll be gone, but I have every confidence in you, Miss Megan. I know you won't let the boy run away again and I'll feel better if he is in your . . . in your gentle hands." He smiled, and I saw there could be humor in the curve of his lips after all.

For the space of a moment I regretted the fact that he did not find me altogether gentle. But what he thought did not matter, so long as he left Jeremy in my care. This was the step I wanted, and I felt elated at the new trust placed in me.

In spite of myself, during the course of this interview certain of my views about Brandon Reid were being softened and revised. Because I wanted to show that my rancor was gone, I spoke to him pleasantly, assuring him that I would do my best for Jeremy. Then, thinking little of it, I mentioned the church I had visited that morning—though I did not mention seeing Leslie there.

"The minister said wonderful things about your brother,"

128

told him. "He spoke glowingly of the Dwight Reid Memorial Home and its opening in January."

My employer stiffened, and I recalled too late what Mrs. Reid had said about her husband's opposition to the Home, and her claim that Brandon had been envious of his brother. Now I saw his eyes return to his father's portrait with an almost passionate pride. Pride in what? Did he really oppose the opening of the memorial? And why?

He turned back to me without comment, his manner indicating clearly that our interview had come to an end. I was not expected to sit here chatting in a sociable manner. I rose at once and took my departure with far less indignation than had ridden me when I came in.

Not until I was out of his company did I realize how thoroughly the wind had been taken from my sails. I had not retreated from any stand I had made, yet I had the feeling that I no longer blamed or condemned him as I had when I entered the room. How this change had been brought about, I was not altogether sure. Nor was I entirely sure that it pleased me. I did not want to be won over against my better judgment. On the other hand, what *was* my better judgment? It was so difficult to know.

11.

THE FOLLOWING day, on the very heels of the snowstorm, New York was enveloped in an unusually early freeze. Before the snow had time to melt, the temperature plummeted and a sharper foretaste of winter was upon us. A jingling of sleigh bells could be heard along the Avenue, and the panes of every window were etched in patterns of frost.

The sub-freezing weather held for several days, and on the afternoon before Brandon Reid was to take his wife upriver to visit her mother he paid an unexpected call upon us in the nursery.

I had scarcely seen him since our interview in the library, but evidence of his plan to put Jeremy into my hands had been made clear. Miss Garth was sulking and casting dark looks in my direction. She was crosser than ever with Jeremy, yet, until the signal was given to put me in full charge, I did not want to stir her to further opposition by the objections I longed to express.

While I bided my time, I planned the history lessons we would do together, Jeremy and I. Andrew, I'd found, was good enough when it came to American history, but he had little interest or knowledge in the ancient world. So I intended to open to Jeremy's bright mind more of the subject of Egyptian civilization and what it entailed for the world of that day. So far his state of apathy had not lessened and he would sit for hours huddled over the pages of a book he did not read—just as he had done when I first came to the house.

That afternoon when his uncle strode into the nursery, the boy was lost in his own troubled thoughts and did not look up. The rest of us—Garth, Selina, and I—stared in surprise, for I had never seen him set foot in the nursery before.

He left the door open so that drafts from the hall cut through the warm stuffiness and Miss Garth shivered pointedly, edging a shade closer to a fire that must nearly scorch her as it was.

"Good Lord, how can you breathe in a place like this?" he demanded. I half expected him to stride to a window and fling it open and I would have welcomed a cold blast of fresh air.

Jeremy glanced at him briefly and then stared at his book again, his face expressionless.

"This is a day to be outdoors," Mr. Reid said, his eyes on the boy. "How would you like to go skating in Central Park, Jeremy?"

Selina squealed at the suggestion and demanded to go too, but Jeremy did not look up or answer. I sat in silence, waiting uncertainly for whatever was to come.

"What of the ice?" Miss Garth asked, ready as always to oppose any plan that was not her own. "There has scarcely been time for it to freeze, Mr. Reid."

"I've checked, of course," Brandon Reid said impatiently. "The flags are showing on streetcars running uptown—white flags with a red ball. Which means the red ball is up on the Arsenal and the ice is firm. Get the children into their warm wraps, Miss Garth. We'll leave as soon as they're ready."

I believe the governess would have liked to refuse, but the master of the house was in no mood to brook opposition. He had made this sudden plan and he would do as he chose. When I glanced again at Jeremy, I was ready to bless his uncle. A faint stirring of interest had come into the boy's eyes, and he had pushed the unread book away. When Brandon pointed a finger at him and said, "Hurry up, boy!" Jeremy followed Selina and Miss Garth willingly from the room.

Once they had gone, Brandon Reid stared at me with a light of challenge in his eyes.

"I shall need you to help me with the children, Miss Megan. Garth is too old for skating, if she ever learned. You are able to skate, I presume?"

I felt a sudden eagerness in me, though I tried to answer sedately. "I learned to skate when I was very young, sir."

"Then into your things at once," he ordered. "You've been looking pale lately. We'll get you out in the cold and whip some color into your cheeks."

"This will be good for Jeremy," I said. But though I ignored the reference to my own appearance, as I left my chair I felt suddenly as young as Selina and as eager for exciting action. If any warning voice whispered in my mind, I shut it away and hurried to get ready.

I still had the skates I had used as a girl and I had sturdy high shoes to fasten them to. I put on my warmest dress and wrap, tied my bonnet ribbons firmly, and wrapped a green muffler about my neck. Then I went downstairs to find the others waiting.

They were prepared for the cold, with Brandon Reid wearing a turtle-necked jersey under his tweed hunting jacket and a red stocking cap on his head. Jeremy's cap was blue and white stripes, with a long tassel down the back. Selina looked like a miniature of her mother, with her hands clasped in a small sealskin muff.

Miss Garth waited downstairs with the children, and I saw that her mouth was set in tight disapproval. When Mr. Reid

133

went out the front door to see if the carriage was ready, the children hurried in his wake, Selina calling to me to come along. Before I could obey, there was a moment in which Miss Garth and I were alone. The governess raised the heavy lids of her eyes and looked at me without evasion.

I will never forget the sense of shock I experienced as she turned her dark gaze upon me. Her look was one of pure malevolence. I had seen her angry and disapproving and resentful before. But I had seen nothing like this. Thora Garth did not merely dislike me. She hated me and I knew in that moment that if the opportunity ever came she would do me harm. Yet no word was spoken between us. She simply stared at me with that ill-intentioned gaze. Then she turned and went upstairs.

I ran down the steps to join the others in the carriage, shaken more than I wanted to admit. Quite suddenly I did not like the prospect of being left alone in that house with only the children and Thora Garth for company.

This time as we drove away, I did not glance up to see if Leslie watched us from her window. If she did, I did not want to know. I was disturbed enough and I desired only to shed the spell of threatening evil Miss Garth had seemed to promise me.

Overhead that day the sky was the color of wet ashes, but the air was clear and cold. The first horsecar we passed on Fifth Avenue displayed the skating flag, and our anticipation quickened. Gradually, with the house behind us and Brandon Reid's electric mood growing contagious, I began to throw off my somber misgivings and regain the earlier sense of excitement that had filled me over this outing.

Even Jeremy began to enjoy himself. His uncle was making up for the disaster of the matinee, and I knew I would have a happier boy to work with when the Reids left on their journey tomorrow.

134

Certainly we could not have asked for a more thoughtful escort that afternoon, nor one more amiable. On the drive uptown Jeremy's uncle entertained the children with stories of winters when he was a boy, and he drew out of me an account of one New Jersey holiday I liked to remember.

In Central Park he chose his favorite pond, and we found that a long wooden building had been erected to offer accommodation for skaters. There was a restaurant inside, counters where skates could be rented, and a room with benches all around where we could sit while putting on our skates. Two potbellied stoves offered rosy warmth to the cold-nipped fingers and toes of skaters.

While Jeremy and Selina put on their skates, Brandon Reid knelt to fasten mine to my shoes. His touch was surprisingly gentle, and I sensed in him an eagerness to please me that I would never have expected him to show. It seemed likely that speaking my mind the other day had accomplished more than I had hoped for. We were dealing today with a man almost boyishly intent on giving us pleasure.

The ice had been newly opened for skating, and its gleaming surface spread smooth and cloud-white from shore to shore. The four of us teetered down a plank walk that led to the pond, and in the beginning we set off with Mr. Reid skating hand-in-hand with Selina, and Jeremy with me. But Selina's efforts required a slow patience that Brandon lacked and before long we had changed partners. Jeremy, who had been taught to skate by his father and had considerable skill, seemed willing to take Selina in hand and set his speed to her capability. Before I knew it Brandon Reid had drawn me away from the shelter where the crowd was thick and we were striking out for the far curve of the pond, our hands crossed, our glides well matched so that we moved smoothly as one.

For this little while I was content. I looked neither backward nor forward, but gave myself into his sure hands and let him guide me as he would. For this one afternoon I would exist in a world of snow and ice, suspended away from all the problems of my life. Or so I foolishly thought.

There was a change in Brandon Reid that I did not attempt to weigh too closely. I knew only that he was not the mocking, impatient man who had taken us to the matinee as a joke. It was as if he too had shed the smothering atmosphere of candlelight and violets that pervaded the house and had become at once a more natural and a kinder person.

When we reached the far curve of the pond, I could have wished for an endless horizon that would never require us to turn back. Though that wasn't possible, I held to my dreaming state, my hands secure in his as we rounded the curve and started toward the place where we had left Jeremy and Selina. Before we had skated far, he slowed our glides and drew me toward the bank. I sensed that he too was reluctant to return and that to Brandon Reid, as well as to me, these moments were ones of blessed escape.

"Here's a place where we can stop and catch our breath," he said.

Up the nearby bank a few skaters had gathered about a chestnut vendor. His cart—a converted baby carriage—had a basket of burning charcoal for a stove set into one end. There was warmth and good cheer around the cart and the delicious odor of roasting chestnuts. We climbed the bank, and Brandon Reid bought a sack of chestnuts that warmed our hands as we shelled and ate them. The group around the vendor changed constantly and paid little attention to us. Standing somewhat apart from the others, our skates balancing us in deep snow, we felt as if we were quite alone.

As I watched the skaters on the pond below, gliding past in the thickening gray light, I became aware that my companion was not watching the crowd or the chestnut vendor. His attention was upon me, and there was no unkindness, no

136

criticism in his look. I had the feeling that in some strange way we had become friends this afternoon, as we had not been before. A curious thought for a woman in my position, yet it was there and it was true.

"Don't think I'm unaware of all you're doing for us, Megan," he said quietly. "You've brought something into that house that is making itself felt. We've had little of kindness for one another, and I'm sure Jeremy has suffered for it. Perhaps this day of skating will get you off to a better start with him. Has he forgiven me, do you think?"

"Oh, yes," I told him quickly. "He would forgive you almost anything. It was good of you to think of an outing. Good for both children."

"And for you, Megan? Good for you—as it has been for me?"

He held my eyes with his own, and yet I could not read his full meaning. Or perhaps I did not want to. I looked away, suddenly perturbed. He thrust the sack of chestnuts into his pocket and took my mittened hands in his. In spite of the sharp, cold wind that blew upon us, I felt the warmth of his hands through wool and longed to let my own hands clasp his as warmly. Some strange chemistry stirred between us, and in the very instant of awareness I knew that we must not be drawn toward ice that cracked treacherously at our very feet. To linger meant danger.

I stepped back quickly and nearly lost my balance. My companion laughed and steadied me. The moment was past, and I did not know whether I felt relief or regret.

"We'd better return," he said, and we went down the steep bank together and started toward the far end of the pond and the shelter. Our steps matched less perfectly now, and I knew my glides were often ragged. When we rejoined the children, we found that Selina was growing cold and ready to start home, though I think Jeremy could have skated till dark.

In the carriage Brandon gave them the bag of chestnuts

and they occupied themselves with shelling and munching on the long drive downtown from the park. It had begun to snow again, and once I saw Brandon glance up at the filmed sky with a look so unhappy that it stabbed me to a pity I had never expected to feel toward Brandon Reid.

12.

THE NEXT morning I wakened to the realization that this was the day when I must meet my new responsibilities.

I tried to put from my mind the insistent memory of that moment near the chestnut vendor when Brandon Reid had held my hands and I'd heard the first faint cracking of the ice. I tried to dismiss the look Miss Garth had given me as something I must have exaggerated. Detest me, the woman might, but there was nothing she could do to injure me and I must not let such imaginings possess me. Malevolence was far too strong a word.

Mr. and Mrs. Reid left early that morning, with Selina sitting between them in the carriage. They would drive to the pier to take passage on one of the river boats that ran between New York and Albany. Miss Garth, having been informed that all control of Jeremy was to be relinquished to me for these few days, slept late and arose sullen. But there was nothing so alarming as malevolence in her. She was pleased, she told me tartly, to have Jeremy off her hands, and she wished me well with him in a tone which implied her true wish that everything possible would go wrong.

Jeremy was up and restored again, and I began to devise

ways in which to keep him busy. There were, of course, the lessons with Andrew in the morning, and I sat through them, not sewing, but taking part in the discussions, and often working out the wrong answers to arithmetic problems, much to Jeremy's superior amusement. Andrew took his cue from me, and we were more frivolous than usual about lessons. I believe we all enjoyed the change and that it was good for Jeremy, even though studies did not progress as well as they might.

Miss Garth did not appear at lunchtime—Kate said she was having a cup of tea in her room—so the meal went well. By the time Andrew left the house, Jeremy was cheerfully ready to interest himself once more in the gift he planned to make for his uncle. I had never asked him what it was, but now he told me about it voluntarily.

When we were again in the schoolroom, which for all its bareness, I preferred to the stuffy nursery, he brought me the book I had purchased on Egypt and showed me the picture of a statue. The figure wore a wide, flat collar of the type so often seen in Egyptian paintings and sculpture.

"I'm making a collar for the Osiris head," he told me, his eyes ashine with pride. "I'll need more of those steel beads you gave me, and I'd like some other beads of the same shape and size. Perhaps in green, and a few red ones too. Mr. Beach brought me the wire, and it's just right for making the collar stiff."

He showed me the plan he had drawn with colored crayons on paper and the work he had painstakingly commenced. The design was attractive, and its execution revealed the boy's creative gift. I was happy to give him my unstinting approval and promise him the beads.

This seemed a good time to urge upon him an interest in making gifts for his mother and Selina as well, but this suggestion left him indifferent.

"Selina likes silly things," he said. "And my mother has

140

everything she wants. When she wishes something new, she buys it. So there's no use trying to give her anything."

I sensed that his resistance was due to more than the difficulties he named and I insisted quietly that some sort of gift for his mother must be thought of. I made various suggestions, but he shrugged them all aside.

Later, when we were engaged in a game of chess, with Jeremy beating me badly, he made one of his unexpected capitulations.

"All right—I'll make a gift for my mother if I can think of something," he offered.

I suspected that his change of mind was due to a desire to please me and I took pains to show my approval. Any positive steps he might make were in the right direction.

"Perhaps if I went to her room and looked around," he suggested, "I would get an idea of what to make. Will you come with me, Miss Megan?"

The notion did not appeal to me, but he had already slipped from his place at the table.

"Do come along," he said, sounding as impatient as his uncle.

The important thing was to encourage him in any sort of generous gesture toward his mother, I told myself. There could be little harm if he looked about her room for inspiration. I would not enter, but would stand in the doorway and watch to see that he touched nothing, performed no mischief.

We went downstairs together, and Jeremy led the way first into his mother's small boudoir. The heavy green velvet draperies that hid the door to her bedroom were drawn across the opening, and before we could approach them, a sound reached us from the room beyond. I realized with a start that someone was moving about in Leslie's room.

Jeremy put a finger to his lips. "Hush," he warned. "I know who it is. She does this sometimes when my mother is away. Come and look."

Before I could stop him, he went to the doorway and parted the velvet curtains to a narrow slit. Puzzled, I stood behind him and looked through upon an astonishing scene.

Miss Garth had her back to us and she was dressed in one of Leslie Reid's beautiful gowns. It was a green satin that went dramatically with Leslie's red hair, and it was too tight for Miss Garth to hook all the way up. The flesh of her upper back showed pinched above the hooking, and, as she moved before us, I caught the scent of the violet spray she had used lavishly upon her person.

For a moment I stood shocked and frozen, watching her in something like horror, unable to draw myself away from the sight. As I stared, she picked up the full pleated skirt of the underdrape, turning and dipping before the long mirror until her heavy dark hair, loosened from its puffs, trembled on the verge of dishevelment. She gave her head a quick toss that sent the tortoise-shell pins flying, and her hair came down in thick profusion about her face and shoulders.

I did not like the glow in her eyes or the smile on her lips as she watched her own image. But when I put a hand on Jeremy's arm to draw him away, I could feel his resistance. I did not want to betray our presence by a struggle, and, as I hesitated, the woman in the green gown swooped toward the bed table and picked something up in her hands. As she turned toward the lamp that burned on Mrs. Reid's dressing table, I saw that she held the double miniature Leslie had shown me on my first visit to this room.

Miss Garth's back was still toward us, and I could not at first see her face, though I knew she was studying the twin portraits—or one of them. Slowly she turned with the framed miniatures in her hand, and now I could catch her expression. It was the warm, glowing look of a woman in love, and my sense of shock and horror increased. This time I bent warningly to Jeremy and put pressure behind my grip on his shoulder. Somehow I managed to get him quietly away, and we did not speak until we had returned upstairs.

The thought came to me that in Jeremy's hands, if he were indiscreet, lay a frightening power to wound and humiliate Thora Garth. For all my distress at what I had seen, an uneasy pity toward the woman moved me. She had gone too far along the road of daydreaming, and sure disaster lay in the course she followed.

Back in the schoolroom Jeremy returned calmly to the chess game and began to study the board as though nothing untoward had occurred. A lecture on the evils of spying would have little effect, I knew, but at least I must express an attitude.

"I don't think it's fair to watch anyone who doesn't know she is being watched," I told him gently.

Jeremy shrugged and began a triumphant move across the board with his red queen. "Garth is crazy," he said. "Crazy as a witch."

I pushed a black bishop absently into a castle's path, unable to concentrate.

"She certainly isn't crazy," I insisted. "You must never say such a thing about anyone."

"Why not?" His dark eyes met mine almost insolently. "It's what they say about me. But Garth is a lot crazier than I am."

I leaned toward him across the board. "Listen to me, Jeremy. Miss Garth must be a very lonely woman. Especially now when your mother and Selina are away. I expect she feels at home with your mother's things because she took care of her when she was a young girl. Since children like to dress up in older people's clothes, why shouldn't older people enjoy dressing up like someone younger?"

"You don't know what she's like," Jeremy said carelessly, unconvinced by my feeble logic. His main attention was still for the game. Deliberately he moved his queen and said,

"Checkmate," ending the contest. "You're too easy to beat, Miss Megan," he added.

I sensed that further argument would not reach him just now and cast around in my mind for something cheerful to do with the rest of the afternoon. It was then an inspiration came to me.

"Let's have a tea party in my room, Jeremy. I can heat water on the hearth in my little kettle, and I've some biscuits I've been saving for a special occasion. I've even a new rocking chair to show you—and my new lamp. Come and keep me company."

He seemed to like the idea, perhaps because I had never before invited him into my room. He helped me with the fire, and we soon had smoke and flames writhing up the chimney. In a little while there would be bright warmth. I lighted the lamp I had recently purchased. A plump china globe sprigged with pink rosebuds circled the chimney and added a touch of cheer to the small plain room. I spread a cloth of Irish linen over the table and set Jeremy to work putting out the blue Lowestoft tea set. When I opened the tin of Huntley and Palmer biscuits, Jeremy took pleasure in arranging small pink and white frosted cakes on a blue plate.

While we made our preparations, I told him of the morning I had gone to church and of the fine things the minister had said about Dwight Reid. Everyone else avoided any mention of his father's name to Jeremy, and I felt this to be unwise. It could only add to the burden of unspoken guilt the boy carried. He listened somewhat warily to my account and I sensed his inner bracing.

"Miss Megan," he said when I finished, "if there's an opening ceremony for the Home, do you think Uncle Brandon would permit me to go?"

"I don't see why you shouldn't go," I told him recklessly, since I had no knowledge of how his uncle might react to this

144

suggestion. "Anyway, it's a month or more away, so we needn't worry about it now."

Absently, he put the cover back on the oblong biscuit tin. "I *must* go," he said, and I wondered what expiation such an act might signify to the boy.

We did not mention the matter again that day, however. To distract him, I went to the mantel where Richard's carrousel sat and while the water heated in a kettle hung over coals, I wound the toy and set the tiny horses and sleigh to whirling as the music box played. Jeremy's eyes brightened as he watched and I sang the old nursery tune for him in French.

> *"Frère Jacques,*
> *Frère Jacques,*
> *Dormez-vous?*
> *Dormez-vous?*
> *Sonnez les matines,*
> *Sonnez les matines,*
> *Ding! Dang! Dong!*
> *Ding! Dang! Dong!"*

He was clearly fascinated, but when I would have taken the toy from the mantel to let him see it more closely, he put his hands behind his back, remembering what I had forgotten.

"I'm still being pun—that is, I'm still paying a penalty, Miss Megan," he said. "I mustn't touch it."

I set it back on the mantel and wound it again, deciding then and there that this toy would be my Christmas gift to Jeremy.

When the kettle had bubbled and the tea was steeped, we enjoyed our little party to the full. Jeremy looked so contented that I wished his mother and uncle had been there to see him. There was nothing wrong with this child that new interests, patience, and a little loving kindness would not cure.

When our cups were empty and a sufficient number of biscuits had been consumed, I told him something about Richard, who had owned the carrousel, and there was an easing in my own heart for the telling. Finally I drew out a book of fairy tales that had belonged to me when I was little, and from which I used to read to Richard. Jeremy seemed delighted at the prospect of being read to, and I realized with a pang that he knew nothing of the companionable experience of reading aloud. He took a cushion from a chair and sat upon it cross-legged before the fire, studying the flames as all children love to do, while I began the story.

I had found a favorite of Richard's, though I was not quite sure how Jeremy would receive it. He did not look at me as I read, but there was a rapt expression in his eyes and a faint smile curled his lips.

The tale was the one of the ugly little toad whom no one could love until the kindness of a beautiful maiden freed him from enchantment and he became again a handsome, shining prince. Jeremy made not a sound until the last word was done and silence lay upon the room. Then he turned toward me and I saw a mist in his eyes.

"Even while he was a toad," Jeremy said, lost in wonder, "he found someone to love him. Someone who didn't mind how ugly and warty he was."

It cost me an effort to speak in the matter-of-fact manner I knew I must adopt. I wanted to kneel on the hearth beside him and put my arms about him, but the gesture must not come too soon or it would be suspect and thus rejected.

"I think that was quite natural," I told him. "The girl in the story was kind and she could see past the toad disguise to the fine prince he really was inside."

Jeremy nodded. "But first there had to be something fine

146

for her to see. What if there hadn't been anything at all? What if he were wicked clear through?"

The lump in my throat was unbearable, and while I sought words to reassure and comfort him, a sharp rapping sounded on the door.

I went to open it and found Miss Garth on the threshold. She was dressed once more in her brown merino, though the breath of violets still clung to her person. Color rode high in her cheeks, and she was furiously angry.

13.

THE WARMTH and gentle happiness of the little room was gone in an instant. The moment I opened the door Miss Garth saw the boy and she pushed past me, entering without a by-your-leave.

"What did you do with them?" she cried, pouncing on him. "Where did you hide them?"

Jeremy went white and sullen beneath the angry pressure of her hand upon his shoulder. He stared at her with contempt rising in his eyes and said nothing at all.

"What is it?" I asked. "What is it you think he has taken? Surely you can ask him more kindly!"

My earlier sympathy for the woman had vanished, and I was ready to oppose her for the boy's sake.

"He knows very well," Miss Garth snapped. "He has taken the gold scissors and thimble that were my mother's. He has played with them before and now he has stolen them from the sewing basket in my room. What have you done with them, you wicked boy?"

He shrugged her hand aside and rose to his full height before her, clearly unafraid of the anger that burned in the woman.

"Why do you try to pretend that you're my mother?" he

asked coolly. "Why do you dress up in her clothes and make believe that you're young and pretty when you're really so very old and ugly?"

Every vestige of color went out of Miss Garth's face. While I stood helpless and alarmed, she gasped as if she could not draw her breath without pain. Then she reached out and caught Jeremy by the arm with fingers turned as vicious as claws. He lacked the strength to resist her, and she pulled him with her out of my room and to his own, next door.

I followed them, my anxiety rising. I had no intention of abandoning Jeremy, but the woman was in so demented a state that coping with her would be difficult.

In his own room she flung the boy from her. "Are you going to tell me what you've done with my things?" she demanded. "Or must I search your room for myself?"

He recovered his balance and would have hurled himself upon her if I had not put my arms about him, holding him back. "Wait," I whispered. "Let her be, Jeremy. You shouldn't have said what you did."

For a moment he struggled, then went limp in my arms. Together we watched as she moved about the room, pulling open drawers, looking into boxes. When she reached the bed she lifted the pillow and pointed dramatically. There beneath it lay the gold scissors and thimble. She snatched them up and held them out accusingly to Jeremy.

"So now you are a thief as well!" she cried. "Don't expect to escape without punishment this time. Your uncle shall hear of this when he returns. A thrashing is what you have coming to you, and a thrashing you will get!"

"My uncle will not thrash me," the boy said tensely. "He wouldn't dare. Nor will you."

Her eyes, glazed by rage, searched the room as if to find some means of punishing him. Her eyes fell upon the collar Jeremy was making for his uncle's Christmas gift, with loose beads and wire strewn around it. With a spiteful, slashing

150

gesture, she dashed the collar from the table, scattering beads over the carpet.

"Trash!" she cried. "Worthless trash!"

Jeremy escaped my arms and flung himself to his knees where he could pick up the collar. Over the shimmering circlet he stared up at Miss Garth.

"When I find the gun," he said in a low, deadly voice, "I will kill you too."

The woman looked at him, and the crazed fury went out of her, replaced by sudden fear.

"I'll not stay in this house tonight!" she gasped. With the scissors and thimble clutched in one hand, she fled from the room without looking back, and I knew she was truly frightened.

Silently I knelt beside Jeremy, helping him pick up the scattered beads. They were small, and the loose ones had scattered widely. I held to my silence until his harried breathing quieted and some of the trembling went out of him.

"I think the collar hasn't been damaged," I said. "And we've found most of the beads. I'll get you more tomorrow."

He emptied his own handful into the empty candy box that served to hold them and did not answer me at all.

While Miss Garth had behaved in an outrageous fashion, the boy was at fault too, and I could not let his threatening words pass without comment.

"Why did you borrow her things?" I asked softly.

He gave me a troubled look from wide, dark eyes. "I don't know," he said. "Do you think it's because I am what they say I am—mad?"

I couldn't endure his white, solemn expression and I made a move to put my arms about him. He stepped back at once, rejecting the gesture.

"Of course you're not mad," I went on as reasonably as possible. "All of us do foolish things we're sorry for afterwards. The next time you feel like doing something you know is wrong come and tell me first. If we talk it over together, perhaps you won't want to do it after all."

"How can I tell you when I'm going to do something like that when I don't know ahead of time myself? How can I not say dreadful things when I don't know I'm going to say them? Like what I said about killing her."

"You didn't mean that threat," I assured him. "She upset you, and you wanted to pay her back. Though paying people back doesn't serve us very well most of the time."

He looked straight at me, his eyes cloudy with emotion. "Once I made a threat like that and I meant it," he said.

So unsettled was the look in his eyes that I shivered involuntarily. At once he noticed this evidence of weakness.

"You're afraid of me, aren't you?" he said, dark triumph in his voice. "You're afraid of me too!"

I suppressed the shiver and shook my head firmly. "Of course I'm not afraid of you, Jeremy. I'm never afraid of someone I trust."

For a moment longer he stared at me; then his thoughts seemed to turn inward and his stare lost its focus. I knew he was slipping away and out of my reach, yet I could not bring him back.

We had supper alone in the downstairs dining room that night, for, true to her word, Miss Garth had left the house. We dined in loneliness at one end of the long table, and it was a somber meal, with no conversation between us. Jeremy scarcely ate, and I did not urge him. I had little taste for food myself, and it was a relief to leave the big room and the watchful eyes of Henry and return upstairs.

How empty the house seemed that night. Not only because Jeremy and I were alone in the upper story, but also because Brandon Reid was away. The vigor of his presence always filled the house and gave it life. When he was not indoors, the house seemed to wait for his coming. When he was home, the noises of everyday living were present and a voice that spoke

152

out with no fear of raising the echoes. When he was away altogether, the house whispered and creaked and murmured, but it did not speak aloud reassuringly.

That evening was long to get through. Jeremy retreated behind the book on Egyptian archaeology, yet he turned the pages so seldom that I sensed how active his mind must be beneath the pretense of reading. There was no way to draw him out, no reassurance I could offer. I sewed on a frock for Selina until my eyes wearied and then I too sat in silence, staring at the plaid wool in my lap.

When bedtime came, Jeremy startled me. He put his book aside and stood beside my chair.

"Miss Megan," he said, "will you please lock me in my room tonight?"

I considered the suggestion soberly and felt the quick beating of my heart beneath my calm reception. It seemed a dreadful thing he suggested. Why should he need forcible restraint when Garth, with whom he was angry, was not in the house tonight? Or did he fear a return to his father's room and a repetition of the wild hysteria of sobbing he had indulged in once before? I knew he still had the key to the room, for I'd seen it in a box on his bureau, though he had not used it again.

Quickly I sought for a counter suggestion. "I've a better plan than that," I told him. "Come and help me and I'll show you."

He followed me doubtfully into his own room and watched while I stripped his bed.

"Now then," I said when the covers were off, "you can help me with the mattress. It's too heavy for me to manage alone."

"What are you going to do with it?" he asked.

"Help me and you'll see," I said with as lighthearted a smile as I could manage.

He took one end of the mattress, and I led the way, backing, as we carried it into my room. With a little rearranging of the furniture, we were able to spread it out on the floor near my bed.

"There!" I said. "This is where you may sleep tonight. We'll keep each other company, since there's no one else upstairs in the house."

He did not answer or come with me when I ran back for the bedclothes, but stayed where he was, staring at the mattress.

"You won't mind sleeping on the floor, will you?" I asked. "It will be like something from a story—like camping out. We'll put an extra quilt over you to keep away the drafts, and you'll be cozy warm."

I glanced at him and saw that he was watching me in a queer, tense way.

"What if I try to hurt you in the night?" he said.

I was on my knees beside the bedding and I could look into his eyes more nearly at his own level. I took his hands and held them lightly in my own. Somehow I even managed what sounded like a laugh.

"Jeremy, you are only a little boy. I'm much stronger and bigger than you are. I won't let you hurt me, and I won't let you hurt yourself. There now—that's a promise!"

For once I had found the right words. The heavy load of anxiety seemed to slip away from him. He gave me a smile that was strangely sweet, and I knew that for the moment he had given me his complete trust. Again I held back an impulse to catch him to me and let him know the feeling of arms that loved and protected. But I could go so far and no farther until he was ready to come to me.

Though Jeremy slept quickly, I could not fall asleep at once. I lay listening to his light, even breathing and thought about the incidents of the last few days. Of Brandon Reid and his apology to me, his change of attitude. Of yesterday, when we had skated in Central Park and everything between us had been strange and different. Beguilingly, dangerously different. My hands knew again the pressure of his, warm

154

despite the cold, and I grew warm again remembering. Such thoughts frightened me because of my very willingness to indulge them. I pulled my imaginings up short and chose another course.

With Mr. Reid on my side, wonders might now be achieved with Jeremy. If only we could weather such setbacks as occurred, real progress might be possible. Miss Garth, of course, should be kept away from the boy. He must be left wholly to Andrew and me.

When my thoughts turned to Thora Garth, it was with sick distaste. Yet I could not entirely condemn her. If Jeremy was caught in a web of circumstances he could not overcome, she too was similarly trapped. Behind all that was unpleasant hid a woman whom life had cheated. Or was it possible for life to cheat us? Did we not do the cheating ourselves when we could not meet with wisdom and courage and joy what befell us? Had Thora Garth allowed herself to indulge too long a fantasy that would now destroy her? Which of those two miniature portraits had attracted the fervent expression I had seen on her face? To what extent did her dressing up in Leslie Reid's gowns mean an identification with Leslie so that she might share vicariously experiences her mistress had known?

These thoughts were not conducive to sleep, and again I tried to change their course. It was of Andrew I must think. He was the one person in this house I could count on, whether I always agreed with him or not. At least he spoke the truth as he saw it, even though his words might sometimes sting and bite. He was fooled by no one. He could find good in a pickpocket and be disdainful of those in high position. There was a sharpness to his view that cut through to the secret self a man might hide beneath pretenses. Or a woman.

I knew he disliked Brandon intensely. I knew he pitied Leslie. Garth he simply detested and tormented. Yet I suspected that he would understand very well if I told him what Jeremy and I had seen today.

Thinking about Andrew did not, after all, help me to fall asleep. I knew Andrew would have been horrified by the fact that Jeremy lay asleep on the floor beside me. I would be in for a lecture tomorrow if I told him. Yet nothing anyone could say would stop me in my course. Some of the love I had given my brother was turning toward young Jeremy. It was there within me to be given, and I must have something human to turn it upon.

So I lay and watched the red coals turn black in the grate and heard the sifting of ashes. I watched the bright glow of the snowy night at my window and listened to Jeremy's breathing as he slept.

It must have been long past midnight when I too slept, dreamed, wakened fitfully, and then slept again. When a clock somewhere in the house struck three I came wide awake, listening for more than a striking clock. I could no longer hear the rhythm of Jeremy's sleep and I turned quietly in the bed so that I could look out upon the cold, still room. Between me and the window something moved, and my breath caught in my throat. The boy was up, silhouetted dark against the snowy light beyond. Softly, almost stealthily, he was moving toward my bed. A thrill of unreasoning terror left me weak and breathless. Fear that this was not the harmless child I had claimed. This was a boy who was given to violent angers and who had once deliberately killed.

"Jeremy?" I managed his name between stiff lips.

The relief in his own voice was very great. "Oh, you're awake? I'm sorry if I wakened you. I was so cold—I couldn't sleep."

I flung back my quilts and carried one of them to his pallet. "Lie down quickly and let me put an extra cover over you. You'll be warm soon. There's nothing to fear."

My voice soothed him, and he slipped beneath the covers, snuggling down into warmth with the sigh of a very young child. I knelt beside him, holding his hand until his shivering

156

ceased, and I sang once more the music box song in French. Drowsily he began to repeat the words and fell asleep murmuring, *"Dormez-vous?"*

There was only peace in this room, the snow gently falling beyond my window, and no fear anywhere in the Reid household.

14.

THE FOLLOWING days were blissfully uneventful. Miss Garth stayed away, and there was no word from up-river. Jeremy went back to sleeping in his own room, again willing to be nine years old and scornful of babyish ways. I did not, after all, tell Andrew of the things that had happened on that very disturbing night.

Lessons progressed well during Selina's absence, and Jeremy seemed to work with a will that surprised Andrew. Once or twice I found the tutor looking at me in a speculative manner as though he were almost ready to give ground a little when it came to Jeremy.

After Andrew had gone, the afternoon hours belonged to us, and Jeremy and I started our studies of ancient Egypt. The boy's mind was eager and intelligent, often ready to leap ahead and leave me, who posed as a teacher, far behind. At least I could open the door for him and that was worth doing. Sometimes we forgot about books and walked in the square or explored the nearby Village, but I saw to it that the boy had time for his private concerns as well. I knew he was working once more on the gift for his uncle.

Something occurred during this period that encouraged me more than anything else. One afternoon Jeremy came to me in the schoolroom where I was reading and dropped something into my lap. I put my book down and saw that it was the green silk I had made for his sister. He spoke to me almost fiercely.

"I felt like cutting it up! See, I put the scissors in my pocket and went into Selina's room to get the dress and cut it up."

"But you didn't," I said.

He shook his head violently. "No! I remembered what you said about coming to tell you when I felt like doing something wrong. So I brought it to you instead. And here are the scissors too."

"That's fine," I assured him. "Now we can talk about what made you want to hurt Selina. You're fond of your sister. You wouldn't truly want to injure her, would you?"

"They took her with them when they went upriver," he said. "I like my grandmother and she likes me. But they left me at home."

I nodded my understanding of his feelings. "It's true they took Selina with them, but that isn't her fault. Besides, you enjoy being with me, don't you?"

"Uncle Brandon never wants me around," he said, putting his finger on the true source of his brooding.

There was nothing I could do about the actions of Brandon Reid. Indeed, I tried to think about Jeremy's uncle as little as possible. I had discovered in myself a tendency to daydream, to recall too often the day we had gone skating, and this I distrusted in myself.

"I want you here," I told the boy. "I'd have been terribly lonely if you had gone away with the others."

When I returned Selina's dress to him with complete trust, he took it proudly to her room, having vanquished temptation. I was pleased with him and told him so.

Once or twice the subject of the Dwight Reid Memorial Home came up. During lessons one morning Jeremy asked whether the date of its opening had been set, and Andrew knew more about the matter than I. There was some dispute,

160

he said, about the setting of the exact date, due to the continued opposition of Brandon Reid. At once Jeremy wanted to know why his uncle did not like the idea of a Home that would take care of some of New York's homeless children. Andrew told him curtly to work at his lessons and leave grown-up affairs to others. I sensed that the tutor was holding something back, and I wanted to know more about the matter.

When Kate served Jeremy's ten-o'clock chocolate and biscuits in the nursery and the boy left us for his recess, I brought the subject up again.

"Is there something wrong about this memorial for Jeremy's father?" I asked. "I keep hearing about Mr. Reid's opposition and the obstacles he seems to be putting in the path of the opening. What does it mean?"

Andrew shrugged. "Preserve me from a curious woman, Megan. Why should I know any more about it than you do?"

"I think you do know more," I countered, and did not deny his accusation of being curious.

"If you want me to guess," he said, "it could be that he's afraid of further publicity. Afraid of having the papers rehash the old scandal. The slightest mention in the papers has a tendency to make Master Brandon nervous. There's been cause enough in the past for him to be sensitive when it comes to the press."

"I suppose there's always the risk of involving Jeremy again," I agreed. "We can't blame him for wanting to avoid that."

Andrew left his books and went to the blackboard, where he stood tossing a piece of chalk in a familiar gesture. I had a feeling that he was concerned about something more, something I did not understand. When he turned to me again he had his impatience in hand and spoke to me more kindly.

"Like your friend Miss Garth, I've taken to feeling trouble in my bones," he said. "In fact, it's probably Garth's muttering that has started me off. She seldom opposes Mrs. Reid in anything, but she's as dead set against this memorial as Reid is himself. She and I have both been smelling disaster in the wind. And when it comes, Megan, I'd like to see you away from this house."

His words made little sense, and I remained unmoved by such unexplained warnings.

"Why aren't you trying to get away yourself?" I asked.

"I can take care of myself," he said.

There was a sudden harsh note in his voice that surprised me. He seemed deadly serious now, with no mockery in him. But if there was trouble in the offing, I had no notion from what quarter it might come. Nor had I any desire to flee from what I did not see or fear. Jeremy needed me. He was improving. That was all I would concern myself with at the moment. So I merely shook my head at Andrew's gloomy words.

On impulse, however, I asked another question, one that I had asked myself many times by now, though without finding an answer.

"What puzzles me most of all is how Leslie and Brandon Reid came to marry. They seem to have so little—"

He broke in without waiting for me to finish. "I should think her appeal for a man like Brandon Reid would be clear enough. Why shouldn't he have been caught by her beauty?"

"But if she still loved her first husband—then why would she marry his brother?"

"Perhaps she had her price," he said carelessly. "Or perhaps he had his. Who can tell?"

I thought his attitude callous and was sorry I had questioned him. He laughed at the look on my face with one of his sudden returns to good humor.

"What a prim expression you wear, Miss Megan! You want to hear criticism only in a direction you choose. When I suggest that the master is less than perfect, you turn your head. Is that it?"

The conversation was out of hand, and it was a relief when Jeremy returned, licking a smear of chocolate from his upper lip. I would know better, after this, than to ask Andrew Beach anything about the Reids and their affairs.

That afternoon, when Andrew had gone and we had done our lesson on Egypt, the idea came to me that before his mother and uncle returned, I ought to arrange some sort of festive occasion for Jeremy. Often I regretted his lack of friends, but there was nothing I could do about it for the time being. Miss Garth had indicated that mothers in this area did not want their sons to play with Jeremy Reid. What had happened, even though it was considered an accident, left them fearful about him as a playmate for their children. Thus he was left in the unnatural position of having no friends of his own age. I hoped the time might come when we could mend this. But for now I would have to serve as a playmate.

When we came into the downstairs hall after our walk, I made my announcement. "By the way," I said, elaborately polite, "I am giving a little dinner party this evening, Master Jeremy, and I would like the pleasure of your company. Though perhaps I shouldn't invite you formally, since you must be the host in your uncle's absence."

He looked at me in such amazement that I had to laugh in his face.

"I really mean it, Jeremy. Come along and let's see what can be managed."

We went into the dining room together, and I rang for Henry and braced myself against the butler's opposition. We would, I informed him, not daring to look straight into that haughty face, omit our early supper tonight. Instead we would dine at eight, with candlelight and the best linen and silver. And Jeremy should have the privilege of choosing the menu.

Henry surprised me. He did not so much as blink an eye.

His haughty mien did not soften, but he made me a suitable bow of acquiescence.

"Yes, miss," he said. "I will see that everything is properly prepared. May I suggest that Master Jeremy consult with Cook concerning the menu?"

I agreed that this would be wise, and we stood on no ceremony with Cook. We ran down to the basement kitchen to find out what would be possible. Jeremy wanted fried chicken with giblet gravy and mashed potatoes. And an apple pie with thick slices of yellow cheese. There was no problem with Cook, in spite of this late warning, and Kate entered with relish into the make-believe, putting herself out to help both Cook and Henry.

Perhaps the servants, more than I realized, were sympathetic toward Jeremy. They were not, of course, fond of Miss Garth, and since the governess did not approve of me, I may have had a place in their estimation I'd not otherwise have held.

I warned Jeremy that he was to wear his best suit that evening, with the round, starched collar and soft tie, and I spent as much time with my own dressing as though I had been going to a real dinner party. This was one evening when I could indulge in such pretense without fear of disapproving eyes upon me, of Brandon Reid to criticize my appearance.

In my room I took out my second good dress, a gown I had seldom worn. It was not altogether in style, but Jeremy was hardly likely to notice. The faille was a soft wisteria color, with black velvet banding for a trim. The fitted bodice was cut with a square neck, and the sleeves came just above my elbows. The tight draping over the hips was edged with accordian pleating, repeated again at the hem and in the fullness that fell away in a small train.

Selina could not have outdone me in primping that evening. Or even Miss Garth, dipping and preening before her mistress' mirror. The latter image was not one I wanted to

164

recall. I too was indulging in make-believe tonight, with only a little boy to admire me.

Since I had no fine necklace, I adapted a black velvet band to wear about my throat and pinned to it a gold brooch studded with tiny diamonds. Dangling jet earrings of my mother's matched the velvet band, and I pulled back the dark curls over my ears to reveal the fall of jet. I was both pleased with my image in the mirror and wistful at the same time. It seemed rather a waste that there would be only Jeremy to see how I looked in my finest of feathers.

I forgot such foolish thoughts, however, when I went to call him to come downstairs with me.

"This isn't our grand entrance," I said. "This time we'll just run down and check to see that everything is right. Then a little before eight you can knock at my door and escort me downstairs."

Jeremy scarcely listened, for staring at me. "You look different," he said. "You look beautiful. But I like you the other way too."

This was as fine a compliment as I had ever been paid, and I thanked him sincerely. We ran downstairs hand in hand to the dining room, to discover that Henry had put himself to the greatest of pains.

The silver gleamed, and the best crystal was in evidence, even to an array of wine glasses we were not likely to fill. Tall white candles were ready in every holder, still unlighted. Henry's one apology was for lack of a centerpiece of flowers at such short notice. Jeremy frowned over this as though we had been faced by a major crisis. Then he glanced at me shyly.

"Your brother's carrousel would make a lovely table decoration, Miss Megan. That is, if—"

"A wonderful idea!" I cried. "Run upstairs and get it, Jeremy. You may touch it tonight, since this is a special occasion."

When he had gone I tried to show Henry my gratitude for

helping in our make-believe, but he was as stiffly remote as ever.

"Thank you, miss," he said and left me alone in the room.

I would light the candles myself, I thought. Tonight candlelight would not mean Leslie Reid and the scent of violets. I lit a taper in the fireplace and had reached toward the first candle when I heard a key turn in the lock of the front door. Had Leslie and Brandon returned? Or Miss Garth, perhaps? Whoever it was, we were caught in our innocent pretense, Jeremy and I.

I blew out the taper and remained where I was, looking across the glittering table toward the open door to the hall. Steps came in the direction of the dining room, and a moment later Brandon Reid appeared in the doorway. His eyes noted the elegant table, the silver candelabra, my own dressed-up person.

"I see you are expecting guests," my employer said gravely. Then, before I could offer the slightest explanation, he turned and went away.

I stood beside the table, fingering the taper in my hands, wondering whether Leslie had come home with him, wondering what course I must now take. After all, this was a small enough pleasure I had planned for Jeremy and there was no reason to cheat him of it just because the master of the house had returned.

As I pondered a course of action, Jeremy came into the room, the carrousel held carefully in both hands, and apprehension on his face.

"Uncle Brandon is home," he whispered. "He just went into the library. Does that mean we can't have our party?"

I made up my mind. "Of course it doesn't," I said. "You stay here and arrange the centerpiece, and I'll go upstairs and speak to him."

I caught up the wisteria silk of my skirt and flew up the stairs. As yet no fire had been lighted in the library and the door stood open. Across the room Brandon Reid leaned upon a window sill, staring out over Washington Square. I tapped upon the open door, and he called to me to enter.

The room was gray with the winter light of early evening, illumined only by a dim radiance from the hall and reflection from the lighted square. Nearing him, I saw that his gaze was fixed upon the scene outside as if he saw something that held him enthralled. There was a strangeness in his face, the look of faraway vision in his eyes.

I coughed gently to make him aware of my presence so that he started and looked at me.

"Oh, it's you, Megan," he said.

"I hope your trip went well," I began.

He seemed not to hear my words. "Do you know what I was imagining out there? Not snow in Washington Square, but sun on desert sands. That blinding, burning, golden light that's like nothing else on earth." He turned his back on the window. "How I hate bleak city streets in the wintertime. At night the desert can be bitterly cold and sand can be harsher than any blizzard. But there's always the return of the sun to look for. Here winter's just started and there are endless gray days, endless dreary cold to be endured before spring comes."

Ordinarily I enjoyed cold weather, but his words made me shiver in my light dress. "How marvelous to have seen those sun-drenched places," I said softly. "I've read of Egypt so often, and I've tried to imagine—but always my vision falls short."

He smiled at me and so quickly was the chill gone from my blood that I was reminded unguardedly of the very sun of which he spoke. It was as if I uncurled a little like some dry plant touched by life-giving warmth.

He seemed to catch the echo of my earlier question about the trip. "My wife has not weathered her travel well," he said, and I noted a hint of impatience in his voice. "Indeed, my presence seemed to make her worse, so I decided to return alone. How have things gone while I was away?"

"Everything has gone well," I assured him. "Though Miss Garth disapproved of my handling of Jeremy and left the house. She hasn't returned as yet."

"Good!" he said. "I shall relish her absence. But don't let me keep you from your dinner, Megan. I saw what you intended. Pretend you haven't seen me; go on with your plans."

"It was only make-believe," I confessed. "Jeremy and I are playing host and hostess. It's just a change in the routine for this one evening. Though of course if we'd known you were returning—"

"You'd have given up your party? What an unkind opinion you have of me. I'd be happier if you were willing to invite me as a guest."

He was smiling again, yet almost hesitant in his manner. My nagging anxiety fell away, and delight surged into its place. Now our dinner would no longer be make-believe. The festive occasion was genuine, and I knew Jeremy would be as pleased as I.

"Will you really come?" I said. "And not be too angry with the liberties I've taken?"

He crossed the room to give me his arm, and the gesture was my answer. We went down the stairs together and I was aware of the fabric of his coat beneath my fingers, of the clean odor of unperfumed soap and the male scent of tobacco. Downstairs the beautiful table awaited us. Tonight I would sit there as though I belonged, and the thought went through me as dizzily as champagne.

15.

JEREMY'S FACE glowed with pleasure at sight of his uncle, and he dispatched Henry at once to set a third place. The carrousel lent a touch of gay color in its place of honor in the center of the table and, as Brandon seated me and took his own place, it caught his eye.

"What have we here?" he asked, leaning forward to examine it.

Jeremy explained. "It's a music box that belonged to Miss Megan's brother. When it's wound it plays a tune and the little horses and sleigh go round and round."

"Wind it for us, Jeremy," I directed.

He picked up the toy as though it were made of glass and turned the key carefully. The gay little carrousel whirled, and the tune tinkled lightly through the room. Brandon laughed aloud and nodded his approval of so remarkable a centerpiece.

So it was that our soup was served to the tune of "Frère Jacques" and it seemed as fine a melody to my ears as though violins had played for us.

Our guest was on his best behavior, the cold mood that had been upon him when he entered the house had faded, and he was ready to join us in our pretense for the evening.

He entertained us with stories of his travels, to Jeremy's delight and my own enjoyment. He told us of the Nile and the great temples of Egypt. He called up before us the Sphinx of Giza, that most mysterious of all Egyptian monuments, and described for us the awesome sight of that stone face, bathed in the brilliance of a desert sky. The Watcher in the Sands, they called it, he said, and made us know the terrible intensity of its gaze as small human figures approached across the vast desert.

"I always feel that the eyes are commanding me," he told us. "I go back again and again to find the meaning of that look, yet I never have an answer. Even today we don't know whether the Sphinx represents a god or an ancient king, or both. And I suppose we will never know what it is it asks of us."

"Like Osiris?" Jeremy said, and smiled a secret smile that made me know he was thinking of the surprise he had fashioned for his uncle's Christmas gift.

Brandon studied him for a moment. "No, not like Osiris. The Sphinx doesn't judge. It merely poses an unfathomable riddle. Perhaps the very riddle of life itself."

How strange an experience was that dinner—perhaps for all of us. At first I was merely happy and pleased and innocent, a little like Jeremy in my enjoyment of a party occasion. I was glad that I had dressed with care and that candlelight lay gently upon me, that the look in Brandon's eyes was flattering. I felt at ease with him, and no longer angry or resentful. No longer abashed, as I sometimes found myself in his company.

Yet how subtly my mood began to change, how inevitably my thoughts began to turn in a direction I did not want to contemplate. Perhaps it was Brandon's comment about my dress that brought everything into focus, so that what lay beneath the surface of my mind thrust itself suddenly forward.

170

"That gown you're wearing, Megan— What do you call the color?" he asked me.

Jeremy was eating like any hungry boy and he paid no attention to this talk of clothes.

"Wisteria," I said, and to my ears the word sounded unexpectedly like a sigh.

Brandon nodded. "Yes, there's blue in the lavender, quite pale and soft. The shade makes your hair seem as black as your earrings, yet it brightens the blue of your eyes as well. It becomes you, Megan."

I dropped my gaze, less sure of myself than I had been, sensing once more beneath my feet the faint cracking of ice. The fire hummed its own song of warmth and contentment beside us, the candlelight shimmered as softly on linen and silver, yet my moments of easy confidence were gone. There was a look in Brandon's eyes that told me more than the compliment he paid me, more than I dared read. There was an eagerness in me to respond, to meet his look openly and frankly with my own. But now, all too sharply, I was aware that I sat in another woman's place, that my hands moved among the silver pieces that were hers to touch, that the stemmed glass I drank from was her choice and her right to handle—not mine. But most of all I was painfully conscious of the fact that the man who faced me down the table's length was Leslie Reid's husband.

"You're a pretty thing, Megan," Brandon said. "But then —there are younger men than I to tell you that."

As if he were old at his age! I might not meet openly the admiration in his eyes, but I did not want him to think I would listen to younger men.

"I know very few men, Mr. Reid," I told him.

"Pretty women should have men to squire them about and admire them, tell them they are pretty. What do you say, Jeremy?"

Jeremy considered the matter soberly. "Miss Megan is beautiful," he said. "She's always beautiful."

"Wisdom from the young!" Brandon laughed. But to my relief and faint regret, he said no more about my appearance.

We came to the pie Jeremy had requested for dessert, and afterwards Brandon and I sipped our coffee. But now, though we talked together of small matters, the awareness in me had blighted my enjoyment of the evening and I no longer wanted it to go on and on. I had sensed danger again and I knew the pleasure and innocence would not return. I believe Brandon was aware of the change of mood as well, for though we kept up a pretense for Jeremy's sake, it was as though a faint and ghostly presence had entered to sit between us at the table, as though a scent of violets drifted through the room.

We were silent when we rose from the table, leaving Jeremy to pick up the carrousel and carry it upstairs. Brandon gave me his arm, and, as we climbed to the second floor, the bleak gray mood weighed heavily upon me.

But Jeremy did not know that something had happened to spoil our gay time. He wound the music box again, and the little tune tinkled out cheerily as he climbed the stairs behind us. Suddenly Brandon laughed and threw off the blight with a snap of his fingers.

"Quick!" he cried as we reached the second-floor hall. "Music like this must be danced to!"

I had not time to hesitate or draw back, even if I had wished to. He drew me into his light clasp, and we went down the hall in the quick steps of a polka. Jeremy held the whirling carrousel and watched with shining eyes while we danced breathlessly down the hall and back. When the tune ran to an end, Brandon did not release me but held me close to him with the fierce quick possessiveness of his arm about me. For an instant my body responded of its own volition, my head touched his shoulder and longed to rest there heedlessly. There was the sweet wildness of danger singing around us to

172

the lilt of a nursery tune. Then, almost as quickly as it had happened, he let me go.

Jeremy had noted nothing, and I stopped him as he was about to wind the music box again. "No more for now," I called to him. "I'm quite out of breath."

I could not look at Brandon again, for now I was frightened. Frightened more of myself than of him. I gave him a somewhat uncertain good night, picked up my wisteria train, and started toward the third floor. As I mounted the stairs, I raised my eyes and saw in dismay the figure on the steps above me. The figure in brown merino of a woman with outrage in her eyes. Thora Garth had returned. She must have slipped into the house under the cover of our gay dinner party and we had not known she was there, watching from the stairway.

Telling myself that I had done no wrong, I forced my look to meet hers, but her eyes chilled me as I went past. I did not know whether Brandon had seen her, and she did not speak to me. All her malice focused upon Jeremy.

"It's well past your bedtime," she snapped, marching to the upper floor behind him. "Does Miss Kincaid know no better than to keep you up later than the hour you should be getting your rest? Now you will be ill tomorrow. Get yourself to bed at once, young man."

With an unexpected pride of manner, Jeremy handed me the carrousel and faced her sturdily.

"I have special permission to stay up tonight. And I will not be ill tomorrow. I am only ill when something has upset me."

In her anger she seemed to have forgotten the threat he'd made that had driven her from the house a few days before. I suspect that her glimpse of Brandon Reid whirling me down the hall had wiped everything else from her mind.

"You are a rude, naughty boy!" she said tensely. "Get to your room at once. I will deal with you there."

I could see Jeremy's new courage begin to crumble before

her attack. But before I could come to his defense, steps sounded on the stairway and Brandon came running up to join us. He disposed of Miss Garth with swift, cruel words, and I listened, both in relief and distress.

"Miss Megan is to have full charge of the boy from now on," he told her coldly. "She has done very well in caring for him during this trial period. He is to take all his directions from her, and you are to give him no orders whatsoever. If my wife chooses to keep you on to care for Selina because of old regard, that is her affair. The boy is my affair now, and I prefer to leave him entirely in Miss Megan's hands."

She inclined her head stiffly and went down the hall toward her own room. Strangely, I felt almost sorry for her, perhaps because I knew how I would have suffered if he had spoken so to me.

Jeremy smiled shyly at his uncle and ran off to his room.

"Are you pleased with me now?" Brandon asked. "The boy is wholly in your charge."

I answered him carefully, not wanting him to guess that I was still shaken, and not only from what had just happened.

"Thank you, Mr. Reid. I will do what I can for him." My words sounded primly stiff to my own ears, and I could not help it.

"What a difficult young woman you are!" he cried in exasperation. "For an evening I permit myself to be managed on every score. I give you whatever you desire, and still you look at me in that grave, disapproving way that sends me off with a guilty conscience. What are you objecting to now, may I ask?"

Disapproving of him? I thought. Was that the way I looked? If it was, the fact was fortunate. I knew his words were a mockery. Brandon Reid would always behave as he pleased and manage his conscience as he saw fit.

I answered him with evasion. "When I hear you speak so

174

cuttingly to another, I can only wonder when you will turn words equally sharp upon me."

Once more he surprised me. He put out a finger and tilted my reluctant chin so that the thin gaslight touched my face. "I would like never to hurt you, Megan. But you would never be fooled by light promises. When the whim moves me, I may very well deal you a blow that seems ruthless. You will be wise never to expect kindness from me for long. Other considerations, perhaps, but not always kindness.

"Only the boy matters," I told him swiftly. "If you will be kind to him, then I shan't so much as wince if you grow angry with me."

"The bargain is made," he said. "At least for now. It's not something I'll promise forever, but I'll try this experiment for as long as I can. Certainly you've effected a remarkable improvement in Jeremy. At this rate, I should be able to leave him in your hands when our next Egyptian expedition makes up early in the year."

Jeremy called to me, and I nodded silently and hurried to his room. I sat down on the bed beside him, and all my movements were calmly automatic. Jeremy reached up and put his arms about me. I held him close, yet even as I kissed his cheek and drew the covers over him, even as I moved to turn out the gas, something cold and heavy weighed within me.

When I returned to the hall, she was waiting for me. The brown figure stood in the shadows before my door and there could be no slipping past her without speaking. I had to brush close to reach the doorknob, and she put her cold fingers on my bare forearm, stopping me there. I winced, my flesh shrinking from her touch.

"I saw," she whispered. "But don't imagine that you can succeed in what you intend. Miss Leslie will be home soon, and then you'll not be allowed to stay in this house—no matter what *he* says." She flicked her head scornfully toward the stairs.

"I've done nothing that requires an accounting," I said. "I will be happy to tell Mrs. Reid every detail of this evening if she wishes it."

Miss Garth did not answer. She folded her hands across her body and turned away. So softly did she move that I heard scarcely a footfall as she returned to her room. Quickly I slipped through my door and closed it tightly behind me.

I lighted no lights, but stood there in the darkness, fighting off the spell of evil that seemed to emanate from the woman. She might well cause trouble. She might threaten my very presence in this house. Yet it was not of her I must think in this sharply lucid moment. It was of the possible truth of her accusation.

I stood before the window, heedless of the cold, looking out upon a clear and starry night. How many were the silent stars. How complete my mortal insignificance. Yet the hurt within me seemed as vast and engulfing as the universe. I turned from the window and began to undress, paying little heed to the movements of my fingers or to what I did with my clothes. My mind was wide awake, and my thoughts were merciless.

I, who had never been truly in love before, had fallen desperately, foolishly in love with Brandon Reid. When he frowned at me, I was ready to tremble; when he smiled, I yearned toward him like any mindless blossom to the sun. When he held me in his arms I wanted only to stay there for always. And when he told me he would soon be away on a trip to far places, I ached with knowledge of coming emptiness, of the loneliness that waited for me when he was gone. Yet all the while this man was married to another woman. Married to the mother of the boy whose presence held me here in this house.

I did not sleep easily or well that night, and there was

176

much that I could not dismiss from my mind. I kept re-membering Brandon's eyes upon me—not always in mockery. Remembering the moment when he had held me so fiercely close. And foolish though I might be, how could I wish *not* to be in love?

When I slept at last, it was because I had relinquished the struggle and was ready to hug to my heart the very things that wounded me most.

16.

IN THE morning I wakened to the soft and dreamy mood of a woman newly in love that no feeble effort of reason could dispel. A remembrance of all that was sweet and unhurtful held me in an unreasonable enchantment. I longed to see the face of my love and quickly found an excuse to run down to the library. But Brandon had gone—up earlier than I, and off on some business connected, Kate said, with the new expedition he was financing.

I was not entirely sorry. Some stern sentinel in me knew that my mood was far too gentle and yielding this morning. My awareness of love, too new to be submitted to Brandon's sardonic gaze. I had never felt like this before and so wonderful a thing was my yearning that I did not want the clear light of reality to touch it. The man was real and for all that I longed to see him, I was afraid.

It was a further relief when Miss Garth, instead of Jeremy, remained in bed, ministered to with smelling salts and physics and peppermint tea. This morning I would not think of the day when my own turn to be cruelly hurt might come. I was young and in love for the first time, and I gave myself up to the all-engulfing knowledge. For the moment I did not look ahead to a disastrous future. I merely gave myself over to being.

While Jeremy did his lessons that morning, I sat in the schoolroom, a book in my hands, making sure that I turned a page on occasion, though my imaginings were far more beguiling than the story I used to conceal them. Only now and then was I aware that Andrew and Jeremy occupied the same world with me. I noted absently that Andrew was busy with paper and pencil and that Jeremy seemed restless and not at all attentive to his lessons. Yet I could not bring myself to chide the boy, or even pay much attention to such prosaic problems.

I came out of my dreamy state to some degree when I heard Andrew speak to him sternly.

"Take your book and go to your room, Jeremy. When you can do your lesson with your wits about you, come back and we'll go over it again."

Being sent from the classroom was a disgrace. Selina was often punished in this way, but Jeremy, oddly enough, almost never. I shook my head at him in mild reproach, though I could not help but sympathize. Jeremy too had enjoyed an exciting evening and was probably living in a fantasy world, just as I was.

When he had gone, I gave my attention determinedly to my book, not wanting the intrusion of conversation with Andrew. He made no effort to speak, but went on for several moments working with his pencil. Then he tore a sheet of paper from his pad and held it off at arm's length. The gesture caught my attention, and I saw that he was studying a sketch.

"How do you like it?" he said and pushed the paper toward me across the table.

To my surprise I saw that he had drawn my own face on the paper. The likeness was not a true one. I would not have expected such flattery from Andrew. He had drawn a girl who was far prettier than I, and a far softer, more yielding person

180

as well. Yet I was pleased that he could see me in such a light, for if he saw me thus, perhaps another man would too.

"You've flattered me exceedingly," I told him.

He regarded me with an unfathomable expression. "Do you think so? I wouldn't call it flattery. The face I've drawn is not that of a particularly intelligent woman. Here, let me show you."

I sighed, resigned to an enumeration of my faults. Andrew came to stand beside my chair. As he bent above me, pointing with his pencil, I found myself comparing him with Brandon. How much shorter he was than the man with whom I had danced last night. How very nearly ugly he seemed at times. Especially when the saving grace of humor had gone out of him. Yet I suspected that he might be a better friend than Brandon would ever be, and perhaps more single-mindedly loyal, if his devotion were once given.

He tapped with his pencil the parted lips he had sketched in the picture. "Note the mouth," he said, as if he criticized objectively the work of a student. "There's too much softness there, too much of giving. This is not the mouth of a woman ready to make up her mind and do what must be done realistically. Again—take the eyes. Too dreamy, by far. There's a lack of sound thinking there, too much of a turning inward to some foolish dream."

I glanced up at him, dismayed, and he took the drawing from my hands and went back to his chair.

"In fact, my poor Megan, what I have shown you here is the face of a woman abjectly in love."

I started to answer him indignantly, to deny and dismiss, but he would not listen. The anger his wry expression had masked came through to astound me.

"Do you think I'm a fool? Do you think I haven't seen it happening? Do you think they don't talk about you in this house? Not that anything else could be expected of Brandon

181

Reid, but I'd have expected better of you, Miss Megan Kincaid."

"Talk?" I repeated the one word blankly.

"Talk!" he mimicked. "Do you think I haven't heard about your dinner party last night, to say nothing of your dancing in the hall, and the way Garth was told off. I am far from being a fool, my girl, but I suspect that you are making a very thorough one of yourself."

I could find only anger with which to answer him. "None of this is your business! Whether you are a fool or not is your own affair and of no interest to me. I haven't asked your opinion of my actions—actions you know of only through gossip."

Andrew subsided as quickly as he had exploded. When he spoke again there was pity in his eyes and that was harder to accept than unreasonable anger.

"Poor Megan," he said. "How could you know about a man like that? Foolish you are, my dear. Perhaps not a fool, but foolish. What else can we think of a dressmaker who falls in love with the grand seigneur? He is to blame. And yet it will be you who will suffer."

"If you please"—I resorted to haughty chill—"I can manage my own affairs."

"Of course," he said. "And you have that right. I apologize. I've a temper like all blazes when it gets away from me. But it wasn't you I was angry with, Megan. It was Reid, who knows very well what he is doing, and has no conscience about it."

He held the drawing up, as if to study it to better advantage. Then he ripped it down the center, tearing it quite ruthlessly into pieces before my eyes. While I stared, he blew at the bits, letting them drift across the table and onto the floor.

"I've shocked you—and that's fine. Perhaps if you're shocked badly enough you'll reject this softness, crush it, no

182

matter what the temporary hurt. You'll be happier in the long run."

I could not endure his lecturing. That he had been watching me more closely than I knew, that he held me in so little esteem that he was willing to show his contempt, left me more upset than I would have expected.

"If you'll excuse me—" I murmured, still haughty, and went to the door, only to meet Jeremy returning with his lesson book in hand. But I could not linger now, even for Jeremy, and I ran past him into the hall. I was just in time to see Miss Garth come out of her room dressed in bonnet and cloak, carrying a traveling bag in her hand.

She blocked my path, and for a moment we stood face to face, neither one giving way. My heart beat more quickly as I met the dark intensity of her look. She did not step aside, and she did not speak. She merely stood there staring at me with such dislike in her gaze that I was once more shaken and not a little frightened. The woman seemed hardly sane at times, and her hatred for me promised nothing but disaster in this house.

"You are—going away?" I faltered.

She drew her cloak more closely about her and turned toward the stairs. "I am going upriver to fetch Miss Leslie home," she said and swept past me down the stairs.

I went to my room and sat down in its quiet haven. Something of an early-morning fire still remained on the hearth, but I lacked the will to add coals to the embers. Indeed, I seemed washed of all power to move or act. The encounter with Garth had sapped me. I knew now what lay ahead. She could not harm me with looks, however malevolent, but she could injure me viciously with words. I knew such words would now be spoken in a torrent of abuse to Leslie Reid. I suspected, too, which one of us Mrs. Reid would believe.

Yet, from this sapped and directionless state into which I had fallen, I must now begin from the beginning and rebuild myself into a woman of purpose and will. I must build, not in the shape of a tremulous girl in love, nor in the guise of the monstrous creature Miss Garth would represent me to be. I must begin with the truth.

And what was the truth?

It was true that there had been nothing outwardly wrong last night when Brandon had joined Jeremy and me at the table. Nothing wrong, indeed, in the moments of our playful dance together down the hall. There had been only that instant when he had held me close and I had felt a fierce exultance in him and an answering response in myself. But was not such an instant enough to destroy my usefulness where Jeremy was concerned? Would it not be better for all of us if I recognized the fact that my work with Jeremy had come to an end, that I could not remain in this house hoping to aid him when my own heart had betrayed me into so senseless a love for his uncle?

Yet—if this was basic truth—I still could not accept it. All that really mattered was Jeremy, and there was still much I could do for him. It was for him that I must fight to remain in this house, and not for my fatal, foolish love. There must now be innocence in my thoughts as well as in my actions if I was to face the boy's mother with the clear conscience which could be my only weapon.

In those few quiet days that remained, I faced my problem alone and I believe I began to win. That I loved Brandon, I accepted. Perhaps I would always love him. But if I were to remain here and help Jeremy, neither Brandon nor any-one else must know my true feeling. When Jeremy's mother came home, she must find in me only Jeremy's instructor and loving friend. There was no other identity I could enjoy in this house.

So did I caution and counsel and steel myself. When Bran-don returned in a day or two, I was at first anxious lest he put me to some strain or test. But he did not, and I relaxed

184

one segment of my guard. Perhaps he too had thought better of the way we had both stepped close to a line of danger that must not be crossed. I had retreated in time. I would continue to do so. Or so I told myself.

By the end of the week when Mrs. Reid and Thora Garth returned from upriver, I had reached a state of near equanimity. If my actions had been somewhat less than innocent on the night of the dinner, my conscience was clear enough now. It was what happened from here on that mattered, and I could meet whatever Leslie Reid had to say with no sense of present guilt to trouble me.

That afternoon there was a bustle of activity about the house, with Selina flying up and downstairs, happy to be home, full of her visit to her grandmother, eager to share her experiences with her brother. Jeremy seemed glad to see her and not at all jealous of her trip, as he had been at first.

About Miss Garth there was an air of triumph I could not mistake, and I knew it did not augur well for me. Yet there was no immediate summons from Mrs. Reid. Nothing happened until the following afternoon. When Selina came to tell me that her mother wished to see me, I knew the moment had come.

I did not find Mrs. Reid alone in her boudoir. Miss Garth was there, standing watchfully behind her mistress' chair. Andrew Beach was present too, putting away his painting things. I saw that the portrait on the easel had progressed since he'd last shown it to me. Leslie's head had come more definitely into being, and I paused to look at the picture, seeking any delay that might further strengthen me in the ordeal ahead.

Andrew's portrayal surprised me, for he had chosen to paint a woman not only of great beauty, but of generous spirit. The eyes of the portrait regarded me with warm understanding as they read my heart and still forgave. I resisted a startled impulse to turn to the real Leslie for corroboration of what the portrait revealed. Instead, I glanced at Andrew. As he removed the canvas from the easel, our eyes met. His back was to Mrs. Reid and the governess, and his expression was derisively clear. It was as if he had said. "What else did you expect?" A man who painted on commission must please his subject if he wanted other work, he seemed to be telling me, even challenging me to condemn him if I dared.

But it was not Mrs. Reid's portrait that interested me most at that moment, and when Andrew had gone, I turned toward the woman who had posed for it.

Leslie Reid lay back in the chaise longue, her eyes closed, dark lashes fringed upon her cheeks. The room had been flooded with afternoon light for the sake of Andrew's painting, but now Miss Garth moved to draw the draperies and light the inevitable candles. From the bedroom she brought the tall brass candlestick and placed it on a nearby table, where it seemed to tower, its flame touching an answering light in Leslie's bright hair. I thought of Brandon's reference to a Turkish seraglio and wondered if that candlestick had ever shed light on greater beauty. I breathed the scent of violets and was faintly sickened, even as my resolve strengthened. This woman held Jeremy's future in her hands and I must not be defeated by whatever was to happen now.

So brave was I in the first moments of our interview.

"Close the door, please, Thora," Mrs. Reid said. She opened her eyes then and looked at me. What I had expected, I don't know, but it was not this gaze, brimming with tears, that she turned upon me. She motioned me to a chair beside her, and I sat down without speaking.

"You could have been my friend," she said softly. "You were doing a fine thing with Jeremy. I know that now. I must try to be grateful for your past effort." There was a break in her voice as though it weakened, and she was silent, her eyelids closed again.

Miss Garth slid the candlestick nearer her mistress with a

186

faint scraping sound across the table. I looked up at her and saw her eyes, bright again with triumph.

At the sound of metal upon wood, Leslie opened her eyes and went on. "You are not wholly to blame, Miss Kincaid. My husband has been given to this sort of thing before. I can only feel sorry for the woman when it happens. I doubted the wisdom of bringing you here in the first place, but I could not prevent him from doing as he wished."

It was clear that Garth had done her worst. I answered, speaking earnestly, steadily.

"You are dreadfully mistaken in your conclusions, Mrs. Reid. My one purpose in this house is to help Jeremy. He is beginning to make some progress. It must continue. Nothing must happen to set him back."

"You should have thought of that before this," Garth put in. But Leslie was still mistress, and she raised a finger in warning, halting the governess' words.

"Can you remain in this house and live with your own conscience, Miss Kincaid?" Leslie demanded, and now her eyes held mine with more strength in them than before.

"My conscience is clear," I said, but I knew I was flushing.

Mrs. Reid sighed and lifted her hand in a gesture of dismissal.

"If you will not leave of your own accord, Miss Kincaid, there is no choice left for me but to ask you to go. Please be out of the house as soon as possible. I shall see that you have a month's additional salary and the necessary notes to help you obtain another position."

I stood my ground for a moment longer. "And if Mr. Reid does not choose to let me go?"

Miss Garth made a faint, choked sound, but again Leslie's raised hand stopped her. The amber eyes—so unlike the eyes of Andrew's painting—met mine without wavering. Her cheeks were pale and unflushed, her voice steadier than my own.

187

"I am afraid, Miss Kincaid, that life would become intolerable for you in this house if you remained. My husband will be leaving for Egypt soon after the first of the year. To whom would you turn for support when he had gone? Would it not be wiser for us all to accept the good you have done Jeremy and see that it is carried on in other hands? Hands, Miss Kincaid, of my own choosing this time."

Bitterly the truth of all she was saying came home to me. How could I fight for Jeremy against such odds and without Brandon standing firmly behind me? Was my conscience so clear after all? Had not this sad, quiet woman put her finger on the very truth I had told myself I was seeking? In that moment I knew defeat and knew I must accept the verdict of her judgment.

"I will be gone from the house as soon as I can pack," I told her and went out of the room without glancing again at Thora Garth.

As I passed the library on my way toward the stairs, I saw a light burning there and Brandon seated at his desk. There was nothing I could say to him now, but at that moment he looked up and glimpsed my face. He rose at once and came toward me.

"What has upset you, Megan?"

He might as well know now as later, even though I could make no plea for myself, and I stepped into the room to face him.

"I am leaving as soon as I can," I said. "Mrs. Reid has just dismissed me. My usefulness with Jeremy has come to an end, and there's nothing else for me to do."

I saw color rise darkly in his face. "Wait for me here," he ordered and strode past me out the door.

There was no time to stop him, to tell him that his wife was right and had I been in Leslie's place I would have made the same decision. The angry violence that drove him alarmed me. Beyond Leslie's door I could hear the sound of raised

188

voices, the whiplash of Brandon's tone. Sickened, I went deep into the library so that I could not hear. I must wait until he returned. Then I must make my own position clear to him, and the fact that, under the circumstances, I would be blocked at every turn in my efforts with Jeremy.

So preoccupied was I that I did not know that Jeremy had come to the library door until he spoke to me.

"May I come in, Miss Megan?" he asked.

"Come in quickly and close the door after you," I said.

He obeyed me with obvious reluctance, closing it slowly upon the sound of angry voices.

"Uncle Brandon is furious," he said with relish. "I wonder if he'll break something this time. The last time he lost his temper with my mother, he smashed a vase to smithereens. Why is he angry now, Miss Megan?"

I had no answer for the boy, and when he saw that I would not discuss what was happening, he moved about the room, pausing to look behind a row of books on the shelf, to open the lid of a carved humidor, and put his hand into it. I remembered the time he had seemed to be searching for something in his father's room. The pattern was repeating itself.

"What are you looking for?" I asked.

He replaced the elephant's tusk on the mantel and answered me readily enough. "I'm looking for the pistol, Miss Megan. I don't know where they've hidden it. But if I keep searching, some day I'll find it."

One part of my mind recognized that the voices across the hall had quieted. The other part was caught by the boy's ominous words. Perhaps I could do one last thing for him.

"Forget about the past, Jeremy," I pleaded. "The gun would only bring everything back and make you suffer all the more."

"But I don't want to forget," he said. "I want to remember it all. Always."

Before I could press the matter further, his uncle pushed

open the door with a bang and strode into the room, the air of fury still upon him. He saw Jeremy and flicked a finger toward the door. The boy gave me a quick, frightened look and went away at once.

Brandon dropped into the chair behind his desk and put his hands over his face while I stood waiting in silence, not knowing what was to come. After a moment his shoulders relaxed a little and he looked up at me darkly.

"Jeremy will remain in your care, Miss Kincaid," he said. "I will not hear of your leaving this house."

I answered him as firmly as I could. "I have no choice but to leave. Under the circumstances there's nothing more I can do here. Your wife has chosen the only wise course. Isn't it better to accept it?"

He threw up his head and stared at me. "Do you think I will listen to such nonsense? I'm still master here, and you are in my employ, Miss Kincaid. The matter is settled; there will be no further trouble."

This I did not believe, but while I sought for words with which to persuade him, he spoke to me more gently.

"Is it your real wish to leave Jeremy, Megan?"

I could only shake my head helplessly.

"Then you shall stay," he told me.

Once more he leaned his head upon his hands, and there was such despair in the gesture that for an instant I longed with all my heart to go to him, to comfort him with my love. But this I must not do. He spoke to me again without looking up.

"Sometimes I am afraid," he said. "Sometimes I am mortally afraid."

"Of—what?" I faltered.

"Of myself," he said quietly. "Of myself more than of any other."

190

17.

IT IS fortunate, perhaps, that we cannot live at a continued high pitch of emotion. The matters of everyday living intervene. The nerves, the very muscles that are braced for disaster inevitably relax their tension when the battle is not joined. The mind turns to lesser problems.

In spite of telling myself that this was only a respite I had been given and that sooner or later Mrs. Reid, with Garth behind her, would have her way—when nothing at all happened, I began to behave as though I would stay here forever, as though nothing had changed.

Christmas approached us swiftly, and, in spite of the dismal mood which lay upon master and mistress, a flurry of activity gripped the Reid household. The servants, at least, knew the proper course events should take at Christmastime and much was left in their hands. There were the children to be considered and plans to make for their delight.

If angry words had been shouted concerning my presence in the house, and an edict had been set down, then countermanded, everyone pretended an unawareness of the fact. Garth might look vindictively in my direction, but for the moment she said nothing more. Leslie behaved as though her dismissal of me had never been spoken, and to a great extent we avoided each other. Eventually I knew she must have her way, Brandon or no, but for the moment there was something like a Christmas truce.

If Andrew knew what had occurred after he left the house that day, he did not mention the fact, and though I was aware that he watched me openly, I held him at arm's length and encouraged no friendship between us. If I told myself I felt only scorn for the way he had sold his talent to Mrs. Reid, I did not speak my mind. Now and then I thought almost wistfully of the evening I had spent with Andrew when we'd dined at Mama Santini's. That memory too was something I must put from me. I must depend on no one but myself.

It was shortly after her return from the visit to her grandmother's that Selina began to annoy us all with a foolish little song.

"Selina's-got-a-secret! Selina's-got-a-secret!" she would chant in a singsong that soon began to get on my nerves.

"Of course you have a secret," I told her. "Christmas is coming and we all have secrets. But we don't have to brag about them."

She wrinkled her nose at me saucily. "It's not that kind of secret. I know something you don't know. And Jeremy doesn't know it either. But I won't tell you what it is because if I did someone would spank me."

I found it best to ignore her chanting and I did not encourage her with questions.

From below stairs these days the odors of baking drifted up to us, prevading all the house. The fragrance of mince and pumpkin pies mingled with the tart smell of pickles in the making. The familiar warm scent of freshly baked bread was laced with the odors of cinnamon and molasses cookies.

A huge Christmas tree had been brought home by Fuller and set up in the drawing room to be decorated later. The arrival of the tree was an occasion for excitement in itself, bringing to us as it did green life out of a dead brown winter world, adding the scent of pine needles to the Christmasy smells of the house.

Yet in spite of such normal preparations and a certain bustle of excitement both above and below stairs, I could not help but contrast the atmosphere of the Reid house with that of Christmases I remembered from my childhood. How warmly loving had been our approach to the Christmas season. It was a special and wondrous Birthday we celebrated and we never forgot the fact, even in our joyous anticipation of gifts to be given and received.

The mistress, it was true, roused herself and began a round of unusual social engagements and plans. I know Garth disapproved and felt these efforts taxed her strength, but Leslie seemed nervously keyed to activity, though without any true core of happiness in her busy coming and going. Brandon remained indifferent to all that went on about him, doing what was required of him, but holding himself remote and uninvolved.

I saw little of him and, however much it cost me, I held to my single purpose of teaching Jeremy, playing and working with him, giving him my friendship. This was enough, I told myself, to occupy my mind and time, and a good portion of my heart.

Between Jeremy and Selina and me there was a great play of secrecy during the days before Christmas. Perhaps I encouraged and abetted these exaggerated precautions because I felt the true emptiness of Christmas in the Reid house. We indulged in much scurrying from one room to another so that each might avoid the recipient of the gift he was wrapping. And it helped a little. In spite of pale gaslight and the brooding darkness of the halls, the house seemed to liven and reflect something of holiday excitement as it existed in the excitement of two children.

Two days before Christmas, Jeremy came to my room with a plea. Selina, he said, was snooping. He had caught her at it twice. She had no honor whatsoever when it came to other people's secrets, and something must be done.

"She snoops in your room too," he warned me. "I saw her coming out of it yesterday when you were downstairs. So let's fool her, Miss Megan. Let's hide our presents where she won't go."

I was more amused than disturbed and not in the least on guard.

"Where do you suggest?" I asked.

Jeremy held out his hand and dropped something into my palm. I felt the cold touch of metal and knew what he intended. My first impulse was to reject the idea of hiding our gifts in his father's room. Yet I had a reason for not refusing at once.

If I'd had my way, I would long since have opened that room, swept everything out, furnished it anew, given it a character and being that would have nothing to do with the past. As it was, locked and secret, with all mention of it avoided and forbidden, it seemed to hold an unhealthy fascination for Jeremy. Silence and averted eyes only contributed to a lingering sense of horror that I felt was injurious to Jeremy. While the boy had not returned to the room alone, as far as I knew, its locked silence still drew his attention and this was something I wanted to lessen. I made a quick decision.

"Why not?" I said. "Bring your packages here and put them with mine. When no one is about we'll find a chance to hide them where Selina will never look."

Jeremy seemed pleased, but not overly excited and I congratulated myself on making the right decision. From time to time during the day he smuggled his small, but now numerous, gifts into my room and Selina did not discover what he was up to. We waited until evening, when she was safely in bed, before we carried out our plan. I will confess to feeling somewhat uneasy by that time. Our conspiracy

194

had begun to seem less sensible than in my early rationalization.

Jeremy did not go to bed at his usual time, but slipped into my room to help me carry the gifts downstairs. It was then I suggested a change in plans.

"Why not leave your packages with mine for now, Jeremy? Selina won't come here again. Tomorrow night is Christmas Eve, and we can put them under the tree."

The boy shook his head reproachfully. "You promised, Miss Megan. Selina is sure to snoop a lot tomorrow."

I was tempted to ask the real reason behind his insistence, but I did not dare. If I went back on my agreement now, he might shut me out and not confide in me again. Surely there was nothing that could happen if I went with him to his father's room. We would leave our gifts hidden there and come out at once. The plan seemed simple enough and harmless, and I wished I could dismiss my inner misgivings.

"*Now* is the time," Jeremy persisted. "Do come along, Miss Megan. Mama and Uncle Brandon will be having dinner, and all the servants are downstairs. Miss Garth has a headache and she has gone to bed. Selina's asleep."

I emptied a sewing basket and let Jeremy pile his gifts into it. Then, with a few of my own larger packages in my hands, I started downstairs with Jeremy beside me. We moved softly, giving each other sidelong conspiratorial looks. It would take more than one trip, and Jeremy seemed pleased that it should. We must not be caught, he whispered, and threw a look of exaggerated apprehension behind him and over the stair rail.

In one sense his behavior reassured me. How little of normal young excitement, how little of make-believe he had in his life. He was starved for the sort of play most children indulge in endlessly without question. Tonight, as I began to realize, we were not merely hiding gifts from a curious little girl. We were playing the role of pirates and brigands. We were desperadoes and highwaymen. We would hide our smuggled treasure in the teeth of the law and likely be hung to yardarm or the nearest gallows tree if we were caught in our derring-do.

The horror of what had happened in Dwight's room had nothing to do with our present escapade, and I found myself less fearful for Jeremy than I had been.

When we reached the room, he opened the door with his key and pushed me hastily inside. Unexpectedly, I found myself abandoned there in the dark with my arms full and the contents of Jeremy's basket dumped upon the carpet at my feet. Before I could object, he had shut the door upon me and darted off, leaving me there in the gloom of that cold and haunted room, while he ran off to get the rest of our parcels.

My eyes could see nothing in the gloom, and I stumbled over one of Jeremy's packages as I tried to fumble my way toward the bureau and a candle I knew was there.

As I moved hesitantly, my hands outstretched, my direction became suddenly uncertain. Which way was I facing? Which way had I turned on entering the room? There is something unsettling about finding oneself in utter gloom with the realization that surroundings have shifted, that nothing stands in its known place.

I moved gropingly and, as my breathing quickened, I caught a scent that was not the usual chill mustiness of the room. The odor choked me into sudden awareness. I held my breath, not daring to stir as the perfume of violets closed in around me. In sharpened realization, I knew I was not alone. Indeed, now that I listened with utter attention, I could hear the sound of someone who breathed as lightly, as softly, and quickly as I. But someone who had the advantage of being here first, with eyes accustomed to the gloom.

Some sixth sense warned me not to speak, not to challenge, not to remain for a moment shut into this dreadful darkness with the woman whose faintest movement wafted a

196

scent of violets through the air. But where was the door in this pitchy gloom? And where was Jeremy? The moment he returned and opened the door, I would be safe, the hider in the room exposed. But he did not come and I heard the faint rustle of silk as the woman moved nearby—perhaps interposing herself between me and the door.

I tried to tell myself that this rising panic was foolish. There were others in the house, and I had only to cry out to bring them to me. But the sense of a presence that meant me harm was so acute that I could not speak or move.

She was so close now that as I put up my hand in a quick gesture of defense, my fingers brushed her gown, and a voice whispered suddenly in my ear.

"Be still!" it warned me in a whisper so hoarse that all identity was lost. Fingers, chill and somehow deadly, touched my face, my throat. I put my hands up wildly to thrust them away, and twisted from her grasp. She fell back for an instant, perhaps startled by my sudden movement, and I felt the tearing of cloth in my hands. The deadly whisper came again, from behind me now.

"If you go away, you will be safe. If you stay in this house, you will suffer for it."

My eyes were growing used to the dark, and now I could make out a faint line of light along the doorsill. I had my direction at last. Kicking Jeremy's packages aside, I ran to the door, thrust it open, then shut it behind me with a ringing slam that must have echoed through the house.

Jeremy was mounting the stairs from the lower floor, coming toward me. I turned the key in the lock with a sense of triumph, feeling that I had trapped something evil and contained it in the room—something that must now betray itself in order to escape.

I ran toward Jeremy and turned him about. "Not now!" I whispered urgently. "Go upstairs at once!"

My manner brooked no argument, and he obeyed me. We

did not speak until we reached my room again. Then he faced me anxiously.

"What's the matter, Miss Megan? You're white and shaking. What has happened?"

"Why didn't you come, Jeremy?" I gasped. "Why did you shut me in there and run away?"

He was clearly startled by my state of fright, but he explained quietly. "Uncle Brandon called me. He was coming out of the dining room and he heard me on the stairs. So I had to go down and tell him why I was not in bed."

The thumping of my heart began to quiet a little, and, when I sat in my rocker, the weakness in my knees ceased to betray me.

"What did you tell him?" I asked.

"Only that we were hiding Christmas presents and it was all a secret. So he let me off without a scolding. He was in a hurry to go out for the evening anyway. Are you afraid of that room after all, Miss Megan?"

It was better to tell the truth than to let him think me fearful of the supernatural.

"There was someone in there," I said. "Someone breathing in the darkness. Someone who—who meant me harm. I came out as fast as I could and locked her in there alone."

"With all our presents?" Jeremy asked, his dismay having little to do with my predicament.

"She won't hurt the presents," I said. "But sooner or later she will have to get out. And then we'll know who it is. I wish your uncle hadn't left the house."

Jeremy's snort of scorn did not flatter my intelligence. He went to my door and opened it. "Come along," he said, gathering up the remaining packages. "There's nobody there now, and we must hide the presents and see if the others are all right. Let's takes the rest of them down."

When I still hesitated, he spoke to me with a forbearance

that was strangely adult and might have made me laugh at another time.

"There are other keys to the room, Miss Megan," he pointed out. "And besides, the second door is locked with an inside bolt. If anyone wanted to get out, he could draw the bolt and go into my mother's boudoir. Let's go down right away. You can take a candle if you like," he added kindly.

In the face of Jeremy's logic, I began to feel foolish. Perhaps the fright I'd had was due mainly to my own vivid imagination. After all, I had given whoever was in the room a thorough chance to frighten me. And she had done it well.

I made no further objection, but accompanied Jeremy downstairs, this time carrying a candle.

When we opened the door and left it wide to the hall light and my candle, I saw that Jeremy was right. There was no one hiding in the room. The bolt to the second door had been drawn to leave it unlocked. Jeremy knelt to count his packages and did not speak until he was sure they were safe.

My attention wandered from him and came to rest on something across the room. There upon the polished surface of a highboy stood the tall Turkish candlestick I had seen so often in Leslie's room.

"Was your mother downstairs having dinner with your uncle just now?" I asked.

He shook his head absently, his main interest for the packages he was storing in the depths of a bureau drawer.

"I don't know—she may have been."

Then she could have been here, I thought. She could have left her candlestick behind as she fled. However, I said nothing to Jeremy. With hands that were far from steady, I helped him pack away our Christmas gifts. No one disturbed us. No one challenged our presence, or, so far as I knew, went past the door while we finished our work. But the scent of violets persisted and with it a hovering fear. There was a growing certainty in me that far more than mere resentment of my presence existed in this house.

Had Garth dressed once more in a garment of her mistress' and worn her perfume? I didn't know. I couldn't tell. It could have been either.

For my own safety, it would seem that I should overrule Brandon and leave this house while I could. But there was still Jeremy, and I knew I would never abandon him for so cowardly a reason. There were stronger causes which might eventually force me to leave him, but what had happened in this room was not one of them, however uneasy it might leave me.

18.

I HAD NO answer the next day to the question of who had left the candlestick in Dwight Reid's room, or who had warned me in that hoarse whisper. The sense of a threat hanging over my head persisted, yet I could do nothing but ignore it. I saw Brandon not at all, and in any event I did not want to tell him what had happened. The violent anger he had already shown toward Leslie had disturbed me. I did not want to rouse it again.

That my usefulness to Jeremy was drawing to a close was becoming increasingly clear. Before long I must face Brandon and make him understand the reality of the situation. Not because of what had happened in that room, but because once he had gone away, my position would be untenable. Perhaps I would wait until after Christmas and then tell him whatever plans I had decided upon by that time.

On Christmas morning the master and mistress would preside at the opening of the packages—as was the usual custom—but on Christmas Eve they were to attend a ball at the Fifth Avenue Hotel. Thus we would have the tree-decorating to ourselves.

It was a relief to know that Leslie would be absent, yet in spite of my stern control over my feelings, I could not help but wish for Brandon's presence. Perhaps the innocence of tree-trimming might have relaxed him a little, lessened his tension. And, at least, I could have been in the same room with him openly, with no sense of guilt. There would have been pain for me in his presence, yet I could have lived for that little time in his company. Away from him, as I was coming to recognize with despair, I merely existed. I was going to have such a long while to exist away from him entirely, once I left the house.

In spite of this heaviness of heart, I tried to give myself to the decorating of the tree. As I told myself again and again, it was Jeremy alone I must think of now.

For days we had been popping corn energetically over the nursery fire and threading white kernels into long strands. We had strung cranberries until our fingers were stained and pricked. Now, on Christmas Eve, we were hanging these decorations on the ceiling-high tree. And not even Miss Garth was present to set a damper on the children's pleasure.

While we were so engaged, Leslie and Brandon looked into the drawing room on the way to their party. Leslie was brightly beautiful, as always, and Brandon made her a somberly elegant escort in top hat and Inverness cape. They stood in the doorway for a moment, looking in upon the long firelit drawing room. With strained gaiety, Leslie blew the children a kiss, and Brandon wished us a courteous "Good evening." Then they were gone to their carriage, leaving a silence behind them in the room. A hollow silence that stilled our noisy merriment.

I turned quickly back to the tree and asked Jeremy to bring me the stepladder so that I could place the decoration at the very top. Jeremy had cut a star from cardboard and covered it with silver paper saved from chocolate-cream wrappers. But now he did not hear my request, for he was studying the small heap of gifts he had piled upon a chair. Together we had brought them downstairs from Dwight's room, and without incident. Not heeding me, he picked up a green tissue-wrapped package and turned it about in his hands. I knew it was the Egyptian collar. For the hundredth time I wondered if Brandon would remember my plea to him concerning Jeremy's gift. Or would his present tension result in ungracious or indifferent behavior? I could not forgive him readily, I told myself, if he failed Jeremy on Christmas morning.

In the end I brought the stepladder from the hall myself and climbed on it while Selina gave me the star. Jeremy came out of his preoccupation in time to instruct me on its proper position. Then the two of them handed up colored wax candles in small tin holders and I clamped them to the upper branches.

As I worked in what should have been contentment, I could not suppress the picture that kept returning to my mind. A picture of Leslie in Brandon's arms as they danced together at the Christmas ball. Was his anger with her based on his own bewitchment with his wife and her rejection of him? She was so lovely, so obviously capable of exerting great appeal.

To my regret, Miss Garth eventually joined us to supervise the tree-trimming. I told myself that she must have felt lonely upstairs and I bowed to her suggestions and let her direct the children. Her dislike for me was in the open now, and she did not hide it. I gave her a quiet courtsey and ignored her rudeness, for this was Christmas Eve.

Some strangeness was in Selina that evening, so that she seemed as keyed-up and as nervous as her mother. She danced about the tree, dropped ornaments she was hanging, and frequently made secret little grimaces to herself. I supposed she was reacting in mimicry to the example set by Leslie. But when the tree was nearly done, she suddenly reverted to her maddening little singsong. She turned from hanging up a paper angel and went skipping around us.

"I know something you don't know!" she chanted. "I've got a secret and I won't tell!"

Even Miss Garth was less tolerant of her darling than usual. "What has you so excited, Selina?" she demanded. "It's not good for you to be this way."

Again the child made her odd little grimace. "I won't tell. I'll never tell. It's more fun to have a secret."

Jeremy threw her a scornful look. "You're being a stupid, Selina. Give me that string of cranberries if you're not going to hang it."

Selina would give up nothing and went back to her decorating, but for the moment we heard no more about her secret.

We had just finished the tree when Andrew Beach rang the bell and was admitted to our midst, his arms full of small packages.

"No one invited me till tomorrow morning when the servitors appear," he said wryly. "So I've invited myself tonight. Do you mind if I put my parcels under your tree?"

The children were happy to see him, and if Miss Garth was not, she at least made her disapproval less obvious than usual. With the decorations done, we all placed our gifts on the white sheet spread around the foot of the tree. The Christmas effect was perfect now, and there remained only the lighting of the candles. This was a careful task for adults, and by way of extra precaution I had brought in a huge sponge in a bucket of water as the same safety measure we'd always used at home in case a branch caught fire.

One by one we lighted the candles with tapers until the whole tree glowed with warm, living fire. In the big drafty room air currents sent the pointed flames dipping and tilting so that all the branches shimmered.

Selina, still overly excited, began to crawl among the gifts, examining this one, then that, sometimes holding a package up so that she could shake it and try to guess the contents.

204

It was thus that she unearthed the package I had wrapped for Jeremy.

"Who's this for?" she asked. "It says, 'For the Prince.' We don't have a prince in this house."

Jeremy glanced at me quickly, and I smiled. "That's a secret between Jeremy and me," I told her, and saw pleasure come to life in his eyes. Bit by bit, just as had happened to the prince in the fairy tale, the ugly disguise was being stripped away and Jeremy was changing. I prayed that all would go well with the gift for his uncle so his happiness might be complete.

When the last candle had been lighted, we stood back to admire the effect. The tree had been placed in a corner of the drawing room, and from the wall opposite, a huge mirror reflected the strands of white popcorn and red cranberries, the bright ornaments and myriad flames.

Andrew held out one hand to me and the other to Selina. Softly he began to sing, and I was surprised at the deep timbre of his voice. Jeremy and even Miss Garth came to hold hands with us as we stood before the tree, our voices raised in "O Tannenbaum." We sang the English words, and they rang out strongly in the quiet room.

"O Evergreen, O Evergreen!
How faithful are your branches . . ."

It was a strangely lovely and healing moment. I ceased to think of Leslie and Brandon dancing together at their party. I let the sadness, the loneliness, the fear of the last few days flow out through my very fingertips as Andrew clasped my hand and we sang together. I had the curious feeling that through the very clasp of his fingers Andrew was offering his own quiet strength to sustain me. Tonight he seemed less cynical and critical. I took something of comfort from the

205

hand of a man clasping mine, even though it was the wrong hand.

When at length our voices died away, Miss Garth broke the circle first and went back to her chair. For an instant I caught the shine of tears in her eyes and the thought came to me that we were all rather a forlorn and lonely lot.

Suddenly I wanted to hold to the Christmas spell that had fallen so gently upon us.

"I know the main gifts are to be opened tomorrow when your mother and your uncle are here," I said to the children. "But perhaps we could make an exception with one or two of our own presents for each other. Then we could have a little more of Christmas tonight."

Miss Garth did not approve. It was not the custom, she said. She did not know what Mrs. Reid would think. I suspected that Leslie would not care one way or the other, though I did not say so. It was Selina who settled matters. She flew to the tree and brought out a package from among those scattered below it. Surprisingly, it was not a present for herself, but the one she had made for me.

I opened it while the others watched and found that she had given me a pomander ball. It was an apple, painstakingly, though unevenly, stuck with cloves and tied with a blue satin ribbon for hanging among my clothes. I exclaimed over it in pleasure, and the gift opening was on.

The present for the "prince" came next, and Jeremy gravely opened the package I had wrapped for him. I watched with a lump in my throat as he slipped off the ribbon and pressed back the paper from about the carrousel. While Selina cried out in wonder and envy, he simply stared at it for a moment. Then he looked at me with such delight, such gratitude in his eyes that I could hardly bear it. Yet still he could not believe that this gift was truly for him.

"It belonged to your brother—" he began.

I nodded. "You are my brother now, Jeremy."

206

He wound the toy and set the tune tinkling, the carrousel turning, while we all watched enchanted. Even Miss Garth offered no criticism and did not warn him not to break it. When I glanced at Andrew I saw his eyes upon me, his look unfathomable as it so often was these days. There was a sadness in the smile he bent upon me. I did not know why, but I smiled back, offering without words my thanks for the quiet support he had given me tonight.

It did not take us long to open the rest of the gifts we had for each other. There were the usual penwipers, pincushions, and darning eggs. Selina had made a charming strand of sealing-wax beads in red and gold for Miss Garth. And Jeremy had carved a small Egyptian head for me from a piece of wood. It appeared to be a replica of the Sphinx and I thanked him for it warmly. Andrew gave me a sketch of Washington Square in a snowstorm, and I sensed that it was something of a peace-offering to make up for the drawing of me he had destroyed.

That Christmas Eve was almost a happy time. Happier perhaps for the absence of Brandon Reid, though this I hated to admit. Before Andrew left we sang "Silent Night," and the words were still singing through my mind, *All is calm, all is bright,* as we extinguished the candles. The odor of evergreen and snuffed candles was a perfume Andrew said he would carry into his dreams that night. I believe it brought to each of the three adults in that room a nostalgic memory of days long past, happier days than those through which we now lived.

With Andrew gone and no more packages to open for the time being, Selina returned to her annoying chant about a secret. I suspected that she would never sleep after all this excitement unless she confided whatever it was she had on her mind.

"You might as well tell us," I said. "Your secret is likely to keep you awake all night unless you do."

"It isn't a secret to tell!" Selina cried. "If you want to come with me now, I'll show you what it is."

Miss Garth broke in abruptly. "All this is nonsense. It's your bedtime, Selina. Come along, and on the way upstairs you can tell me about your secret. You needn't make a performance of it. Say good night, dear."

I was almost pleased when Selina laughed at her instruction and turned to Jeremy and me.

"If I'm going to tell, I want to show it to everyone!" she cried and ran through the door ahead of us, her fair hair bouncing against her back.

Jeremy left his carrousel beneath the Christmas tree and came beside me up the stairs, while Miss Garth followed gloomily, once more preoccupied with her role of Cassandra. This was not a good idea, she insisted. The child was too excited. The whole thing must be stopped.

My first misgivings came when Selina went to the closed door of her mother's boudoir. When Miss Garth would have stopped her from entering, she laughed mischievously and slipped out of the governess' grasp, darting into the room ahead of her. In the thin light from the hall I saw her run to the velvet draperies that hid her mother's bedroom and push them aside.

"Do light the gas, Miss Megan," she called. "It's dark in here."

"You'll do nothing of the kind," Miss Garth told me sharply. "The child has no business in this room while her mother is absent and neither have you."

She was right, of course, but now, in spite of a certain uneasiness, I was curious to know what so excited Selina. I went to the mantel, found matches, and lighted the gas Leslie so seldom used in this room of scent and shadow.

Kate had apparently been in to put things to rights after her mistress had dressed for the ball, for there was no disarray in the room. The bedclothes were turned down neatly, and Leslie's nightgown lay across the coverlet. All was in its usual place, and any dusting of powder had been wiped from the top of her dressing table, her perfume bottles and silver-backed brushes set in order.

For a moment the four of us stood looking about. Then Miss Garth moved decisively toward the gas I had just lighted and turned it out. But in the instant before the light vanished, Selina cried out.

"It's gone!" she wailed. "It isn't here at all. So how can I show you?"

Miss Garth gave Selina no further chance to explain. She took her by the arm and whisked her off to bed in such high indignation that not even her charge protested. Jeremy and I found ourselves in the hall, looking at each other in bewilderment.

"What do you suppose all that was about?" I asked.

Jeremy shrugged. "Just Selina being silly," he said.

I was willing to leave it at that.

"Perhaps it's bedtime for us too, Jeremy," I said. "This has been a long, happy evening."

He came upstairs with me and went to bed without objection. But when I returned to my own room, I found I had no desire to go immediately to sleep. A restlessness possessed me. To amuse myself, I sorted out the small gifts I had brought up to my room—Jeremy's sphinx, Selina's pomander ball, Andrew's sketch. I'd felt a sense of friendly companionship tonight while Andrew was there. For a little while I had been able to shut Brandon Reid away in a hidden compartment of my mind. But now I remembered, and remembering, I knew what it was to be lonely on Christmas Eve.

As midnight neared, I could endure my gloomy thoughts no longer. I slipped my dolman about me and tied a woolen scarf over my head against the chill of the night. Then I went softly downstairs and out the front door, taking my latchkey, so I might return without disturbing the servants.

I stood on the high marble steps and lifted my face to a cool wind blowing from the harbor, as if its very touch would clear my troubled thoughts and brush away longings that frightened me. The square lay peaceful and bright beneath the quiet sky. Through recent snow diagonal paths ruled long brown lines. Here and there about the perimeter a lighted Christmas tree brightened a window, and friendly lamps burned where occupants were still up on Christmas Eve. Along one edge of the square the Gothic buildings of the University formed a gray border without illumination, though lights gleamed in the windows of the church next door.

From downtown I heard the clock bell of old Trinity begin to strike the midnight hour and I knew that Christmas Day was nearly upon me. One by one I counted the strokes, and, when they came to an end, a hush seemed to fall upon the air. It was as if a concerted breath were held, as if all the city waited. Into this breathless pause came a burst of rich, sweet sound as the bells of Trinity began to peal their joyful welcome to Christmas Day.

My heart lifted in spite of myself, and I looked up at heavens deep and blue and spangled with stars. The words of the song we had sung earlier returned to whisper softly through my consciousness: *All is calm, all is bright* . . . Something of the night's peace descended upon me, and I returned more calmly to the house and started upstairs to my room.

Gaslight still burned on the second floor, and, as I followed the hall to the upward turn of the stairs, I caught a slight movement in the shadows. For an instant I was startled and thought of Jeremy. Then I saw that it was Miss Garth who had placed a chair outside her mistress' door and sat there, alert and watchful. She saw me, but she did not speak, and I went up the stairs quickly, wanting no encounter with Thora Garth in that lonely hallway.

210

The sense of peace was suddenly gone. It was a long while before I fell asleep. Sometime during the early hours of Christmas morning I wakened to hear horses being stabled in the mews beneath my window and knew that Leslie and Brandon had come home.

19.

EARLY THE next morning, before I'd had break-
fast, I went downstairs, meaning to go for a walk in the winter sunshine of Christmas Day. More and more the atmosphere of the house weighed upon me, oppressed me.

But though I moved quietly, someone else was up as early
as I, and, as I passed the library, Brandon heard my step and
called to me to come in. I paused just inside the door. Here
was my opportunity to tell him that I could not remain in
his employ much longer. I must form my own plans soon and
act upon them.

As he came toward me, however, I saw his face, haggard in
the early morning light, the eyes sunken in the sockets. It
could not be the late hours of a ball that had done this to
him. With his vitality he could have danced the dawn in with
ease, had the occasion been a joyous one. I put my intent
aside, knowing I could not add to whatever trouble had set
this stamp of suffering upon him.

"Merry Christmas, Megan," he said, but there was no merriment in the words. He put a hand into the pocket of his
burgundy dressing gown, then drew it out, extending it
toward me. In his fingers he held a small blue box, a jeweler's
box.

I stared at it blankly, taken aback.

"It's for you, Megan," he said. "Today is Christmas, and this is my gift to you."

I did not want him to give me anything. I did not want him to be thoughtful and kind. I kept my hands behind my back like a willful child.

"We're opening our gifts under the tree later this morning," I told him stiffly.

With a quick gesture, as though I exasperated him, he caught my hand and drew it from behind my back, pressing the little box into my fingers and holding them closed about it so that I might not refuse.

"Under the tree you will find a proper gift chosen by Leslie. This is my own gift to you, Megan. It is a very small way of thanking you for all you've done in this house. You can't deny me so trifling a pleasure. Open it; I want to know what you think."

With uncertain fingers I pressed the catch of the box, and the lid flew up. Pinned to the white satin inside was a pale green scarab set in a simple silver brooch.

"That wasn't bought in the streets of Cairo," he said. "It is from the tomb of Queen Hatshepsut. I thought it might please you, so I had it set in a brooch."

It pleased me so very much that I did not want him to guess the extent of my delight.

"It's beautiful," I said in a low voice.

He touched the scrollwork of the design with his forefinger. "The material is glazed steatite. The marks it bears spell the queen's name. I wish you could see Deir-el-Bahri at Thebes where this came from. All those rows upon rows of great steps leading to higher levels where the gigantic enthroned figures sit. Images of the queen on every hand—the same broad-cheeked beautiful face repeated again and again. The place is both temple and tomb."

As I listened, studying the tiny scarab, my mind conjured

214

up a vast temple set against bare brown hills. He broke the spell of my vision abruptly.

"What did you do on Christmas Eve?"

"We trimmed the tree," I told him.

"And—afterwards?"

I told him of how I had been unable to sleep and had come downstairs to stand on the front steps. Of how I had heard the bells of Trinity on Christmas Eve.

"I wondered if you'd hear them," he said. "At midnight I found an open window where I could breathe fresh air and be alone. I thought of you then, Megan. While the bells were ringing."

I had come into this room meaning to tell him that I could stay no longer in this house, but I knew I could not speak at this time. There was a burning of tears behind my lids, and I dared not remain in his company. I turned from him quickly and fled the room.

I ran upstairs with his gift held tightly and in my room I cried over it a little. No matter what this house held for me in the way of pain, I would keep this small brooch always and remember that Brandon Reid had thought well enough of me to want me to have it.

When I went to breakfast that morning I could not resist pinning the delicate brooch at the collar of my dress.

Miss Garth, the children, and I breakfasted together in the nursery. Only Selina still seemed excited about Christmas. Miss Garth appeared morose and greeted me with the news that poor Miss Leslie had danced beyond her strength last night and was too ill this morning to join in the Christmas-tree festivities. Though the governess said nothing openly, I caught the implication that Brandon Reid was to blame.

During the meal Jeremy inquired about the date for the opening ceremonies at the Dwight Reid Memorial Home, and Miss Garth answered him impatiently.

"Why don't you ask your uncle? I know nothing at all about it. And care less!"

"I want to be there," Jeremy said with the same persistence he had shown before. "Do you think my mother will take me?"

Garth glowered at him. "I hope your mother will stay home. If your uncle has his way, there'll be no ceremony."

Jeremy sighed and did not question her further. He and Selina left the table ahead of us, both eager for the opening of presents. Ordinarily I would have followed, loathe to be left alone with Miss Garth. But now I found myself regarding her with open curiosity. It was so seldom that she sided against Leslie. Only in this matter did she oppose Mrs. Reid.

"Why don't you want to see a ceremony held at the opening of the memorial?" I asked.

She was angry enough to answer me. "Because the whole thing is a mockery—that's why! The boy's father wasn't always the hero they make him out to be. There was bad blood there, I can tell you. The boy is like him. For once his uncle knows what's right and what isn't. But my poor Miss Leslie is completely deluded and won't listen to reason. If Master Brandon hadn't been away in Egypt—" She paused, and I pressed her quickly, wanting to hear more of this astonishing revelation.

"What brought the older brother home from abroad that last time?"

"He came because Master Dwight sent for him! He wanted his big, strong brother to rescue him from the results of his own weakness of character."

"What had he done?" I asked bluntly.

"Enough to put the Reid name under a black cloud and perhaps land himself in jail in the reform wave that was picking off those in high places. Enough to ruin all he had built, and undoubtedly kill his father with shock over the disgrace."

216

"But—what was it he did?"

I had pressed too hard. Miss Garth's dark gaze returned from a stormy distance to focus upon me. "None of this is your business, my girl. It's past history now, and the only thing that matters is not to revive it and stir things up all over again. If you had any sense, you'd not stay around to be mixed up in it. You'd not wait for your next dismissal—you'd leave this house to save your own reputation . . . and perhaps more!"

Animosity toward me marked every line of her face, but I stood my ground.

"I don't like to be threatened," I said. "Neither by daylight, nor in a dark room."

Miss Garth pushed back her chair and left the table without another glance in my direction.

I sat on, thinking of the surprising things she had said. That the brilliant, successful young Galahad, Dwight Reid, might have had feet of clay. That he had sent for Brandon to come home and rescue him from some scrape of his own making. What did all this portend? I sensed some significance here, some meaning that would make everything clear, but I could not put my finger upon it.

There had been spite in Garth's eyes, in her voice when she spoke of Dwight. A memory of that day when I had seen her in Leslie's room, wearing Leslie's gown, with the double miniature in her hands, returned to me. I had wondered which brother her look of adoration had been for. Now it appeared that, unlike her mistress, she had harbored only contempt for Dwight. Could it be that a secret infatuation for Brandon throbbed beneath the stiff façade she presented to the world?

Selina called to me then, and I put aside these new troubling thoughts as best I could in order to join the children in their opening of Christmas presents.

It was as well that we had enjoyed a taste of real Christmas last night, for nothing was the same this morning. The tree was gay and bright, the candles shone with a lovely radiance, and the air was scented with evergreen. But the warmth that made all this important was lacking.

Brandon Reid's mood was far from festive. He stood with his back to the mantel, above which we had draped a string of red tissue-paper bells purchased from Stewart's store. The gay bells, unfolded to plump accordian pleating, presented a somehow ludicrous contrast behind his somber head, seeming frivolous to an improper degree. When Miss Garth told him that his wife would not be down, he looked increasingly displeased.

As their gifts were doled out, the servants offered polite thanks to the master and went off with their unopened packages. Brandon was courteous enough, but clearly remote. I could not help wondering what had happened at the party last night to result in Leslie's illness and this dark, angry mood of her husband's. Miss Garth's excuse that too much dancing had brought such a result did not convince me.

Now and then I glanced uneasily at Jeremy and saw that his attention was fixed mainly on the gift he had wrapped so carefully for his uncle.

When it came to giving out the family presents and those for the governess, Andrew, and me, Miss Garth employed Selina to fetch packages to her from beneath the tree. She would read off the name, and Selina would take it to the recipient. Jeremy's package had still not been chosen, and I could sense the boy's anxiety whenever his sister went near the tree. If it had been possible, I believe he might have taken the gift away and hidden it upstairs, rather than face this chill, indifferent mood of his uncle's.

Except for Andrew's occasional efforts, Selina was the only one with any Christmas spirit that morning. She had forgotten about her "secret" and bubbled gayly along, with no awareness of the pall that lay upon the room.

When the child at last picked her own gift for her uncle and carried it to him down the long room, I saw Jeremy's interest quicken. Perhaps he thought the reception of this gift might be some indication of how his own might fare. Brandon, to do him credit, endeavored to play the game. He held up the bright fluff of varicolored embroidered felt that Selina intended as a penwiper, and remarked over it as he was supposed to do. But the effort rang false, and even Selina sensed that her gift had not been received with a proper Christmas enthusiasm.

"I made it very quickly, Uncle Brandon," she apologized. "I know it isn't very neat, but there was no time to make another."

Her uncle did his best. "It's very pretty, Selina. I'll keep it on my desk and think of you whenever I use it. Thank you, my dear."

She seemed satisfied and skipped back to the tree to find a gift for Miss Garth. Nervously I fingered the scarab pin at my throat and caught Andrew watching my fingers. The look he gave me was mocking, and I knew he guessed where the pin had come from. It had been a mistake to wear it, I thought, and let my hand fall to my lap.

My own gift from Mr. and Mrs. Reid was a muff of gray squirrel—a luxurious present. Yet this had been chosen by Leslie and it did not mean to me what the little scarab meant. It was merely a conventional gesture, since Mrs. Reid wanted me out of this house.

By that time I believe Jeremy thought that his sister might overlook his gift for Brandon altogether and leave it there among the unopened gifts for their mother. But she crawled among the remaining packages on her hands and knees and saw it at last.

"Oh, look!" she cried. "It's for you, Uncle Brandon. Jeremy made it for you, and I know what it is."

The room was oddly still as she ran to put the package

into her uncle's hands. Perhaps we all sensed in one way or another how much hung in the balance with this particular gift. All, perhaps, except Brandon himself. Ever since she had dashed the beads to the floor in his room, Miss Garth had hated what Jeremy was making and undoubtedly wanted to see no good come of it. Andrew had admired the collar more than once and shown some surprise at Jeremy's workmanship. Selina had been proud and admiring from the beginning.

I watched as tensely as Jeremy did and wished that I might catch Brandon's eye and send him a pleading glance to remind him of his promise. But he did not look my way at all. With maddening deliberation he fumbled with ribbon and paper, perhaps postponing the moment when he would have to pretend a role he had no heart for just now.

Jeremy sat on a low footstool near the fire in utter stillness. Only his eyes were alive and anguished.

"Oh, do open it!" I cried, unable to contain myself.

Brandon threw me a look that told me he did not care for impatient women, and at last opened the cardboard box in which Jeremy had nested the gift in tissue. Silently, without expression, he drew it from the box and held it in his hand. I saw again the wide, flat collar with its rows of beads strung on thin wire. Further spokes of wire around the wheel held it flat. Here and there the dark pattern of cut steel was broken with touches of red and green and turquoise blue.

Brandon held it up to examine it more closely, and I saw his eyes light with an appreciation in which there was no pretense. He knew what it was at once, and his smile of approval for Jeremy was surprisingly warm.

"It's for the Osiris, isn't it?" he said. "A fine piece of work, Jeremy."

"I'm not sure when those collars were in fashion," Jeremy said worriedly. "I'm not sure this is right for Osiris."

"That won't matter," Brandon assured him. "Long after the broad collar went out of style it was used as a funerary

220

ornament, and the dead were Osiris' business. I suppose you've tried it for fit?"

Jeremy nodded as though he found it difficult to speak. Since I felt a little lightheaded with relief myself, it was easy to guess how he must feel.

Selina danced about them in delight, clearly pleased that their uncle liked her brother's work.

"Jeremy let me go with him when he tried it on Osiris," she said. "Since the beard sticks out from the chin, the collar goes right under it. It looks beautiful."

"Miss Megan helped me," Jeremy said, finding his voice again. "She wouldn't let me give up when I got discouraged."

Brandon looked at me across the room. His gaze flicked from my face to the pin at my throat and back again, and there was something as gentle as a caress in his eyes. It was almost as if he reached out to touch me as a lover might. The look was so unexpected that it disarmed me completely. For an instant my guard against him went down and I gave him look for look. By the time I recovered and steadied myself, Andrew was watching me. I knew he had seen the exchange and I could feel his disapproval almost as if it were a tangible thing. I could not have cared less.

When the last present had been opened, Brandon suggested to Jeremy that they take the collar to Osiris. Selina wanted to go with them, but Miss Garth called her back. She was attending a Christmas luncheon party today, and it was time for her to dress. Jeremy went eagerly with his uncle, and I was glad to see them go alone, without interference. Selina, remembering the party, was now impatient to be off and went away pulling Garth along with her.

Andrew and I were left with the debris of Christmas, and this was a tête-à-tête I had no taste for. I went to work as busily as possible.

20.

"HELP ME snuff out the candles, will you?" I said to Andrew. "Then I'll ring for Kate to clear up the trash."

I gave him a snuffer on a long handle, and he came to assist me. As we circled the tree he reached the place where Leslie Reid's packages were heaped unopened.

"They look a bit forlorn, don't they?" he said.

I was surprised to hear such sentimentality from Andrew and I glanced at him in surprise. He was regarding me with a look that was odddly intent and a little pitying. I wanted neither his pity nor his interest and I turned my back and reached for a high candle.

"Why don't you take her packages upstairs to Mrs. Reid?" Andrew asked.

Was he baiting me? I wondered. Didn't he know that Mrs. Reid had wanted to dismiss me? I turned from the tree to face him. "Miss Garth says she doesn't wish to be disturbed. It's not my place to take her presents to her."

The wry, familiar smile twisted Andrew's mouth. "You're a kind enough person ordinarily, Megan. You're thoughtful toward everyone in this house. Even toward me at times, and toward poor old Thora. Toward everyone but Mrs. Reid." He reached a finger toward the scarab brooch at the throat of my dress. "But of course you can't be generous to Brandon Reid's wife."

I moved from his touch. "I don't know what you're talking about. I seldom see Mrs. Reid. It would be ridiculous for me to carry her packages upstairs and disturb her while she's ill."

"Would it?" Andrew said.

I began to suspect what he was doing and why. Whether I wished it or not, he was intent on protecting me from Brandon. Deliberately, cunningly, he was turning me to face the possible suffering of Leslie Reid. What he could not know was that I had settled all this with myself in my own way. I did not need the effort he was making.

He must have sensed my resistance, for he changed his approach. "Will you come for a walk with me, Megan? I'd like to tell you what I mean. We can't talk here without interruption."

There was an earnest persistence in him, and I realized again how little I really knew Andrew Beach. When he roused himself to action, he could be thoroughly determined. Perhaps it would be best to go with him and hear him out. Only then could I defend my own position against his misconceptions. Besides, there were certain things I wanted to tell him, and a question I meant to ask.

"I'll get my cloak and bonnet," I said and went upstairs.

When I came down ready for the street, he was waiting for me near the door and his eyes brightened at the sight of me. I could not help but think that all might have been easier for me if I had felt some answering response.

As we went down the steps, he tucked my hand into the crook of his arm. "It's pleasant to walk with a pretty girl on Christmas morning," he said.

The mood I remembered from that night at Mama Santini's was upon him again, but now the spell of a darker, more desperate love held me in thrall and I had nothing to offer Andrew Beach.

After a bright early morning, the day had turned gray and there was once more the smell of snow in the air. All about us bare branches etched a delicate brown tracery against the snowy area of the square, and I studied it as I walked in silence at Andrew's side. It was he who wanted to talk, and I could only wait for what I feared would be a lecture.

He began, however, with ancient history—with the time when Leslie Rolfe had fallen in love with Dwight Reid.

"Not that I knew either family then," he said. "But I learned a great deal about them when Dwight Reid died. And more has come to light since. Dwight fought in the war, as you probably know. Brandon didn't. Though it wasn't Brandon's fault that he saw no action. He went as a civilian aide on a mission sent to England for the purpose of swinging British sympathy toward the North. From what I've heard, it was a post he served well. I've no quarrel with him on that score.

"While he was away the Rolfes, in trouble financially, moved next door to the Reid house on Bleecker Street, and Dwight, home on leave, fell in love with Leslie. Perhaps she had a special aura of romance around her then—at least in Galahad's eyes. Before the war began her father's fortune had been ruined. He was trying to recoup with war profits, but the family was still in straits. I fancy that old Rolfe must have been more than pleased with Dwight's interest in his daughter."

"Brandon Reid was still in England at the time?" I asked.

"He came home after Dwight had rejoined his company. Garth says he met Leslie at a party and didn't know who she was, or that she was all but engaged to his brother. He followed suit, falling in love with her too."

We had reached the Washington Square fountain, and Andrew stared absently at icicles dripping in spears from the low rim of the basin. His story had roused my interest. I wanted to learn all I could about Brandon Reid, no matter how much pain such knowledge might bring me. Only through knowledge could I understand him now.

"Go on," I urged. "What about Brandon?"

Andrew reached down to touch a dagger of ice, and it shattered with a glassy crackle. "Brandon learned the truth, of course, and he accepted the assignment of a mission to France and got out of the country. His background of experience in England was useful to the government. When the war was over he went to Egypt and managed to be away on one expedition or another after that for years at a stretch. Leslie married Dwight, and, I suppose, should have lived happily ever after, since he was the better man."

That I would not accept. "*Was* he the better man?" I challenged. "Or is Dwight Reid's reputation a myth? Is it something Leslie clings to and the public was fooled about?"

Andrew threw me a questioning look, and I told him what Garth had said that morning at breakfast. He did not speak until I concluded with the matter of the letter Garth claimed had brought Brandon home from his last expedition. Then he nodded with no great surprise.

"I've wondered sometimes if too much perfection was claimed for Dwight. And I've heard an unpleasant rumor or two. About the letter, I wouldn't know. At any rate, the great traveler, who had once been in love with Leslie, came home to his brother's house. And by great coincidence the brother died and the young wife was left unprotected."

I heard the bite of scorn in his words and stiffened. "You've no right to make veiled accusations!"

"I'm making no accusation of any sort," Andrew said.

"Why did you bring this up?" I demanded. "What has any of it to do with me?"

Andrew smiled and again drew my fingers into the crook of his arm as we walked on, crossing a path that led over what had been the Washington Parade Ground, and before that Potter's Field.

226

"You know very well why I've brought it up," he said. "I don't want Reid to accomplish with you what he has accomplished with other women. There's time to turn back, Megan, if only you'll try to see him as he is. There's a ruthless quality about him that drives through to get what he wants, no matter what the cost, or how long it takes. I want to see you sorry for Mrs. Reid as well as distrustful of her husband. You can afford to be more generous and kind."

This was too much. "As you are being generous and kind in that portrait you're painting! Do you really believe that *she* is so gentle and generous?"

He answered me quietly enough. "No, I don't. But perhaps she needs to see herself in a more flattering light. Sometimes I think we tend to become what others believe we are."

Since he had an apparently low opinion of me, I grew still more annoyed. "Mrs. Reid is a woman who married her husband's brother a year after the man she loved died. A woman who, you say, has never loved anyone but the younger brother. Give me the answer to that, if you will, instead of condemning Mr. Reid."

"You ask me questions I can't answer," Andrew admitted. "Whatever either of them may have hoped for in this marriage, each appears to have suffered disappointment. But it's you I'm thinking of now, Megan."

I was still angry. "You take too much upon yourself! You're not the keeper of my conscience. I know very well what I should or should not do, but I have very little sympathy for Mrs. Reid."

"I suppose that's natural enough," Andrew said.

I saw once more the hint of pity in his eyes and flared out against it. "Do you know that she tried to dismiss me?" I asked. "That she told me to leave the house? She believed whatever Garth told her and would not listen to me. It's only because of Mr. Reid's intervention that I've stayed on."

"Garth saw to it that I was informed," he said shortly.

227

"What else could you expect but dismissal under the circumstances?"

"Expect? I expect nothing! But I did hope that I would be allowed to help Jeremy in my own way. And without being blocked by his mother or Miss Garth. As it is, who could be more unwelcome than I, if I were to take those gifts upstairs to Mrs. Reid?"

Andrew's steps had slowed beside me. "Can you give her no reassurance at all, Megan? Have you no sympathy for the humiliation of her position?"

"Perhaps there's humiliation for me too," I said, "when I'm given no chance to do the right thing as I see it."

He swung me suddenly about, his hands upon my elbows so that I was forced to look into his eyes. There was an insistence in him that I had never seen before.

"What I'm suggesting is the right thing. You've known what loneliness is like. Go back and take Mrs. Reid's gifts upstairs to her. She needs a friend in that house—a woman nearer her own age than Garth. You can help her if you will."

I did not want to be swayed by him. "Why do you involve yourself in this?" I asked.

For a moment he hesitated, the wry smile lifting a corner of his mouth. Then he did an unexpected thing. He leaned toward me and kissed me in a light quick caress.

"Perhaps that's why," he said. "Perhaps because of how I feel about you, Megan. Though that is something you've been too busy otherwise to notice." He laughed and was himself again, setting me gently from him.

For a moment I could only stare—perhaps not so much in surprise as in dismay. Had I not sensed the direction in which he was moving and even wished at times that I could respond? The reassurance he sought was not so much for Leslie, I suspected, as for himself, and I wanted very much to be kind to him.

"If it will please you," I said, making the only small offer I could give him, "I'll do what you ask. I'll take the gifts to Leslie, if you believe this will help."

I did not fool him. We had been walking in the direction of the house, and, as we neared the front steps, he paused.

"I won't try to tell you what you must do, Megan," he said quietly. "It's true that I have no right to advise you. Or to condemn any course you choose to take, for that matter."

He turned my gloved hands palm up and held them for a moment. I think he meant to say something more, but instead he let me go. He waited there motionless while I ran up the steps and let myself in the door. When I glanced back, he was still there, staring up at the house.

I let myself in and went to the drawing room, where Kate was at work clearing up. Whether it was foolish or not, I must keep my promise to Andrew, and when I had gathered her presents into my arms, I started upstairs to Leslie's room.

21.

MY ARMS were so well filled with packages that when I reached Mrs. Reid's door I had not a free finger with which to rap. I called to her softly, half hoping that she would be asleep and never hear me. Then I could return my armload to the tree, my conscience silenced, with nothing further for me to do. I had no belief that this action was right or would in any way be welcomed by Mrs. Reid. Yet if it would show Andrew that I did not mean to follow my love in Brandon's direction, then this was what I must do.

In a faint voice Mrs. Reid called to me to come in. The door was ajar, and I pushed it open and went into the darkened room.

"I've brought your Christmas gifts," I said. "I thought you might like them here where you can open them comfortably."

She looked at me so blankly that I felt impelled to offer something more.

"You were missed at the tree this morning," I added as I put my burden down on the foot of her bed. "I hope you're feeling better."

She remained listless, indifferent, offering no response. How dreary this dim room seemed in spite of its luxury. The lack of air and light must surely affect the woman in the bed.

"Do you mind if I open the draperies?" I asked.

"Do as you like," she told me without interest.

When I had let in the light of late morning, I poured her a fresh cup of tea from the cosy-covered pot beside her bed and helped her to sit up. She did not resist me, but sipped the tea and watched me gravely over the rim of the cup.

Dark circles showed beneath her eyes, and there was no dusting of powder, no blush of coloring in her cheeks. The merciless daylight made her look wan and tired, and I saw the beginnings of fine lines at the outward corners of her eyes, the first etching of permanent unhappiness about her mouth. It would be possible, I thought, to pity her, as Andrew did.

I moved the packages where they lay tumbled across her feet and spoke cheerfully. "Which one will you open first?"

After a moment's hesitation she reached across the satin quilt and made a selection. It was her gift from Brandon.

She read the card and dropped it aside. I could not help but see the first words of the bold handwriting: "To my adored wife . . ."

She held the package in her hands and looked up at me. "Why are you doing this, Miss Kincaid?"

I did not want to tell her that the task had been thrust upon me and that I had begun to feel a little sorry for her.

"The packages looked forlorn under the tree," I said. And that was true enough.

With little interest, she untied the ribbon about the package. The wrapping opened to reveal a large flat box with a Tiffany label, and as she touched the lid it sprang open.

I caught my breath. Against rich black velvet lay a parure in chased gold, rubies, and diamonds. The set consisted of necklace, pendant earrings, and a bracelet. I had never seen anything so handsome and I was astonished when Leslie pushed the box from her and burst into tears. In utter devastation she wept without concealment.

Dismayed, I searched her dressing table, found a lace-edged

232

handkerchief, and gave it to her in some concern. She dabbed futilely at tear-drenched amber eyes.

"It's always like this!" she cried. "He thinks money can make up for emptiness! Once I knew what love was like. Once I had a husband who adored me. That's why I know now what emptiness is."

Her outburst shocked me, not only because of her meaning, but because it meant a relinquishing of all pride. If she lost her pride, she would have nothing.

"At the ball last night he humiliated me dreadfully," she choked. "He would not even pretend to be pleased with my company. It was no better than our trip up the Hudson, when he was constantly impatient with me."

I could well imagine how Brandon might humiliate a woman if he chose, and I could not help but pity his wife. Yet he was not a man who would willingly endure in a woman endless headaches, vapors, and self-pity.

She must have sensed my softening toward her, for she grasped at it. "Sit down, Miss Kincaid. Now that you're here, you must listen to me."

I seated myself on the edge of a chair beside her bed, wishing myself anywhere but in that room and blaming Andrew for placing me in this predicament.

Her words began to pour out in complete abandonment. "There was nothing to live for when Dwight died! Yet I had to go on living. Can you understand what such a loss might be like, Miss Kincaid?"

I thought I might very well understand and I nodded.

"In order to live, I snatched at anything that seemed to offer me sustenance. Brandon had been in love with me before I married Dwight. He was Dwight's brother. They had been devoted to each other. So why shouldn't I find in him something of what I had lost? Instead—" the life went out of her voice, leaving a heaviness of despair, "instead there is only this!" She flung a gesture of rejection at the

233

jewels Brandon had given her. "This and a prison from which there is no escape."

Nevertheless, I thought, I would fight back if I were in her place. She was allowing herself to be submerged. Yet I did not know how to offer her strength in this moment of appalling weakness.

Perhaps my silence seemed to spell condemnation, for she began to speak again, a little wildly now.

"You know why I married Brandon, Miss Kincaid," she said. "But haven't you ever wondered why he married me?"

"That is none of my affair," I said evenly.

"While that is quite true, I shall tell you. And it will be something for you to think about in the night hours, something for you to ponder when his face comes to your mind. He married me to buy my silence. Because if he did not, I would have told the truth he is so terribly afraid of. And now that I am bound to him in this empty marriage, I cannot speak out as I might like to do."

I made no response to her words as I moved quickly to gather up packages that lay in bright mockery across her quilts. I said nothing at all as I carried them into the boudoir and left them on the chaise longue, where she might later do as she liked with them. Then I returned to her bedroom and drew the draperies to shut out gray daylight and leave her once more to darkness. All the while she lay very still, her eyes closed, the lashes dark upon her pale cheeks. She did not speak as I went silently from the room and closed the door behind me.

Where the truth lay in any of what she had said, I did not know. It would be best not to think of her words at all, or try to sift truth from self-delusion. She was ill, not only in body, but in mind as well.

As I moved toward the stairs, Jeremy came from his uncle's library, pouncing upon me eagerly the moment he saw me.

"Come see how the collar looks, Miss Megan," he invited.

234

I had no heart for his request and no desire to see Brandon at that moment, but Jeremy was insistent. In the library Brandon stood at the window, his back toward me, and I went no more than a step or two into the room.

The fanciful collar looked a little strange against the stone from which the head had been sculptured. The tall white crown with its stylized plumes at each side made the patterned beads seem too bright by contrast. Yet in the expression of carved lips and eyes I fancied an understanding of all that had gone into the making of the collar. Osiris wore the gift with dignity.

"It's very beautiful," I told Jeremy, and turned toward the stairs before Brandon could speak to me.

When I reached my room I removed the pin that bore Queen Hatshepsut's name and put it among other trinkets, not daring to look at it again. Now that I was alone, the words I had thrust away as being the ranting of a sick woman, returned to plague me. What silence could Brandon have bought? What truth could Leslie speak out against her husband?

These things had no meaning for me, and I must not think about them. I must profit by Andrew's warnings. I must seek recovery of my own pride.

It was not for me to weigh the truth or falsity of the matters she had touched upon. They were no concern of mine. Brandon was out of my reach and always would be. I must tell him that I was leaving. I would wait only until the New Year had begun. That seemed a logical time for decisive action.

Leslie, having flung herself into the depths, roused sufficiently to undertake a further social round that must have left her exhausted almost every night. Perhaps that was what she wanted—the oblivion of exhaustion. She seemed to alternate between coolness toward Brandon and a trembling appeal for his attention, if not his affection. I was relieved to see little of either of them. And ashamed of that relief.

Miss Garth and Selina were away with Leslie much of the time, and I had Jeremy to myself. His mood of exultant happiness over his uncle's acceptance of his gift relaxed into something resembling contentment, and I was glad to see him come down from the heights. For the time being, at least, his uncle's manner toward the boy had changed encouragingly and I wished I had not the sensation of waiting for the unforeseen to happen when it came to the master of the house.

During that week when all was outwardly peaceful, only one small incident ruffled our daily calm. It was no more than a child's quarrel and of little consequence, had it not pointed to trouble ahead. The incident came about because of the carrousel I had given Jeremy.

It was the custom of the house for the family to leave all gifts beneath the tree during the week between Christmas and New Year. If they were taken away to be worn or played with, they were put back when the owner was through. Thus it was that Jeremy somewhat reluctantly left the little music box among his other presents under the tree. He warned his sister not to touch it, and this of course increased its fascination for Selina.

One afternoon when I heard wails of anguish from the drawing room, I ran downstairs to find that Jeremy had slapped Selina for playing with the carrousel. Though Jeremy had the toy safely back in his own keeping, Selina was screeching as only she could screech, while Jeremy watched her in anger and disgust. Miss Garth too heard the uproar, and we both reached the drawing room from different doors at the same time.

There were an unpleasant few moments in which I had to stand up to Miss Garth for Jeremy's cause as being just, while still condemning him for slapping his sister.

"The toy is fragile," I said. "Jeremy had a right to say who may touch it and when. He is very careful with it, and it would be a shame if Selina or anyone else broke it. Selina isn't always careful with her things, as we all know."

If I had not been there, I think Miss Garth would have returned Jeremy's slap and upheld Selina. But she saw that I would not retreat from my stand, so she carried the weeping Selina away to distract and quiet her. The immediate result of the incident—which the children quickly forgot—was an increased tension between Thora Garth and myself. I had a feeling that the woman was merely biding her time, waiting for an opportunity to catch me in some ill-advised moment when I would be at a disadvantage. Then she would raise heaven and earth to get me dismissed. That I did not intend to have happen. When I left, I wanted it to be by my own will, not because I had been put out in disgrace.

As New Year's Day approached, the house itself lent weight to my forebodings of calamity ahead. The holidays had not dispelled its atmosphere of gloom and hidden tragedy. Except for Selina, who wore her feelings lightly on the surface, every member of the household seemed possessed by some dark blight of emotion, hidden or disguised, but ready to burst into the open at a touch.

Had it been like this, I wondered, in the days before Jeremy's father had died? I did not like to entertain such a thought, but it returned more than once to haunt me. New Year's Eve seemed especially hard to endure. Since this was a time of facing both past and future, my thoughts were far from cheerful.

Leslie had long been planning a party for New Year's Eve and she hurled herself into feverish preparation which I could only view with new alarm. She could not go on like this, yet Brandon made no effort to stop her. He seemed to regard her behavior with a cold amusement that had no kindness in it.

On New Year's Eve I sat in my room and tried not to hear

the sounds of gaiety two stories below. I read until eleven o'clock, then braided my hair and went deliberately to bed, pulling the covers well over my ears. I did not want to know when the New Year began. I did not want to hear the bells and I determined fiercely to be well asleep by the time they sounded.

I did not sleep, and I heard the bells quite clearly.

Not only the bells and the tooting and whistling from a distance, but racket from the immediate neighborhood and from within the house as well. Downstairs fringed paper crackers were being pulled with a bang and paper hats undoubtedly donned. One rapping noise came very close, and I realized with a start that someone was knocking on my door.

It must be Jeremy, disturbed by the noise. I flung a wrapper about me and opened the door. Brandon, elegant in evening dress, his shirt front stiff above a white waistcoat, his tie faultless, stood there smiling at me. Beneath dark brows his eyes were alight with a reckless gleam and in each hand he held a glass of champagne. He seemed more vibrantly alive than I'd ever seen him, and I sensed danger in him as never before. In quick remembrance I recalled the first time I had seen Brandon Reid. Even then he had drawn and compelled me, and now I found myself stirred by an excitement I was helpless to resist.

"Happy New Year, Megan," he said. "I wanted to toast the New Year with no one but you. Will you do me the honor?"

All caution was lost to me. I took the glass and held it up by its slender stem, raising it to his.

"To a way out for us," he said and touched the rim of his glass to mine.

My eyes did not drop from his as I drank the sparkling wine. I could not think or weigh or question. I could only feel.

I took no second sip, however, for he removed the glass

from my hand and set both aside on the table near my door. I knew what was to come and I had only one will, one desire. As simply as though no other course of action were possible, I went into his arms. Their clasp hurt me, his mouth bruised mine, yet I reveled in pain.

When he released me without warning, I was startled, for there was sudden anger in him and it alarmed me.

"I'll force her hand. I'll make a way!" he told me, and the roughening in his tone spoke again of violence scarcely restrained.

I drew away, shaken and no longer yielding. He saw that he had frightened me and spoke more gently.

"Give me time, Megan. A little more time to find a way out of this trap I'm caught in. But don't run away. That's one thing I will not have. Do you understand me, Megan?"

I could only nod in agreement. I was held by a compulsion I could not resist. He accepted the answer my eyes gave him, picked up the glasses, and strode toward the stairs. But when he had gone the sound of his voice continued to ring through my mind and I heard the echo of fury driving him.

Shivering, I turned back to my room. Yet my body was warm with fever heat. I went to my window and flung it open upon the cold dawning of the New Year. Though the outward chill did not touch me as I leaned my arms upon the sill, a trembling I understood very well went on and on within me, and part of it was fear.

Outdoors the bells had pealed their way to silence. The last horn blast died raucously. Down in the mews one of the servants banged a final derisive clatter upon a dishpan, as if mocking this arrival of a year in which hope could be so little justified.

The chill I felt lay deep within me. Fear had its roots in a sense of unknown danger. Danger and betrayal. "Don't run away," he had said. Yet even then I knew I had no other choice. Not only for my own sake and for Jeremy's, but for

Brandon's as well. If I remained where he could see me, find me, the violence would erupt into some desperate act. I knew this as surely as though he had told me so. The ingredients for tragedy were building, and I must be well away before an explosion could result.

Chilled at last through all my body, I closed the window upon the New Year and went back to bed. Brandon's kiss had burned itself out on my lips, the memory of his arms no longer warmed me to life. For me this coming week must be one of decision and action. Unhappy decision, action that would cause me endless pain. Yet I knew now what must be done.

22.

THE COLD light of morning brought a strength-
ening of resolution. Brandon had no right to order me not to
run away. Nor could I obey him. Last night I'd learned
enough about myself and about him, about the inexorable
force that drew us together, to warn me thoroughly. The
very fact that deep within me was an ache of longing to
speak my love, to acknowledge it and let it rule me, no
matter what the consequences, made the need for action
all the more urgent.

Fortunately, I had saved most of the salary I'd received in
the Reid household and I would have enough to keep me
until I could find another position. My first thought was to
tell Mrs. Reid that I would heed her wishes, then slip away
without seeing Brandon again, and give him no chance to
stop me. But the more I considered such a course, the more
cowardly it seemed. If my own courage were as strong as it
must be, then nothing he might say could alter my decision.
Today was the time.

The master of the house arose in a mood so stormy that it
made itself heard up the stairs. I began to suspect that he had
regretted his actions of the night before and was thus angry
with himself and perhaps with me as well. All of which

played into the hands of my intention. Tenderness, pleading would be harder to face than anger.

Jeremy, playing the endless tune of "Frère Jacques" on his music box, incurred his uncle's wrath early that morning, and I heard Brandon shouting at the boy to turn it off. I ran to the stairs, meaning to call Jeremy up to the quiet and safety of the third floor, but Brandon saw me there and stared as though I were another child to be reproved.

"Where is the pin I gave you for Christmas?" he demanded. "Why aren't you wearing it?"

So unreasonable a question was exactly what I needed to brace me against any faltering, even though this was not the time to ask for an interview.

"I will return the pin to you," I told him coolly. "Come, Jeremy. Bring the carrousel upstairs."

Brandon scowled at me, but at least it was to his credit that he noted Jeremy's face and apologized to the boy, if not to me.

"I'm sorry, Jeremy. I've a beastly headache. I didn't mean to snap at you like that. Just play your box upstairs for now, will you, my boy?"

Jeremy accepted his words with good grace and came cheerfully upstairs with me.

By custom New Year's Day was a time when ladies remained at home to receive, and the gentlemen of New York, young and old, went from house to house, often imbibing so freely and so often that it was wiser for women to remain indoors and avoid the public streets. Brandon, however, had shut himself early into the library and showed no sign of leaving for a series of calls.

With Selina beside her, Leslie had gone to the drawing room to receive, and, as the doorbell began its constant pealing, servants hurried back and forth, and the day went into its full social swing. Miss Garth busied herself supervis-

242

ing the activity, and, as a result, Jeremy and I had the long day to ourselves.

We passed some of the time watching visitors from the front windows and speculating about them. I tried not to remember that soon this little boy would no longer be a part of my everyday life. It was all I could do to hide my feelings when the thought of coming loneliness engulfed me. Whatever we did, I could not forget that it might be for the last time.

Not until late afternoon, when the calls had wound to an end, when Mrs. Reid had retired, and Garth and Selina were once more upstairs, did I leave Jeremy and seek the opportunity to speak to Brandon Reid.

At the library door the tormenting reminder returned. This, too, was for the last time. He invited me in pleasantly enough and offered me a chair. His manner seemed faintly apologetic, as though he regretted his early-morning temper. But I wanted no relenting from him. It would be better for us both if only I could detest him.

I had brought the pin with me and I laid it upon the desk before him. "I have come to a difficult decision," I said. "But a necessary one. The only course of action remaining to me is to leave your employ as soon as possible. As you know, there are reasons why I cannot remain in this house any longer. Tomorrow I will look for a room and move out as soon as I can."

It took only a moment for the apologetic manner to vanish and anger to take its place. He picked up the scarab brooch and held it out to me.

"You need not insult me into the bargain. This belongs to you."

I took it from him in silence, waiting.

"I might have known you would run away," he continued. "The woman doesn't live who has the courage to stand by when she's needed."

Since I was exerting all the courage in me at that moment,

his words did not help my own temper. "I know where I am needed," I told him with some vehemence. "Jeremy needs me. But there are other matters to be considered first, and my decision will stand."

It was at this unfortunate moment that Jeremy came unwittingly into the room with the carrousel in his hands. Bent on his own concern, he did not sense the atmosphere of the room. With the growing trust he had in Brandon, he held the toy out to him.

"Something is wrong with it, Uncle Brandon," he said. "See—it will play only when I shake it."

He proved this by shaking the toy so that it began the tinkling, monotonous little air I had once found so merry. Brandon flung out a hand in a gesture of impatience. His fingers struck the carrousel, and it flew from Jeremy's grasp and fell with a clatter on the bare hearthstone. The tune whined on for a moment and then clicked to an abrupt stop. I stared in dismay at the crumpled sleigh, the dented canopy.

Jeremy cried out in anguish and rushed to pick up the toy. All his hard-won confidence in his uncle had vanished. The carrousel was the finest treasure he had ever owned, and it was he who was angry now. He turned furiously upon Brandon, pummeling him with his fists until I came to put quieting hands on the boy's shoulders.

Shocked by his own impatient, but unintentional act, Brandon apologized for the second time that day. "I didn't mean that to happen. Give it here and let's see what damage is done."

This time his retraction had no effect. Jeremy held the toy behind his back. "You *did* mean it to happen! You were angry about it this morning and now you're glad you've broken it!"

White and stricken, he clasped the toy tightly to him and rushed out of the room. I stepped to the door and called after him, but he ran unheeding up the stairs.

244

His shrill voice had brought his mother to the door of her bedroom and Miss Garth part way down the stairs. He moved as though he saw neither of them, and Garth stepped back against the wall to let the small furious figure rush by.

"Let him go," Brandon told me, impatient again. "I'm sorry this happened, but I've had more of that tune than I can stand. When he recovers, we'll see what can be done to mend the toy. Right now I want to talk to you."

I was very nearly as upset as Jeremy. The incident had shaken me, and I could not remain to be argued down by Brandon Reid. Without replying, I went into the hall to follow Jeremy upstairs.

Leslie had thrown a loose yellow gown about her shoulders and she looked pale and worn from the festivities of last night and today. I could not face her either just now and I ran up the stairs, brushing past the looming figure of Thora Garth.

Jeremy had closed his door and he did not answer when I tapped on the panel. I stood for a moment listening to the pounding of my own heart, trying to quiet my trepidation. Then I turned the knob and went in.

The boy sat on the edge of his bed with the broken toy in his hands, staring at it intently. I took it from him and tried to minimize the damage.

"I think it's not too serious," I said. "If your uncle can't mend it for you, perhaps we can find someone who can. Or I'll go back to the shop where this came from and try to get another for you."

"He smashed it." Jeremy spoke evenly, without emotion, without expression. "He smashed it because he hates me."

I put my hand on his forehead and found it burning hot. He did not resist when I helped him to undress and get into bed. At suppertime he would eat nothing, and I sat beside his bed until he fell asleep. Only then did I tiptoe away to my own room.

245

I lay down fully clothed, meaning to get up from time to time and make sure all was well. But I was bone-weary. The emotional turmoil I had been through, the hard decision I had come to, all had taken as great a toll as physical action. I fell so deeply asleep that only some deafening sound could have awakened me.

The sound came during the night hours, shattering the quiet of the house. I sat bolt upright in bed, attending with all my senses the echoing crash.

I knew what had wakened me, though I had never before heard such a sound inside a house. The air still trembled with vibration, though otherwise all was silent. I went to my door and opened it a crack upon the dark hallway, waiting for the outcry that must surely follow. But now there was no sound, no sound at all—and that increased my alarm. The silence seemed too intense until I heard a creaking on the stairs. Was someone coming up, or going down? I could see nothing in the blackness. A terror I had not known I could feel washed over me, and I closed my door and stood trembling with my back against it.

Nothing happened, and reason slowly returned to steady me. I must not cower here because I thought I had heard a pistol shot in the house. In his room next door Jeremy would be awake and in need of reassurance. I must look in on him, make sure of his safety. Then, if no one else stirred, I would go downstairs and investigate for myself. Perhaps the sound had come from outside after all. Perhaps a forgotten dream had magnified it.

Lighting a candle, I opened my door softly. At once I saw Jeremy. He stood halfway down the hallway in his nightshirt, and I could hear the chattering of his teeth.

"Go back to bed, dear," I said firmly. "Get in where it's warm and I'll go downstairs and see if anything is wrong. I promise to come back and tell you as soon as I can."

He did not seem to hear my words. He raised his hands

and held them away from him, staring as if they did not belong to him, as if he had never seen them before.

"I've done something terrible," he said.

His tone chilled me far more than the icy air of the hall-way. I pushed him toward his room.

"Quick now," I said. "In bed with you; you're dreadfully cold."

I left my candle on his bureau, lighted another, and started downstairs. Dread of what I might find slowed my steps, yet I must go down. Where was everyone else? Why hadn't the servants come upstairs? But then—would they? Once before there had been tragedy in this house following a shot at night. Might not the servants take the course of wisdom and remain below stairs unless they were summoned?

As I descended toward the second floor, my feeble candle flame pushed back the darkness a bit at a time. When I reached the lower steps I saw that the sound had, after all, aroused others in the house—others as frightened as I.

23.

IN THE door of Leslie's bedroom stood Miss Garth, an arm about the woman who had been her charge as a child. Leslie's face was washed of all color, her eyes enormous. Both women stared at me as I came down the stairs. Neither looked as though she would be of any help, and I had to bolster my own courage.

"Do you think that was a shot?" I asked.

Leslie clung weakly to the governess, and it was Miss Garth who answered me.

"Of course it was a shot and it came from the library. I rushed downstair at once to make sure Miss Leslie was unharmed. Where is Jeremy?"

"In bed," I said, my lips barely forming the words. My fingers tightened around the candleholder lest I drop it. Where was Brandon? Why hadn't he come out of his bedroom?

I could not endure this new terror. The door of the library stood open, a blank oblong of darkness that gave way dimly before the pale thrust of candlelight. Shadows swayed across the room as I held my candle high. At first glance nothing seemed amiss. I moved toward Brandon's desk and stumbled over something that lay on the floor beside his chair.

It was all I could do to hold the candle nearer and look down at what lay at my feet. For a moment no sound came from my lips. Then I called to the two women in the hall.

"Come here and see what has happened!"

Leslie was still afraid and would not come, but Thora Garth stepped into the room and stood beside me. Together we stared at the debris before us. Someone had shattered the Osiris head. Broken pieces of it lay strewn across the carpet, and I knew it must have been smashed by a shot from a pistol.

"Where is Mr. Reid?" I asked. "Why isn't he here?"

"He went out before dinner," Miss Garth said stiffly. "As far as I know he hasn't returned. And a good thing for him it is!"

A sick understanding of her meaning swept through me. She meant that Jeremy had come into this room with a pistol in his hands, perhaps seeking his uncle as he had once sought his father. Not finding him, he had vented his anger upon the stone head his uncle treasured. This was his retaliation, his revenge for the breaking of the carrousel.

Miss Garth turned back to her charge. "It's all right, Miss Leslie dear. It's only that heathenish head that's been broken. You can breathe again, lovey."

Leslie came hesitantly into the library, and it was then we heard the turning of a key in the front door downstairs. Brandon Reid had come home. We waited for him, as still and posed as the inanimate objects in the room. He climbed the stairs, saw the light in the library, and came through the door.

"What has happened?" he asked.

I held out my candle to him and gestured toward the floor. He took the holder from me, staring in disbelief at the shattered bits of stone.

"Light the gas, Megan," he said over his shoulder.

I hurried to do his bidding, and he searched the room swiftly, purposefully. Almost at once he found what he was looking for and picked it up from beneath the desk. When he held it out to us, Leslie gave a cry. It was the pistol from which the shot must have been fired. An ornate weapon with elaborate fittings.

"Wait here," he said to us. "I want to have a look downstairs."

When he had left the room, Miss Garth spoke, her tone deadly cold. "This has gone too far. Something must be done about the boy."

"Yes," Leslie said helplessly, "something must be done."

I thought of Jeremy, trembling upstairs, waiting for punishment to befall him—perhaps asking for it again? I had promised to return quickly, but now I must wait.

Brandon rejoined us in a few moments, carrying a towel filled with slivers of glass. "It's as I thought. Someone wrapped this towel about a fist so as to make no noise and smashed the glass front of the cabinet that holds the pistol collection."

Leslie began to weep softly. Perhaps the memory of that other, more dreadful, shooting had returned to devastate her. But Miss Garth made no move to comfort her now.

"The boy would have killed you if you'd been here," she told Brandon fiercely. "Now perhaps you'll listen to reason."

"Get her to bed." Brandon's words were curt.

Miss Garth made a despairing gesture and then took Leslie by the arm. "Come, lovey. You must get your rest."

When they had gone, Brandon turned to me. "I'll talk to the boy," he said and went out of the room.

As I followed him up the stairs, I tried to plead for Jeremy, but there was so little I could say. If Brandon had been home, would it have been the Osiris that Jeremy smashed? Garth's terrible accusation silenced me.

At the head of the stairs Brandon spoke to me. "I'm partly to blame for this. Because of the carrousel. But that doesn't excuse the boy. Such outbursts are too dangerous, too violent. What if I had been working in the library tonight?"

Whatever I might say would only make matters worse, and I was silent.

For all his chill, Jeremy had not returned to bed. He sat on the floor cross-legged, as if he were trying to make himself so small that no one would find him there. Bleak misery looked from his eyes, and I was reminded of the time when he had fled to the Memorial Home and hidden himself there.

Brandon spoke to him, not ungently. "Tell me exactly what happened, Jeremy."

The boy stood up to face his uncle. He wavered for a moment, then flung himself across the bed in the same wild fury of grief I had seen before.

"I didn't mean to!" he cried. "I never meant to do it! Never, never! I only meant to frighten him. Never to kill him. I was just going to wave the gun at him; I never meant to pull the trigger."

Brandon and I looked at each other. It was not of the Osiris head Jeremy spoke. His mind had fled back in time to the killing of his father.

I sat beside him on the bed and tried to soothe him, but he would not let me touch him. He hurled himself wildly from me, staring in terror at his uncle.

"Listen to me, Jeremy." Brandon spoke quietly. "It's not what happened long ago that we're talking about. Someone broke into the pistol collection tonight. Someone went into the library with a loaded gun and shot a bullet through the Osiris head."

The terror in Jeremy's eyes did not subside, but he stopped crying and sat up, stricken to silence, unable to speak at all.

"Don't question him now," I said to Brandon. "You can see he's in no state to answer you sensibly. You can talk to him tomorrow."

For once he heeded me. He told Jeremy a grave good night and started toward the door. Jeremy found his voice and spoke up in a high, strained tone.

252

"You'll punish me now, won't you, Uncle Brandon? But you won't keep me from going to the memorial service for my father? You *will* let me go to that?"

We were both startled by this sudden turn Jeremy's thoughts had taken. I believe Brandon hesitated on the point of immediate refusal. Then he said, "We'll see," and went out of the room.

I followed him into the hall. "Be gentle with him to-morrow. He's going through a dreadful time."

Brandon shook his head. "There's no use in keeping on with this, Megan. Especially since you're going away. I've given the boy every chance, but this is beyond our handling. He must be placed where he can do no further harm."

This was more than I could bear. "Then put him in my charge! Let me take him away and care for him. If he could be given a new life in different surroundings—where no one knew anything about him, where such terrible things hadn't happened, he would improve. He has been better lately. I know he has!"

For a moment Brandon stared at me coldly. When he spoke there was no kindness in his voice. "You are thinking only of the boy. Do you believe it fair to turn this violence loose on others who cannot even expect it, or defend them-selves?"

For a moment I was held by a doubting that his words awakened in me. Was he right? Was there too much danger to others involved in keeping the boy in normal society? After what he had done tonight, it would seem that Brandon was justified. Yet I knew I could not abandon Jeremy to be put out of the way in some dreadful institution.

I returned to his room, where he still lay across the bed, and persuaded him to get under the covers. Then I sat be-side him and talked to him for a little while. He was quiet enough now, with the emotion drained from him by the out-burst of weeping.

"I think you are old enough to understand that what happened to the carrousel was an accident and not deliberate," I said. "An accident to be forgiven. It was wrong of you to try to pay him back by hurting what he treasured."

He nodded his agreement, wide-eyed.

"Would you like to tell me about it?" I asked gently.

His gaze did not move from mine. "I can't remember," he said, and I heard despair in his voice. "I don't remember anything about it. Miss Megan, I can remember when I shot my father. But I can't remember taking Garth's scissors and thimble, and I can't remember this. It frightens me that I do things I can't remember afterwards." He sat up and flung his arms about me. "Help me not to do them, Miss Megan! Help me not to!"

I remembered the comfort he had taken that time when I'd told him I would not let him hurt either himself or me, and I wished I could give him some similar assurance for the future. But how could he be guarded every moment when one never knew what he might do next?

"I know you love your uncle," I persisted. "Yet you tried to hurt him. You worked so hard to make the collar for the Osiris. How could you destroy the head?"

His eyes were dark with anguish. "How *could* I?" he echoed blankly. "How could I do such an awful thing?" And he looked at me fiercely. "I don't even remember leaving this room."

I held him close, comforting him as best I could, while a flicker of astonishing suspicion ran through me. Was there something here I had missed entirely? Something we were meant to believe that might not be true? What if Jeremy was not guilty of all the mischief attributed to him? He admitted quickly enough the deeds he remembered. If he could not recall the others—had they been his doing?

Such suspicion opened frightening possibilities, and I dared not so much as hint my thoughts to the boy.

254

"You'll be able to sleep now," I assured him. "I'll sit by your bed. You're perfectly safe. Nothing can harm you."

He closed his eyes with such trust in my words that I was shaken. There was so little real assurance of safety I could give him.

The candle on the bureau dipped and guttered, burning low. I went to my room for a shawl and came back to continue my vigil beside Jeremy's bed. I knew I could not sleep if I tried.

What if some of Jeremy's supposed mischief had really been managed by a malignant adult? Someone who wanted the boy put away, who hated his presence here in this house. If the boy could be made to seem increasingly unstable and dangerous, then a purpose might be accomplished. If he went, I would go too—that could be a part of this purpose.

Such a suspicion was shocking to contemplate. Whoever in this household was willing to let a child be blamed for something he had not done, indeed to place evidence at the child's door, was a person driven by a malevolence that knew no bounds.

Jeremy stirred and opened his eyes. "Miss Megan, I do want to go to the ceremony when the Memorial Home is opened. It's to be soon—only about ten days now. Will you speak to Uncle Brandon so he won't choose that for punishment?"

"Why does this mean so much to you?" I asked.

For a moment he seemed at a loss to answer. Then he struggled to explain.

"Since the ceremony will be to honor my father, perhaps he will be close by that day. Perhaps I'll be able to feel him there, and then I can tell him I didn't mean what happened. I've tried to reach him in that room downstairs, but I think he is truly gone from there."

I wanted to put my arms about him and hold him tenderly, lovingly. But I sensed that it was wiser to be matter-of-fact.

255

"I'll speak to your uncle," I promised, though I had little confidence that Brandon would listen now to anything I said.

My soothing and Jeremy's own weariness took effect at last. I sat beside him as he slept, a new force of determination growing within me. All my plans must now be changed. I would not look for a room tomorrow. I could not possibly leave this house until Jeremy was safe. I would stay, and, if someone was using the boy for a hidden, iniquitous purpose, I would expose whoever it was once and for all.

24.

AFTER SPENDING the remaining hours of the night in the chair beside Jeremy's bed, I felt thoroughly bedraggled and weary by morning. Nevertheless, I caught Brandon in the library immediately after breakfast and confronted him with my new resolve. I dared not tell him of my vague suspicions, but I said that I would stay on at my post if only he would not send Jeremy away.

Brandon was a sober, troubled man that morning. He too looked as if he had slept little. The maid had not yet come in to clean the room, and the broken pieces of the stone head still lay upon the floor. The tall white crown had cracked through and broken away from the serene brow of Osiris. The head of the snake—that mark of royalty—clung to a broken fragment, still alert and eerily raised, as if it had life of its own.

I had made it clear that it was Jeremy's interest alone that had caused my change of mind, and Brandon was coolly formal. Perversely, there was an aching in me because he had moved far beyond my reach, but I told myself this was what I wished and I faced him with a manner equally impersonal.

"I'll grant you time," he said. "But not a great deal. I'll grant it only because I want to investigate possibilities more carefully than I've been able to so far. It would be better to put the boy in some private home where he could be assured of good treatment and care. The Bloomingdale Asylum is not to my taste. At least I'm relieved that you'll stay for the time being."

This was not a great deal of assurance, but I must live from moment to moment while I sought an answer to the questions in my mind.

I bent to pick up the flat collar where it lay in the midst of shattered stone and held it out to him.

"It's hard to believe that Jeremy would destroy something he admired so much," I said. "Not after all this work on the collar he made for the head."

"Exactly," Brandon agreed. "The very fact is further evidence of an irrational pattern. I respect your feeling for the boy, Megan, but you mustn't be blinded by your own emotions."

There was no defense I could offer. For all I knew, I might well be blinding myself. Yet there was no other course I could take until I was sure. As I prepared to leave, I remembered Jeremy's request and put it to his uncle.

"Will you allow the boy to attend the opening of the Memorial Home? His heart is set on being there. It seems a small favor to grant him."

As had happened before, Brandon seemed to freeze at mention of the memorial, his disapproval clearly evident.

"That is something I can't allow," he said. "Why should he want it?"

"Perhaps it's a—a penance he wants to make," I suggested not wishing to betray Jeremy's confidence. "Why must you punish him in this particular way?"

Brandon knelt to pick up portions of the shattered stone head. "I'm not punishing him. The boy's behavior is too emotional, too uncertain. We can't have a scene at this ceremony. The papers will be eager for any sensational tidbit

258

they can feed upon. I don't want them raking up what happened in the past because of the boy's presence."

I could understand this, but I felt that the effect upon Jeremy was more important and I said so firmly. Brandon had found a portion of the stone profile—a large piece with part of the brow and cheek, most of the nose, and the entire mouth almost intact. He rose with the piece in hand, and it was strange to see the stone lips with their tolerant smile still untouched by destruction.

"A paper weight for my desk," he said wryly. Then he looked at me again. "The matter is closed. The boy cannot be allowed to attend. If you can't make that clear to him, I will."

"I'll try to make him understand," I said.

All seemed to be at an end between us, and I would have gone from the room, but he put a hand lightly upon my arm and I remembered with a pang the warm clasp of his hands on that cold happy day when I had skated with him in Central Park. How long ago that seemed to me now.

"When did you last have a full night's sleep, Megan?"

I managed a stiff smile. "Not last night. But I can sleep during lesson time this morning." I moved from his touch because I did not like the way a weakness I decried started through me.

He noted my withdrawal as he had noted it the first day I had come to this house.

"I've granted you time with Jeremy," he said. "So now you must grant me time as well, Megan. Believe in me for a little while. I am not without ingenuity. A way out must be found. Do you understand what I mean, Megan? A way out for us."

But there was no way out with honor and without harm to others. His words broke my heart a little, and I knew I dared not stay, dared not listen, lest I be in his arms again. I gave him a quick, governess' bow and would have hurried away, had it not been for a sudden interruption.

Henry came to the library to say that a telegram had come for Mr. Reid, and the messenger was waiting for an answer.

Brandon opened the wire and spoke quickly to Henry. "It's my father. He is gravely ill. Will you pack my bag at once and call the carriage. I'll take the first train I can catch."

I wanted to offer my sympathy, ask if there was anything I could do, but he had forgotten me and I slipped quietly away and went upstairs to the schoolroom, where lessons were about to begin.

Miss Garth was with Selina, and Andrew and Jeremy were seated at the long table, their books spread before them. I had not seen Andrew since our walk around Washington Square on Christmas Day.

I told them the news about Brandon's father, and Miss Garth dropped her embroidery and stood up.

"I must tell Miss Leslie," she said, and hurried from the room.

"It's a wonder the old man has held on as long as he has," Andrew said. But there was something that interested him more, and he cocked an eyebrow in my direction. "Garth has been giving me an account of your exciting night," he told me. "With possible embellishments. Sometime I'd like your version, Megan."

I knew by the way Jeremy bent over the pages of his book that Miss Garth had let vitriol flow and he had retreated from the flood.

"I'll be happy to give you an account of what happened," I said. "It may be different from other accounts you've received."

Jeremy looked at me, suddenly intent. "Have you asked my uncle about attending the memorial opening?"

In the face of his anxiety I made a sudden resolve. "Yes, I have," I admitted. "For reasons that have nothing to do with any punishment, neither you nor Selina may attend. However, I am going in your place, Jeremy. I know it won't ac-

260

complish the same purpose, but at least I will be there *for you* and I'll come home right after it's over and tell you everything that happened. And later I'll take you there on a special visit. Will that help a little?"

He was far from content. Disappointment lay upon him heavily, but he returned to his book without argument.

Andrew was openly displeased with my plan. "If Reid had any sense, he would see that the affair was canceled. It's no place for you, Megan, or for anyone else from this house. Let Reid be the one to make a target of himself if he wants scandal to break again. The rest of you should stay home."

"He doesn't want it," I said. "He is very much against the whole thing."

"Yet he allows it to go on. Even Garth is worried about the outcome."

What could happen other than further unpleasantness in the papers, I did not know, and I was not at that time particularly interested. I left them to their lessons and returned to my room, where I lay down to rest.

It was disturbing to realize that Brandon would now be away in New Jersey and I would be left alone with two women who hated me.

Nevertheless, the days passed quietly enough and nothing untoward happened. Word that his father had died came from Brandon. He would return immediately after the funeral, and in time for the opening of the memorial.

I began to count the days.

During this period Jeremy was not well. The destruction of the Osiris head was taking its after-toll in his own concern about his actions. I longed to offer him reassurance, but I did not dare because I could not be sure. My belief was something that seemed reasonable to me, but I had no shred of evidence to support it. With Jeremy's curious trick of absenting himself from the world around him, it was still possible that he had destroyed the head in a moment of fierce anger

261

against his uncle and then blanked the incident from his mind.

The fact that after the occurrence Leslie, too, was ill, offered me nothing in the way of proof. These days she seemed increasingly upset by the slightest thing, and I wondered that she insisted upon attending the opening of the memorial to her first husband.

Garth refused flatly to go. Not even for her beloved Leslie would she attend this affair. My own intention of going I meant to keep to myself until the time came.

Brandon returned home a day ahead of the affair, and while he expressed grief over the death of his father, there was something strange about him that had nothing to do with his loss. Something suppressed and restrained, as if he held himself back with difficulty. I know he was closeted with Leslie for some hours on the day of his return.

On the morning of the memorial ceremony I hurried through the house looking for him, to announce my plan. I found him alone in the dining room, finishing breakfast. He invited me to join him, and I sat down reluctantly. I knew he would regard my purpose as sheer obstinacy and I wanted to get through the announcement of what I meant to do as quickly as possible.

He gave me no immediate chance, but began to reminisce about his father, telling me more of the old man and his fierce family pride, of how he had worshiped his younger son and taken satisfaction in his every achievement.

"I kept that intact for him, at least," Brandon said. "I let nothing destroy it, no matter what the cost. And he never knew the cruel truth about—about what happened. He seemed content to have me with him at the end, even though I've never taken the course he wanted me to follow."

Brandon fell silent and when I knew he did not mean to continue, I told him what I had come to tell him.

"I've made a bargain with Jeremy," I said.

He began to watch me with an odd intensity, and I saw that some elation kindled him this morning. When he made no comment, I hastened to explain my plan.

"Since Jeremy cannot go to the ceremony, I've promised that I will go in his place, and that later I will take him there on a visit. Naturally I will not join the family. I'll slip in quietly and sit somewhere at the back of the room."

"As you like," he said with surprising indifference, and I sensed the excitement in him, barely restrained.

Suddenly he leaned toward me across the table. "Megan, I've talked to Leslie. I've told her that she must release me from this impossible marriage. She has cause enough, and it's hopeless to go on living together under the same roof when we detest each other."

I sat very still, saying nothing.

"She took it rather well," he went on. "At least she indulged in no fits of temper or weeping. In fact, she said very little, one way or another. How she will react when she's had time to think my proposal over is a matter for speculation. There may easily be a scandal if she chooses to make one. Or there may be nothing at all. In any case, I've decided to leave this house as soon as I am able."

In spite of my own involvement with his plans, I had to think of Jeremy. "If you leave, what of the boy?"

He set his coffee cup down sharply. "If the boy were normal, I would consider him to a greater extent. He is not. There's no further doubt on that score. At least I promise you that he will be placed in better circumstances than he lives in under this roof."

"But he will be a prisoner?" I said. "An—an inmate?"

"What would you have? If I leave him to the tender consideration of his mother, he'll be packed off to Bloomingdale at once. And you will be dismissed the moment I am out of the house. I give you my word, Megan, that I'll see the boy well cared for before I take any step to work out my own freedom."

"What if you're doing Jeremy an injustice?" I asked. "What if it was not he who did that dreadful mischief the other night?"

"What are you talking about?" Brandon's disbelief was evident.

I made a helpless gesture. "I can give you no proof. But while he remembers other things he has done, he doesn't remember this. I think he would tell me if he did."

"Nonsense! The boy is too unbalanced to know what he has done after he does it. Who would play such a trick? And why?"

"The person who most wants to see the boy put away without further delay. The person who has now succeeded—or believes he has succeeded—in proving Jeremy too dangerous to remain in this household."

Brandon made a sharp, quick movement, and his hand struck the coffee cup, spilling brown liquid across the linen. I was reminded of the quick gesture that had broken the carrousel. How could I love so angry and irritable a man? Yet love him I did and I watched miserably as he rang for Henry. When the butler came to clear up, I made my escape. For the moment there was no more to be said between us.

At least I had planted my seeds of doubt. Let Brandon consider them and perhaps nurture them into growth.

I went upstairs to dress for this morning's affair, feeling myself in a strange state of suspension. I could not believe that Leslie would easily let Brandon go, whether she loved him or not. No matter what he had said to her, I did not dare to hope. And whichever way I turned, there was always Jeremy. Even though she might detest the sight of him, Leslie was his mother and in the long run she would decide his fate. Perhaps it was she to whom I must talk. Perhaps if I went to her outright and told her that I would make an

264

accusation if she tried to put Jeremy into an asylum, I could frighten her into a change of attitude.

But though my thoughts were never still, I could fix upon no sound course of action. The moments slipped by, and I moved with them as though I were carried by some sea current that held me inactive for the moment, yet would inevitably hurl me upon a rocky and dangerous shore.

25.

DRESSED IN my wren's brown, I left the house ahead of the others, saying good-by only to Jeremy, and took a Broadway car to my destination. My few months of riding in the Reid carriage had given me a greater distaste than ever for the dirty, vermin-ridden horsecars. I held my reticule tightly, for pickpockets often rode the cars in this crime-infested city. It was a relief that I need not travel far.

At my stop I left the car and hurried across the street. The sidewalks were rimmed with soot-strewn snow, and there was gray mud everywhere in this mucky thawing. Already there were carriages drawing up before the new brownstone building and people were thronging inside. The scaffolding and workmen were gone, the home ready for occupancy. No one questioned me as I stepped into the wide main hallway and followed others toward a long room that had been set up for this occasion with rows of wooden chairs. A small platform had been placed at the head of the room, with a lectern and several chairs upon it. The front rows, except for a section saved for the Reid family and dignitaries in charge, were already filling up.

Speaking to no one, I found my way to the rear and sat down to wait, trying to make myself as inconspicuous as possible. I was here merely as a spectator, to report to Jeremy all that I saw. At least there seemed no cause for the foreboding Andrew Beach had entertained about this affair.

The long room, perhaps a dining room under ordinary circumstances, was almost full by the time Brandon Reid came in with Leslie on his arm. I could not help but note once more what a deceptively fine-looking couple they made together. He, tall and impressive in appearance; she, so slight and lovely in the black that gave her pallor an ethereal look. Various persons came forward to greet them and show them to their seats in the front row. A buxom, motherly woman, perhaps the matron of the Home, stepped up to shake Mrs. Reid's hand.

After a slight delay the speeches began. There was an impassioned eulogy for Dwight Reid, given by the minister whom I had heard in the little church on Fifth Avenue. From where I sat I could see both Brandon and Leslie in profile and I watched them as the words rang out over the assemblage. Brandon looked grim and uncomfortable, as if he longed to be anywhere else than here. Leslie's profile looked as pure and cool as though it had been chiseled from ice. She was following every word that was spoken, with the intentness of a sorrowing widow, and the black plumes of her hat trembled when she bowed her head. An inappropriate role, surely, and inappropriate mourning, since she had been married for some time since Dwight's death.

When the minister completed his words of praise and sat down, a member of New York's judiciary stepped to the lectern and spread before him the papers of his speech. I had heard of this man, had read about him in the papers. I wondered that he had been selected for this occasion. There was so much scoundrelism in high places these days, for all that Tweed had been sent to prison, and there had been much buying and selling of justice. Someone farther removed from the breath of scandal might have seemed a wiser choice, even though this man had been introduced as a friend of Dwight Reid's.

So dull was his speech that the listeners began to stir restlessly and there was disrespectful whispering. My own attention had wandered when I heard someone murmur, "Oh, the poor lady!"

I whipped my gaze to the front of the room and saw that Leslie was on her feet, facing the audience. She had flung out her hands in entreaty, as if asking to speak, and the man at the lectern paused in astonishment, gaping at her. She swayed a little as she stood there, and her pallor was alarming. The interruption occupied no more than seconds, for Brandon was at her side at once. He caught her lightly up in his arms and spoke to the chairman as he hurried toward the door with his burden.

"Forgive us, please. My wife is ill. She has fainted."

I did not think she had fainted, but at least she did not struggle as he carried her through the quickly opened door. As the buxom matron hurried after them, the speaker sought his place in his notes once more and droned on above the rustle of the room. I left my seat unnoticed, and fled through a rear door. Ahead of me the matron led the way to a room across the hall, and I followed as Brandon carried Leslie into it and laid her upon a sofa. After a moment of hovering, the matron said she would go for aromatics and hurried away. I closed the door behind her, and Brandon noted my presence with a quick glance, though he did not speak.

Leslie needed no aromatics. Her cheeks were no longer pale, but flushed as if she were feverish. She sat up and pushed Brandon away from her.

"How dare you stop me!" she demanded, and I heard the rising hysteria in her voice. "Why didn't you let me tell them the truth? All of the truth—while everyone was there to hear!"

"You're out of your senses," Brandon said coldly. "This sort

269

of behavior will merely get you into the scandal sheets." He glanced at me. "Let no one in, Megan, until she recovers enough so that I can take her home."

I opened the door a crack to the matron, took the bottle of smelling salts from her, and said that Mrs. Reid wished to be alone with her husband. She did not challenge my presence, and I was able to close the heavy door before Leslie's voice made itself heard beyond the room.

All the stored-up emotion in her was finally spewing out, and it was a dreadful thing to behold. Her beauty had vanished in this ravishment of her features; her voice was high with tension.

"It's time I spoke the truth! It's time I told the world that it was you who killed Dwight. You, who were so determined that nothing should smear your precious family name, that you shot your own brother to death and used the boy to hide your crime."

Her voice broke, and a dreadful silence lay upon us. Horror possessed me. For one shocked moment I almost believed her. Then denial and incredulity washed through me and I knew Brandon must be protected from such madness. I braced myself against the door, knowing that I must let no one into this room.

His face had gone deathly white, and a muscle twitched in his cheek. When his hands closed into fists I thought he would do her bodily harm. Then his fingers opened slowly and he did not touch her, even though her words ran on in a wild stream of accusation.

"The boy had a pistol in his hands, yes! But it was your gun that fired the shot, not the one he held. Have you forgotten that afterwards I helped you to get rid of the extra pistol so that it would never be found? I protected you! Because I was foolish enough to love you in spite of everything."

She would have struggled up from the sofa, but he took her by the shoulders in a grip that must have hurt and held her

270

there. Now, surely, he would deny her words. He would laugh at this vicious nonsense that could have no basis in reality. In silent anguish my thoughts pleaded with him.

He said nothing. He held her in that crushing grip till her head fell back and she stared up at him with a dawning of realization in her eyes. I think she knew then how close she was to death. And knowing, she went limp in his hands. He let her fall back upon the sofa and stepped away from her. I longed to be anywhere but in that room. I had seen and heard more than I could bear to live with, if Brandon did not deny her words. Yet still he said nothing.

Released from momentary danger, Leslie sat up and again her voice took up the tenor of dreadful condemnation.

"Do you think you can silence me now? Do you think I'll let you escape me for one of your light-o'-loves? Never! You'll stay with me and suffer as you've made me suffer. If you take a step away, I'll tell the truth to the world, as I nearly told it today!"

Brandon's hand flashed out, and the slap of it across her cheek sounded sharply through the room. Leslie crumpled upon the sofa cushions, silenced at last. He stood looking down at her, and, if there had been hot anger in him before, it had now turned to icy disgust.

"Get her home," he said curtly to me. "I can't trust myself if I listen to her longer."

He opened the door and went past me without reassurance or denial, and I closed it behind him, turned the key in the lock. I was torn in a dozen ways. I wanted to leave Leslie there and escape the very sight of her. I wanted to run after Brandon and beseech him to tell me that none of what his wife had said was true. But there was in me as well a primitive impulse to force a denial of her words from this woman by sheer force. That I should be so shaken by an instinct to injure, shocked and steadied me. For a moment longer I stood with my back

271

to the door, waiting for my breathing to quiet so that I could act. There was, of course, only one thing I could do.

A quick look about showed me that the room opened upon a small service area, with a cellar staircase leading down. If I could rouse Leslie, perhaps we might escape without being halted for questions or sympathy. This was the only purpose I could cling to with certainty in my state of sick shock.

I went to the sofa and took her hand, pulling her up without gentleness. To my relief, she offered no resistance, more like a rag doll in my grasp than a woman. I could not speak to her with any kindness, and the sound of my voice was harsh in my own ears.

"Come," I told her. "You are ill, and we must get you home at once."

She came with me blindly, as though she scarcely knew my identity. On the stairs she stumbled and might have fallen if I had not put an arm about her to steady her as we went down. My flesh crept at the touch. I could have no task more abhorrent to me than to give aid to Leslie Reid. Yet even as I shrank from contact with her, my wayward mind heard again the torrent of her words and began to question of its own volition.

Could there be the faintest truth in anything she had said? For if there was, who was I to shrink from Leslie Reid? I, who loved a man who might have committed a murder and allowed a child to shoulder the blame?

No! I thought. No—never! Not Brandon.

Once down the stairs, I found a rear door easily and in a moment we were out upon the sidewalk. The hall had been drafty and we had both retained our wraps, so we were ready for the street. I made no attempt to find the Reid carriage, but hailed a passing hansom cab and bundled my companion into it. In mutual silence we sat side by side in the leathery-smelling dimness. The weight of shock still lay upon me, and I was fearful of my own traitorous thoughts that would not give unquestioning belief in Brandon as I wished them to.

The cab jounced along over uneven pavement, and Leslie began to recover. She sat up and fastened her plumed hat more firmly upon her head with its long skewer of a hatpin, thrust her tumbled red hair into place beneath the brim. Her breathing had gone faint after Brandon had slapped her, but now it quickened and she seemed aware of me for the first time.

"How queer that it should be you who rescued me," she murmured. "Have you ever thought of how we've been drawn together under strange circumstances, you and I? If you had trusted me, I could have helped you, I could have saved you from the trouble you are in."

"I am in no trouble," I told her unsteadily. I wanted none of her deceptive gentleness.

She went on, her voice soft as a whisper, and I remembered that day when she had stood in the window of her room and watched us drive away, that day I'd gone to the play with Brandon and the children. I had thought of her then as a ghostly presence in the house. How wrong I had been.

"You are in very great trouble, Miss Kincaid," the soft voice insisted. "You are in the same trouble I was in from the moment I first saw him. You are in love with him, and any woman who loves him must suffer."

I ignored her reference to me. "How could it be from the first moment? You were going to marry Dwight."

She nodded, and the plumes on her hat ruffled gently with the movement. "Yes. And I married Dwight. Because he loved me and always would. And because my father was ruined and everything had crashed about my head. But I never stopped wanting Brandon. Afterwards—when Dwight was dead and there was no safety to cling to—what choice did I have? Even to becoming an accomplice after the fact. And what could he do but marry me and thus assure my silence? Believe me, Miss Kincaid, he was not above buying that protection. Otherwise

273

he would never be tied to one woman. Once he has what he covets, he grows bored and there's an end to it. Perhaps an end to everything for the woman. Do you think that would not happen to you also?"

I wanted to put my hands over my ears to shut out her words. Instead, I tried to deflect them.

"It was you who wanted Jeremy out of the house," I said. "You, most of all."

She made no attempt to evade the accusation. "Naturally. Because sooner or later the boy would convince someone that a second pistol existed and Brandon would be convicted. I still loved him. I still wanted to save him from the results of his own act. There would be no injustice to Jeremy. He is unbalanced and violent."

It was safer to think of Jeremy.

"He is your son," I said. "Yet you have no love for him."

"Selina is the child I love. Jeremy has always frightened me. He was so much his father's son, and I could never love him. You've seen for yourself how dangerous he is."

"I've seen nothing of the kind," I said. "I've seen only the aftermath of his self-blame." I turned my head and looked at her there beside me in the dim interior of the cab. How pure her profile, how deceptively lovely. "It was you who smashed the Osiris head, wasn't it?"

Faint laughter brimmed to her lips. "How clever you are! Yes, of course it was I. Brandon would never believe in his own danger. His sense of guilt has caused him to be overly generous to the boy. Your presence and influence on Jeremy has made everything worse, and I had to prove that we could keep the child with us no longer."

I could feel only loathing for the woman beside me. "Then it was you who took Miss Garth's scissors and thimble and hid them beneath Jeremy's pillow." I did not question; I stated. "But now the truth must be told," I went on. "All of it. Jeremy must understand his own innocence."

274

Her eerie laughter bubbled again, and afterwards the silence between us was potent with meaning.

To think of Jeremy was no longer safe. Freeing him from the years' weight of guilt might mean to seal Brandon's fate. Yet Jeremy must be cleared. There was no other choice. My heart contracted at the thought of his long helpless suffering. Surely, surely Brandon would never have taken his own freedom at so great a cost to a child. I would never believe that of him. He might kill in hot anger, but this he would never do. And he must tell me so himself.

I had only one purpose now. As soon as it was possible I would see him and ask for the truth. He would tell me that Leslie was a liar, that she held nothing over his head. He *must* tell me that he was innocent of his brother's death, of this long torturing of Jeremy. I could live only for the moment of seeing him. Nothing else mattered.

When the ride ended, Leslie got out of the cab and went up the steps without my help. She rang the bell insistently while I paid the cabby. When Henry opened the door, I followed her into the house.

26.

THE MOMENT Leslie was inside, she turned limp and helpless again. Garth was summoned to take her upstairs, and the household was in a stir of concern over her state. Such histrionic ability no longer amazed me. This was the way she kept everyone jumping through her hoops.

When I found that Brandon was not yet home, I went directly upstairs. I hoped to avoid Jeremy for the moment, but he was watching for me on the third floor.

"Come and tell us everything that happened, Miss Megan," he invited eagerly.

There was no escaping him, and I went into the schoolroom, where morning lessons were coming to an end. Selina and Andrew sat at the table. Andrew saw my face and brought me a chair, but I would not sit down. I wanted only to satisfy Jeremy and make my escape.

"I'm sorry," I told the boy, "but I have little to report. Dr. Clarke, the minister, gave a fine talk about your father, and there was a great crowd of people there. But the strain was too much for your mother. She became ill, and I had to bring her home. So I've no idea of what went on at the ceremony after that."

"Why you?" Andrew asked. "Why didn't Reid bring her home himself?"

I could not stand there and quibble. Fear and anxiety were building up in me, and Andrew recognized the fact that something was wrong. He did not press his own questions and he checked Jeremy.

"No more now," he said. "Miss Megan is tired. I'll see her to her room."

Not even the reassuring pressure of Andrew's hand beneath my arm could save me from my frantic fears. I wanted only the solitude of my room, where I could wait until Brandon returned to the house.

Andrew opened my door for me, but he did not let me go at once. "Tell me what's troubling you, Megan," he pleaded.

I was near the breaking point and I looked at him a little wildly. "Mrs. Reid has accused Brandon of his brother Dwight's murder. She is out of her mind—completely mad. What happened was dreadful—dreadful and nearly disastrous."

"So it's come at last," he said. "The lid has blown off with a vengeance. You'd better tell me about it, Megan. Perhaps it will help you to talk."

Even in my distraught state, I saw his concern for me, but I could only shake my head. "I don't know the truth yet. Perhaps I can tell you later—when I know. Let me go, Andrew, please let me go."

He put a hand on my arm in a quick, comforting gesture and released me. I went into my room and flung off my wraps, letting them fall where they might. I could not lie on the bed, or settle myself in a chair. I could only pace the small room. I heard the summons to the midday meal, but I did not go down. Would anyone in this house ever again be able to eat a quiet meal? The thought of food sickened me.

Once I paused in my pacing and summoned Kate, to ask if

278

Mr. Reid had yet returned to the house. She told me that he had come home and was now closeted with his wife. I could not refrain from questioning her. I no longer had any pride.

"Are their voices angry?" I asked. "Do you think they are quarreling?"

There was pity in her eyes, and I wondered how much of my "secret" was known to the servants.

"I couldn't hear a thing," she told me frankly. "Though I listened outside the door. Garth came out soon after the master went in and she nearly caught me there. But their voices were low, miss."

When she had gone, I left the shelter of my room. The children were in the nursery, and Garth was with them now, Andrew gone. Like Kate, I listened at the door to make sure. After that I paced the third-floor hall instead of my room. Up and down, up and down, pausing occasionally at the stair rail to look down at the floor below, or to hold my breath and listen. Now and then a murmur of voices reached me, but they were not raised until the very end. When I heard the door of Leslie's bedroom open, I went a few steps down without care for being seen. Thus I heard his words and saw them both in that angry moment.

"You can do your worst!" he flung at her in a voice that was deadly to hear. "It doesn't matter any more."

In her yellow gown, Leslie seemed as stiff as a dressed-up doll. But her face, as I saw it before she closed the door of her room, was that of a woman who would stop at nothing.

I waited only until Brandon went into the library. Then I flew down the stairs and entered without knocking. Entered and shut the door behind me. I would not let him send me away.

He stood before the window, where I had seen him so often, and he did not know I was there until I spoke his name. Then he turned and looked at me down the length of the room.

Again I was aware of the high sweep of dark hair above his forehead, the gray eyes, the nose with its faint hump of bone, the mouth that could be cruel as well as kind. I knew only that this was the face of my love and that I must suffer now as he so plainly was suffering. Yet when I took a step toward him with my hand outstretched, he left the window and put the desk between us.

"What are you here for?" he asked coolly.

"I want only to understand the truth," I told him. "I will believe whatever you tell me."

His short laugh was far from reassuring. "The truth? That is a very large term. Do you, for instance, know the truth behind every action of your own, Megan?"

I had often enough had doubts of my own motivation, but now I wanted concrete reassurance—not of motives, not of reasoning behind some troubled act, but the truth of the act itself. There were exonerating facts, I was sure, if only he would reveal them, if only he would deny.

"What did she mean about there being a second pistol?" I asked.

For an instant I thought he would dismiss me angrily from the room. But he seemed to think better of it. With an absent hand he picked up the jagged stone, all that remained of the Osiris head. He spoke without looking at me, his fingers moving down the nose, touching lips that still smiled serenely.

"Leslie has always been a skillful fabricator of lies," he said. "She will invent any fantasy that suits her need, or play any part her fancy dictates. There was no second pistol that night, Megan. I was there when Jeremy fired the shot, as I've told you before. I picked up the pistol he used and found it still warm. You can take no hope for the boy's sake in this fantasy of another gun. She will say anything she could to condemn me."

He seemed to recognize the object in his hands and set it

down as though the face of a judging Osiris repelled him. I leaned forward to touch the broken piece of stone.

"Mrs. Reid told me it was she who smashed the head with a pistol shot. Not Jeremy."

My words seemed to break through the guard he had raised against me. He stared at me for a moment and then nodded.

"Yes, I suppose that's possible. There's no end to what she may try. But I'm done with her now. Done with this house and everything in it. I'll be away as soon as possible. I've told her she can do her worst."

"I know," I said. "I heard." Once more I stepped toward him, wanting only to offer him my belief and trust. "Brandon, take me with you!"

His look softened. Then he shook his head, not unkindly.

"No, Megan. You must leave the house too. But you must leave alone. I'll involve you no longer. What is coming will be desperately unpleasant for everyone. It may destroy me completely. I'm ready to face that now."

"I would stand beside you, if you'd let me," I said.

He came to me then and took me by the shoulders. He shook me with something of his old exasperation and yet gently, with great tenderness.

"You will do nothing of the kind. You will go out of this room and out of my life and you will never look back. You will go now, Megan, while there is still time."

I saw there could be no fighting him at this moment. I would not be put aside forever if he wanted me, but I could not oppose him now.

"Why did you marry her?" I murmured despairingly. "*Why?*"

His hands dropped from my shoulders, and there was a dark opaqueness in his eyes. "You've asked for an answer," he said, "and I'll give it to you. I married her to keep her silent. Are you satisfied now?"

281

I knew that he was speaking the truth. No matter what concealment he might have attempted earlier, what he had just told me was true. He had corroborated Leslie's words. I turned without speaking, suddenly empty of emotion, able to say nothing more.

He made no effort to stop me as I went out of the library and fled upstairs to my room. There I flung myself upon the bed, and, as feeling and painful realization began to return, I think I died a little.

The afternoon went by in a strange, breathless quiet. With so much of terror and hatred stirring under one roof, it would seem that it must surely explode into sound. But on through mid-afternoon the house was still.

I did not die entirely, for my lungs continued to draw breath and my body went on living. I could not lie there on the bed forever, rejecting life, even though that was what I willed. Responsibility remained, and I rose at length and went to seek the children. They were alone in the nursery, playing checkers. Selina said Miss Garth had gone to her room with a headache. I sat with them, distraught and absent-minded, and Jeremy watched me gravely. Once he sought to distract me.

"Selina has told me her secret," he announced.

Selina laughed slyly, but I had no interest in secrets just then.

Jeremy went on. "She has found where the other pistol was hidden, Miss Megan. She has known where it was for a long time."

My attention focused abruptly, and I began to listen.

"I kept the secret!" Selina cried. "I didn't tell!"

"I always knew there was another one," Jeremy said reproachfully. "I tried to tell Captain Mathews and Uncle Brandon that the pistol I brought from the collection *wasn't* loaded. I'd checked it to make sure. I only meant to frighten my father. But then there was a terrible explosion and he fell. Afterwards Uncle Brandon picked up the pistol that had been fired. But, Miss Megan, it wasn't the pistol I'd taken from the collection. It was the same size, but it was a different one. So I kept looking and looking—even though I began to believe I must have shot my father. Everyone else kept saying I had, and after a while I didn't know what was real and what wasn't. Now Selina has found the pistol."

I had not died at all, I found. Every nerve was exquisitely atune and ready to throb with pain. Leslie's words were being proved true once again. The pistol whose existence Brandon denied was real and within reach. For two long years it had lain in concealment while a child pitted his futile child's strength against the disbelief and cruel concealment of adults.

Jeremy was looking at me strangely. "You're very pale, Miss Megan. Are you ill?"

I rallied strength to ask a question and was astonished that my voice did not crack with strain.

"How did you know where the pistol was?" I asked Selina.

She pushed a checker absently with a finger. "I was watching Mama one time when she didn't know. I was peeking between the boudoir curtains. And I saw her take it out and hold it in her hands. She was behaving as though she didn't know what to do with it. She put it in the drawer of her dressing table. Then she changed her mind and hid it in the first place again."

"What place?" I said. "Where is it now?"

Jeremy answered. "It's in that big brass candlestick that always stands on the hearth in Mama's room."

"Let me tell!" Selina protested. "It's my secret. Miss Megan, the top part of the stick unscrews and there's a big hollow space down inside the base."

"The pistol I took upstairs that time had an ivory handle," Jeremy said. "It wasn't the one they found."

I shook my head from side to side dazedly. Not in disbelief, but in pain and confusion.

"Show it to Miss Megan, Jeremy!" Selina cried. "You said someone put the candlestick in Papa's room, didn't you? Get it then, and show her the pistol."

"It's not there any more," Jeremy said. "Miss Megan, after Selina told me this afternoon, I went to Papa's room to find out about the pistol. I didn't notice that the bolt on the boudoir door was off. While I was there the door started to open and I didn't want to be caught in that room. I went down on my stomach and slid under the bed. Someone came into the room, walking softly, and went over to the bureau. I could hear the steps pause and then go back to the door. I looked out from under the bed, and there was enough light coming from the boudoir so I could see. It was Miss Garth, and she was carrying that big candlestick in her hands. So now I suppose it's back in Mama's room. And I can't show it to you. But we must do something about that pistol soon, mustn't we, Miss Megan? We must make my mother tell."

"Yes, we must do something about it." I could barely manage the words. "But wait a little while, Jeremy. We must—we must find the best way to handle this."

He nodded solemnly. "Now someone else will be in trouble," he said. "We have to think about that."

He pushed away the game board and went to look out the nursery window. Watching him miserably, I was reminded of his uncle, staring out at the winter bleakness of Washington Square, longing for escape. There was no comfort I could offer Jeremy. Fear was growing in me. And profound despair.

By late afternoon the wind began to rise—that dark, cold wind that made the square its playground. Shutters rattled, and there was a whining at every window crack the gale could find. Beneath its oval skylight, the stairway was a funnel that sucked up the stormy flow of air.

We had an early supper—just the children and I. Garth did

not join us, but remained locked in her room, as Leslie did in hers. For once, I gathered, Mrs. Reid had refused the ministrations of her former governess and sent word by Kate that she wanted to rest and be alone. I dared not think what dark plans Leslie Reid might even now be concocting.

Though the children could not know the full cause, the sense of foreboding, of waiting for disaster to fall, made itself felt in them as well. Selina was less than her usual exuberant self, and Jeremy was quietly watchful, with an air of waiting about him. Now and then I caught his eyes upon me and knew what he waited for. But I could not yet decide what action was to be taken about the pistol. More than once that afternoon I wished for Andrew's presence in the house. I was ready to confide in him now. There was justice in Andrew. He would know what to do with this knowledge of the pistol's existence and its hiding place. He would help me to do whatever was right.

Had Brandon left the house? I wondered, and listened for his step, for the sound of a door. When would I see him again? Even while my mind tried to cope with his possible guilt, my heart dismissed it and would not believe.

As I descended the stairs from the third to the second floor, I saw that Andrew had not, after all, left the house this afternoon. Leslie must have chosen to recover from her earlier theatrical efforts and sit for her portrait, because Andrew was ahead of me, approaching the door of her room, some of his painting materials in hand.

I hurried when I saw him, intending to ask for a chance to talk to him. But by the time I reached the foot of the stairs, he had gone into Leslie's room and I determined to catch him later, when the sitting was over. As I followed the second floor hallway toward the lower stairs, I met Kate carrying up a supper tray.

"For Miss Leslie," she said as I went past her down the stairs.

I did not reach the front door, however, for the crash of Kate's tray resounded through the house. Startled, I stood at the foot of the stairs, while above me, over the sound of the wind outdoors, I heard a scream, followed by an eerie, wailing cry of terror, a keening that chilled my very blood.

I whirled about and ran upstairs.

27.

THE KEENING ceased, but now I could hear the desperate, terrified sound of a woman sobbing.

Kate was on her knees outside Leslie's room, her overturned tray nearby, its broken china and spilled food on the floor beside her. It was she who was sobbing, rocking back and forth with her apron over her face.

I shook her by one shoulder, shook her hard. "What's the matter? What has happened?"

She raised a tearful, frightened face. "I was just bringing the tray to Miss Leslie, as Miss Garth told me to do. And—and—"

She broke off with such horror in her eyes that I did not wait for her to finish. I started toward the door to find out for myself what had happened. At once Kate reached out and caught me by the skirt, holding me back.

"No, miss! Don't go in there! I saw, God help me. And I'll remember it in my dreams forever. He's still there, miss. Perhaps he's gone mad and we should run away before he kills us all."

She started to her feet, but I held her by the arm and would not let her go. "Don't be foolish," I said. "I saw Mr. Beach go into Mrs. Reid's room only a moment ago. Wait a moment—wait!"

How fearfully sharp every detail of that scene will always be, stamped forever upon my memory. The long hallway, half lost in the gloom of faint gaslight, just as I had seen it on my first visit to this house, the very pattern of the wallpaper, raspberry repeated endlessly on cream. There was a moaning of the wind and an accompanying rattle of shutters, the cold, dusty smell of the unheated hallway.

I heard his steps before they reached the door of Leslie's room, and the sound of them told me how dreadfully something was wrong. Kate heard them too and she gave a little shriek and clutched me tightly as Andrew stepped into the doorway, pale and shaken and sick with shock.

A cry from the staircase above jarred me into life. I released myself from Kate's clutch, and the girl began to weep out loud again. I whirled to see that Garth had come halfway down the stairs. Her attention was fixed upon Andrew, and she must have read in his face that something terrible had happened. He shook his head at her, but she darted down the remaining steps and would have gone past him had he not caught her by one arm.

"Don't!" he said. "There's nothing you can do for her now."

The woman struck away his hand and went directly into the room. I heard her gasp as she saw whatever was to be seen and caught her breath. But she made no other sound and in a moment she returned to the door. All color had vanished from her face, and her dark eyes were sunken hollows, her lips bloodless. She fought to command herself, but she could not speak. Only her eyes spoke for her, staring accusingly at Andrew.

"No," he said. "No!" and made a faint movement of denial with his hands, as though warding off the accusation she did not speak. Then he swallowed hard and went on. "I stayed to complete the portrait. She said I might come in for the finishing touches. But when I went in just now—" He put his hands over his face as if to shut out the image of what he had seen in that room.

At our feet Kate sobbed aloud and Garth touched her with the toe of a shoe, recovering her power to act.

"Stop sniveling at once! Go downstairs and send Fuller for the doctor. Send Henry for the police. Move, now—hurry!"

Kate scuttled away, clearly glad to escape. I stood where I was, stunned and bewildered, while a new, dreadful fear set up a clamor within me.

Garth turned again to Andrew. "I've never had much use for you, it's true. I thought her kindness to you misplaced. But you loved her, and I believe you. You wouldn't have done this. I think we both know who did."

Andrew nodded numbly. "Yes, we know. Is he still in the house?"

Garth moved at once. She flung open the library door upon emptiness and then went into Brandon's bedroom. Her voice came back to us, stronger now, as she gained mastery over herself.

"He's gone, and his bag's gone. He had it packed this morning."

Through my daze and confusion two things began to come clear. Whatever crime had been done, both Andrew and Garth meant to accuse Brandon of committing it. And Garth had said to Andrew, *You loved her.*

"Tell me what has happened," I pleaded as Garth came out of Brandon's room.

She spoke without looking at me, and there was venom in her words. "Go and see for yourself what you've brought upon this house!"

Andrew put out a hand to me. "Don't go in there, Megan. She has been beaten to death. Beaten in violence and anger."

"With that heathenish brass candlestick," Garth said. "He

must have used it in both hands—like a club. Oh, my poor pretty lady!" Her control broke for an instant, but weakness was not for Thora Garth and she recovered at once. "He will pay for what he's done. I'll see to that. The police will find him; he'll never get away!"

This was worse than anything that had gone before. Dwight's death and a hidden pistol had no meaning for me now. I had only one instinct, and no matter what my fear, I followed it.

"Brandon didn't kill her!" I cried. "You can't make such an accusation! What proof do you have?"

"Proof!" Garth echoed the word scornfully. "Do you think there's no proof? Do you think we haven't all known what was going on between you and my poor lady's husband? Do you think he hasn't wanted her out of the way?"

Andrew tried to come to my aid, tried to spare me something of Garth's wrath. "That's not the whole of it," he said. "Reid had a stronger motive than that. She knew he killed Dwight. That's why he married her—to keep her quiet. But he must have pushed her too far, so that she was ready to go to the police. And he killed her to save himself."

Miss Garth flicked his words aside impatiently. "That's nonsense. It was the boy who killed his father; we've never had any doubt of that. It's true the older brother married her to keep her quiet. But not for that reason."

"Then for what reason—what reason?" I demanded.

She seemed not to hear my question, following the trend of her own thoughts in a bitter reviling of Brandon. "She was so sure she could win him, once she had him for a husband. And with any man who was human she might have done so. But he never touched her after they were married. He was off chasing other women within the week. Oh, he was gallant enough to his wife in public. He overdid his ardent attention and laughed in her face when they were alone. I know. She told me many times the truth about their marriage." Her voice rose, shrill now with fury. "But he'll pay for all the wicked things he's done. Now he will pay."

There was no reason left in me, but only unreasoning fear and a determination to help Brandon, whatever the cost.

"He didn't do this thing," I repeated mindlessly. "He didn't, he didn't!"

Miss Garth ignored me and returned to the room where Leslie lay.

"Don't, Megan," Andrew said gently. "Get yourself in hand and start using your mind. You needn't believe everything Garth says. She was in love with him too. She has always identified herself with Leslie, and, as her mistress began to hate him, she did as well. But she's wrong about there being another reason why he married Leslie."

I cared about none of this. "It's not what happened in the past that matters now. You were always just, Andrew, even though you didn't like him. You can't turn against him like this."

Andrew put the heel of his hand against his forehead as if there were a throbbing there. When he spoke, his voice had turned to a monotone, devoid of emotion.

"What's past breeds the present. Who else do you think has done this thing, Megan?"

The frightening thought was in me that there was no one else, no other choice, and I could not answer him.

He pressed me in the same toneless voice. "Do you think it was Garth then? After all her years of devotion?"

I wished I could believe the governess guilty of this. But I could not. She might have killed Brandon, who had scorned and hurt her mistress, but I did not think she would have raised a violent hand toward Leslie. It would have been like injuring herself.

"Was it you, perhaps?" Andrew said. "Or me? Do you think I killed her, Megan? Do you think I could have?"

Again I did not think so. Andrew was capable of strong

purpose, perhaps of deep love. But there was nothing of violence in him. In my mind I could see Brandon raising that candlestick in fury to crush out something that maddened him, but not Andrew. My skin grew clammy with terror, and my throat closed as though I were the victim of nightmare.

Andrew went on in the same dull tone. "I've loved her for a long time. I loved her as she was. I asked of her only what she wanted to give. Her games and pretenses never fooled me. I knew I was no more than someone to whom she could turn for solace. I loved her anyway."

Through the nightmare that held me in its grip I stared at him, and he must have seen my look.

"Forgive me a little, if you can, Megan. I've been fonder of you perhaps than I was of her. What I felt for Leslie was something different. How many times I've thought how much simpler life would be if you and I had met each other before we knew Leslie and Brandon Reid."

Who was I to condemn him? There had been times when I'd turned to Andrew Beach in the same way, wishing I could love where my heart was not truly given. But none of this mattered now.

"Where are the children?" Andrew asked.

For the first time I remembered them, upstairs in the nursery, undoubtedly frightened by Kate's screaming.

"I'll go to them," I said. "Andrew, you'll stay in the house, won't you? Until—"

"I'll stay," he said grimly. "I want to see him caught as much as Garth does. Besides, I'm the one who found her. They'll want me here for questioning."

I turned from the tragic recollection in his eyes and ran upstairs to the nursery. When I opened the door, I found a scene surprisingly peaceful. Selina lay on the red carpet before the fire, listening to the story of the Toad Prince that Jeremy was reading aloud. He paused as I came into the room and gave me the grave look of one adult questioning another. An

292

adult who has taken on the responsibility of distracting a child in a time of trouble.

I tried to sound natural and bright. "It's bedtime, my dears. Let me see how quickly you can get into your night things."

"We heard Kate drop her tray of dishes," Jeremy said guardedly. "She sounded awfully upset about it."

I offered him my silent approval and agreed that was exactly what had happened.

Selina went to bed with a minimum of delay, and, when I had tucked her in, I hurried back to Jeremy. He was in his bedroom, the gaslight on, waiting for me.

"Something bad has happened, hasn't it?" he asked at once.

I would not dissemble to the extent that I had done with Selina, but I could not tell him the truth.

"It's your mother, Jeremy. There's been an—an accident."

The gravity of his look dismissed my words as an evasion. Jeremy was all too sensitive to the climate of disaster.

"She's dead, isn't she?" he said, and then went on calmly. "I knew by the way Kate screamed. She's a silly girl sometimes, but the screaming was real."

"Yes," I agreed, "the screaming was real. You were good about Selina—keeping her from being frightened. Will you help me now, Jeremy? Will you stay here quietly. I'll have to go downstairs and I don't want to worry about you."

All I wanted just then was to escape his grave, questioning gaze. There had not yet been time for me to face the full horror of what had happened. I was still too dazed to think clearly. Fear stood at my elbow, waiting, and my heart beat so thickly it was hard to breathe. Strangely enough, it was Jeremy who had a calming effect upon me as he went quietly on.

"When I was little I loved her as much as I loved my father. But she never liked me. She didn't really like my father, either. The way she acted about him was only pretending. Because I looked so much like him, she couldn't love me. Once she even told me so when she was angry. When I grew older

293

I didn't mind very much. That's why I don't feel now the same way I did after—after my father . . ." He broke off, his young face expressionless.

"I understand," I assured him, loving him all the more for this attempt to be honest with me.

He was not through. "I can remember when I was little. I used to like the way she smelled of violets. I could have loved her very much, if only she had liked me."

His words accomplished at last what my single-minded concern for Brandon had prevented until this moment. The full realization that Leslie Reid was dead, that her cool beauty was forever destroyed and all that was evil in her as well. I could almost catch the scent of violets as Jeremy spoke and I knew I would dread that odor for the rest of my life.

The boy was in bed now, and I drew the covers gently over him and moved toward the light. But before I could turn it out, he asked another question.

"Miss Megan, did someone shoot her? The way my father was shot?"

"I don't think she was shot," I said. "We'll know more about it tomorrow. A doctor will be coming soon. And—other people who will know what to do. Shall I leave a candle burning when I go downstairs, Jeremy? I can look in and blow it out after you're asleep."

"Not a candle," he said. "Nor the gas either. Gas is cold-looking, and sometimes it whispers. And a candle makes the shadows jump. Would you lend me the rosebud lamp from your room just for tonight, Miss Megan?"

"I'll fetch it right away," I promised and went quickly to my room.

How deceptively quiet and untouched by tragedy the small room seemed—as though no one had told it of death.

When the lamp was alight on Jeremy's bureau, I kissed him on the cheek and went downstairs.

Outside Leslie's room Kate was on her hands and knees,

cleaning up the mess from the spilled tray, working as if by her very industry she would keep from flying into hysteria. Andrew paced the hall as I had done upstairs—up and down, not pausing when I appeared, though he spoke to me as he paced.

"The doctor's in there now. And Garth's with him."

"Have the police come yet?" I asked.

"Listen!" Andrew said and leaned upon the hall rail above the stairwell.

Below Henry was opening the front door and I heard a voice that seemed familiar. A moment later Captain Mathews mounted the stairs in Henry's wake, a police sergeant trailing behind him. I remembered him as the man who had met us at the Home that time we had gone in pursuit of Jeremy. He nodded gravely to Andrew and me.

"Is it the boy again?" he asked.

28.

THIS WAS one contingency I had not thought of, and I answered a little wildly.

"Oh, no! Not the boy, Captain. Jeremy has been upstairs all day long."

"Don't worry," he said kindly. "We're only here to find out exactly what has happened."

Miss Garth heard our voices and came to the door. Her tremendous control had not forsaken her, though her color by now was ghastly. She looked first at Kate, still working on her knees.

"Go downstairs," she said curtly, and once more Kate fled with all dispatch. "In here," she told the captain, and he and the sergeant went into Leslie's room.

Andrew stopped his pacing and sat down at the foot of the stairs, resting his head in his hands. I felt sorry for him, but there was nothing I could do or say.

The doctor and Captain Mathews came out of the bedroom together, and a few moments later the doctor took his leave. Miss Garth crossed the hall to Brandon's library and motioned to Captain Mathews.

"You may use this room, if you like," she said.

He thanked her and glanced at Andrew, still sitting at the

foot of the stairs. "I understand you found her, Mr. Beach. Will you come in and tell me about it, please?"

Andrew went into the library and Garth followed them, not waiting to be asked. No one closed the door, and I could hear the voices within quite clearly. The questions were routine, and Andrew was explaining dully what his own role had been. I could not relax enough to sit on the stairs as Andrew had done. Alternately I walked the hall, or leaned upon the rail, listening for any sound from upstairs or down.

Thus I saw Henry as he started up from the floor below. The butler still carried himself with dignity, but I caught the concern in his eyes as he looked up and beckoned to me with a secretive gesture. I asked no questions, but ran down to meet him on the stairs.

"Please, miss," he said. "In the kitchen. If you'll come right away."

I did not hesitate, but ran down to the basement at once. Brandon waited for me in the big warm kitchen. He nodded his thanks to Henry, who went away at once, leaving us alone.

I said the first thing that came into my head. "Why did you come back? They'll be looking for you now. If they find you here, you'll be in dreadful danger."

He put his hands upon my arms, steadying me, stilling my outburst. "I came because Fuller had the good sense to try the club, looking for me, and found me there. Tell me exactly what has happened, Megan."

Impatient though I was over the delay, I told him of how I had come downstairs and heard Kate screaming, and of how Andrew had come out of Leslie's room.

"He was in love with her," I said. "He has admitted as much."

Brandon brushed the information aside. "Of course. She could never rest unless she subdued any young man who came her way. She had to play at love-making constantly, since there was so little love in her. What of Garth?"

I told him of how she had come downstairs and gone into Leslie's room. Of her iron self-control that sometimes cracked a little around the edges.

"They both mean to accuse you," I said. "Please, please get away while you can. Leave the city before Captain Mathews knows you are here."

"My loyal Megan," he said. "I think you would stand by and sacrifice yourself to help me, even in the face of murder."

I was growing frantic. "Don't stay; don't talk! There's no time!"

"There is the rest of my life," he said quietly. "However long, or however short that may be. I am not going to run away, Megan. Come, we'll go upstairs together. Don't look so frightened. They have no evidence against me. Let them look to Thora Garth. Or to Andrew—the jealous lover who found her! I'm not the only one the police will think of."

For all the mildness of his tone, I knew that granite lay beneath his resolve. There was nothing to do but go upstairs with him.

We could hear Miss Garth before we reached the library, and it seemed that her control was failing as her vituperation mounted.

"Let them both pay for this terrible crime! It's the girl's fault as much as it is his. But *he* is the one who did the act. You can't sit here and let him get away while you ask us foolish questions."

Brandon stepped through the doorway, and the captain looked up calmly, noting his presence without comment. Miss Garth rose from her chair, her face working, but Brandon spoke before she did.

"I left the house earlier and didn't know what had happened until Fuller came to the club to tell me. I'm at your service, Captain, to help you in any way I can."

The captain bowed courteously. "Please sit down, Mr.

Reid. You too, Miss Kincaid. Some serious accusations have been made here this evening and—"

"He always wanted to kill her, and now he has!" Miss Garth cried in rising hysteria. "You have the proof in your hands— What more do you want?"

The captain frowned at her. "Will you please wait in the hall until I send for you. You too, Mr. Beach."

Andrew took the governess gently by the arm, and, after an angry moment in which I thought she would shake him off, she gave in and let him lead her from the room.

Captain Mathews nodded to me. "You may remain, Miss Kincaid. The accusations concern you as well. Possible motives have been claimed. Perhaps you may have information that will help us."

Brandon seemed alert now and caught up in a tide of excitement, as though he scented battle and was willing to meet it halfway.

"There are plenty of motives," he said. "I can give you any number myself. But I didn't touch her and you'll find no evidence that I did. Rather than waste time on me, why not explore the motives of others who may be involved."

"I'll do that in good time," the captain said with the air of a man who knew his business and did not intend to be deflected. "For the moment we will consider something which has just come to light. A search of your room has been made, Mr. Reid. Have you any explanation for this?"

He reached into a drawer beside him and drew out something which he spread upon the desk. I leaned forward, anxiously. The object was a white shirt of the type Brandon always wore, and, as the captain opened it before us, I saw the bright red stains upon it.

Captain Mathews' tone was even. "This shirt was found wrapped inside a clean one in a drawer in your room. There was also pinkish water in the slop jar, where it must have been poured after you washed your hands."

I stared in growing alarm at the thing upon his desk. Brandon was no murderer, but someone wanted desperately to make us think he was.

Brandon spoke my thought aloud. "The murderer is very anxious that I should be blamed, but I know nothing of how those stains come to be on my shirt. Do you think I would be so foolish as to hide such evidence in my room and leave it behind if I were really guilty?"

"Rational and coolheaded behavior is seldom achieved at such a time," the captain said gravely. "This is a serious situation, Mr. Reid. A claim has been made by Mr. Beach that there was a second pistol at the time of Mr. Dwight's death, and that the boy did not fire the shot that killed your brother. That, indeed, the fatal shot was fired by you."

Brandon snapped out his answer, but I saw his color change and knew he realized the growing danger of his position.

"That is a story Leslie developed recently," he said. "I've heard nothing about it before. She undoubtedly took Beach in with her rantings. There was no second pistol. After all, you solved the case to your own satisfaction at the time, Captain."

Captain Mathews studied him thoughtfully for a moment. "I remember that the boy made some seemingly wild claim concerning a second pistol. Perhaps we'd better talk to him. Miss Kincaid, will you bring Jeremy downstairs for a moment?"

I had no choice but to do as Captain Mathews requested.

In the hall a chair had been found for Miss Garth, and she sat bolt upright against its straight back, her hands clasped tightly in her lap. Andrew still sat at the foot of the stairs and he raised his head from his hands as I came out of the room.

At the sight of those two, anger flowed through me. "What

301

are you trying to do? What have you to hide that you are trying to incriminate Brandon?"

Andrew looked up at me sadly. "Poor Megan. Don't you know by now that he killed her? If you let him, he will do to you all the harm he did to Leslie."

I left him and ran upstairs to Jeremy's room. The boy slipped into his clothes reluctantly. His memory of encounters with Captain Mathews were far from happy, and he was not anxious to see him again.

By the time we went down, the coroner had arrived and Captain Mathews was in the hall, talking to him. The captain greeted Jeremy kindly and returned to the library with us.

"There's nothing to be frightened about," he assured the boy. "I'd like you to tell me in your own way what you know about that second pistol you mentioned at the time of your father's death."

Jeremy stood up so straight and tall that I was proud of his courage. His voice did not falter as he spoke.

"I tried to tell you, sir. I never fired the pistol they found. The pistol I took had ivory set into the grip. If you want to see it, it's hidden now in the brass candlestick in my mother's room. Maybe you've noticed that candlestick, sir?"

I shivered, remembering that Jeremy did not know how his mother had died.

The captain nodded. "Yes, I've seen the candlestick."

"There's a big hollow in the base," the boy told him. "The pistol is hidden there."

Captain Mathews spoke to the officer in the hall. I stole a look at Brandon and saw that he was frowning at Jeremy.

The police officer returned carrying the huge candlestick in both hands. It had been partially wrapped in a cloth and there was no candle in its socket now.

While we watched, the captain unscrewed the upper section from the lower. It turned, as Jeremy had said it would, though the threads squealed faintly in protest until it came free, exposing a deep, shadowy cavity in the base of the stick. He set the top section on Brandon's desk and turned the base over. Nothing fell out. When he reached a searching hand into the hollow, he drew out some cloth padding that might have wrapped the pistol and kept it from rattling around. If anything had once been hidden there, it was gone now.

Jeremy told the captain the same story he had told me—of how he had gone to his father's room after Selina had confided her secret, and of how Miss Garth had come in and he had hidden under the bed. From beneath the counterpane he had seen her carry the candlestick into his mother's boudoir.

"Miss Garth will know about it," Jeremy finished. "She is the one who took the candlestick away."

But when the captain summoned Miss Garth to explain, she said she knew nothing of any pistol.

"Miss Leslie sent me for the candlestick. She had put it away in that room for some reason. I remember she put it there two days before Christmas."

Two days before Christmas, I thought, and remembered the touch of hands that groped in the dark, recalled the whiff of violent scent that had so frightened me. So it had been Leslie that evening in Dwight's darkened room.

"She sent you for the candlestick this afternoon?" the captain prompted.

"Yes, she asked me to bring it to her. So I carried it into her room and set it in its usual place beside the hearth."

"Did she tell you why she wanted it?"

Miss Garth began to sway a little. She put her hands to her temples in a distraught gesture. "No! I always sensed something queer about that candlestick, but I never knew what it was. She told me nothing. When I'd set it down, she asked me to go away and leave her alone. I—I never touched it again."

"The boy says there was a pistol hidden in its base. His

sister claims to have seen Mrs. Reid take it out of the hiding place and put it back again some weeks ago."

"This is children's nonsense," Miss Garth said, shaking her head.

"I agree," said Brandon quietly.

Jeremy would have spoken, but there was an interruption from the door Miss Garth had left open. Andrew had roused himself and come into the library. The skin of his face looked yellow and drawn, and the dazed look had not left his eyes. He spoke with an effort.

"I've heard you mention a pistol hidden in the base of the candlestick. It wasn't in the candlestick today. It hasn't been there for some time. Mrs. Reid took it out several days ago and gave it to me to get rid of. She still had some notion of destroying evidence that might involve her husband in his brother's murder."

Jeremy's outraged cry made itself heard. "Uncle Brandon didn't kill my father. Of course he didn't!"

"Wait, Jeremy," the captain said. And to Andrew, "Where is the pistol now?"

"I have it," said Andrew. "I have it here."

He drew from the pocket of his coat a small pistol with an ivory-set handle and laid it on the desk before Captain Mathews.

29.

"THERE'S YOUR evidence," Andrew said. "That was the unloaded pistol Jeremy brought upstairs that day."

It was Jeremy who moved first. He slipped from my side and ran to the desk. Captain Mathews made no move to stop him as he picked up the small, deadly instrument and balanced it knowingly in his hand.

"This is the one!" he cried. "It's the pistol I took from the collection and carried upstairs that night. And it wasn't loaded, it wasn't fired. I know that now."

"Exactly," Andrew said. "The pistol Mr. Reid fired was cleverly substituted for the one Jeremy dropped."

"Uncle Brandon couldn't have fired at all!" Jeremy protested. "I'd have known if the shot came from across the room where he stood. It came from where I was standing. Close to me. That's why I began to think that I must have fired the pistol after all. Only I know now I didn't. Someone standing behind me held that other pistol and pulled the trigger. Someone hidden from Uncle Brandon by the curtains shot my father. And I know who it was."

In startled silence we watched as the boy replaced the pistol on the table. Without fear he looked at each person in turn, all about the room, and I found myself following his eyes. I looked at Brandon, on whose face bewilderment struggled with disbelief. Than at Andrew with his yellowish pallor. And at Miss Garth, who looked strangest of all—as if some restricting hand had closed about her throat, cutting off her breath so that it came in a choking gasp.

The captain reached for the pistol, turning it about in his hands, though his eyes did not leave Jeremy's face.

"It is best not to guess about a thing like murder," he said. "If you name a name, you must be sure."

Jeremy hesitated. "I don't know if I can be absolutely sure, sir. I didn't see the person. I never looked behind me at all. But the pistols could have been changed while Uncle Brandon and I ran to my father."

Miss Garth managed a strangled cry. "No—you mustn't listen to him! The boy is demented, unbalanced!"

"He is neither," said Andrew quickly. "But he is lying. He would do anything to save his uncle."

Jeremy flung a quick, scornful look at the tutor and leaned earnestly upon the desk, reaching a pleading hand toward the police officer.

"I'm not the one who is lying, sir. There's something I didn't tell you. When I went looking for the pistol today, I had time to open the candlestick before Miss Garth came in. The pistol was there. I still have a piece of the paper that was wrapped around it. I was in a hurry, so I didn't wrap it up again. I just dropped the pistol back in the cloth and screwed the top on the base. When I heard someone coming, I stuffed the paper in my pocket and hid under the bed. Here it is, sir."

From his pocket Jeremy drew a torn scrap of newspaper and handed it to the captain, who opened it on the desk before him.

"Yes," he said, "this might have been wrapped about the pistol. The date is here—the week of Dwight Reid's death." He looked at Andrew. "Have you anything to say about this,

Mr. Beach? If the pistol was in the candlestick today, as Jeremy claims, then it must have been today that you had the stick in your hands."

Andrew said nothing at all. He stared at the pistol, the glazed look in his eyes again.

Miss Garth made a sudden violent gesture and would have left her chair, but Brandon moved to stop her.

"Wait," he said. "Give him a chance."

The governess fell back in her chair and began to weep uncontrollably, her handkerchief to her eyes. All her earlier self-control had vanished.

"A chance?" she moaned. "He gave my poor lady no chance!"

Andrew seemed not to have seen her movement toward him, nor to hear her words. He stared at the pistol on the desk as though it held his attention above all else.

"I never understood her vacillation about the pistol." He spoke as if to himself. "One moment she would threaten to use it as evidence against Mr. Reid. The next, she would plead with me to get rid of it entirely. I took it to satisfy her. It's true that she gave it to me today. She said it wasn't strong enough evidence to use against Mr. Reid. But I thought she was wrong."

The captain would have spoken, but Andrew turned suddenly to Jeremy.

"Who was it that stood behind you and fired a shot the night your father died?"

The boy answered without hesitation. "It was my mother," he said. "I know it was my mother because I caught the smell of her perfume. Like violets. That was the thing I kept trying to remember afterwards. But by the time it came back to me it didn't make any sense, because I thought I'd fired the gun."

Andrew made a brushing gesture across his face, but he

spoke to Jeremy again. "Garth often uses your mother's perfume. How do you know it wasn't Garth?"

"Because her father was ill and she'd gone to be with him that night. She wasn't even in the house when it happened."

"That's true," Miss Garth said brokenly. "I wasn't there."

Captain Mathews fixed Andrew with his keen, steady gaze. "You are ready to admit that you were with Mrs. Reid the afternoon before she died?"

"Of course he was!" Miss Garth shrilled. "I see it all now. He even tried to fool me, but it was he who beat her so cruelly and horribly."

"What have you to say, Beach?" the captain urged.

Andrew shook his head as if he tried to clear his mind from some confusion of thought.

"I didn't kill her," he said. "I'd never have laid a finger on her. I was the one who loved her."

"She's dead," Brandon said grimly.

A long shivering sigh went through Andrew.

"Send the boy away," he said.

I took Jeremy to the door of the library. "Go upstairs, dear, and get ready for bed. Make sure that Selina is all right. I'll come to you when I can."

After he had gone, I closed the door and returned to my chair near Brandon.

Andrew had not moved and he did not look at any of us. "You're wrong in what you think," he said dully. "If she couldn't have what she wanted, she wouldn't live. She died by her own hand."

The emotion had drained out of his voice, as though he had reached the limit of any ability to feel. No one spoke as his monotone continued.

"After Megan brought Mrs. Reid home from the ceremony this morning, I stayed on in the schoolroom, pretending to work on the portrait. I pushed a note beneath Leslie's door saying I would come when I had a chance to slip in unnoticed

I wanted to know what had happened, and perhaps to comfort her. I didn't get to her until sometime in the afternoon. When Garth brought her the candlestick, Leslie didn't let her know anything was wrong. But she'd taken the laudanum even then. Enough to be sure of death. She told me when I went to her.

"The death of Brandon's father settled matters for her, I suppose. As long as he lived, her husband might stay with her to avoid scandal. But now she knew she couldn't hold him, though she must have brought up the accusation of Dwight's murder in a last desperate effort. Now I can understand why she always pretended devotion to Dwight, devotion to any cause that honored him. It was her own guilt she wanted to hide."

Miss Garth sobbed into her handkerchief. No one else made a sound.

"There could have been no saving her," Andrew went on. "At first I was wild with despair. I felt it was Reid who had killed her with his indifference and scorn. He was to blame for all her unhappiness. The drowsiness hadn't come upon her yet. Her thoughts were clear, and she spoke to me quite rationally. She told me there was a way in which Brandon Reid could be made to pay for all he had done to her.

"She sent me for a shirt from his room. He had already left the house by that time. She gave me the pistol and told me to get rid of it. Then she asked me to light the candle in the big stick on the hearth for the last time. I remember how she watched the flame while she talked to me.

"She told me what she wanted me to do and how I must do it. I had to promise— There was no other way to let her go in peace. Besides, I felt that Reid was her murderer in actuality and I wanted to see him hang for what he had done to her. He had all I wanted, and he valued it so little.

"She talked until the drug started to take effect. When her tongue began to slow, she told me to blow out the candle because she wanted it to be dark. I did as she told me and held her in my arms until she was gone. Afterwards I took up the candlestick."

He bent his head and covered his face with his hands. Behind the guard of his fingers his voice went on.

"After the first blow was struck, it wasn't hard to do. I closed my eyes and struck at Reid with every blow. I could take satisfaction in that. Afterward I took off his shirt that I'd worn and hid it in his bureau. I washed my hands in his basin. I had carried some of my painting equipment as a blind in going in and out of Leslie's room, lest I be seen, and I took it with me when I returned for my coat. I would have left the house if Kate hadn't chosen that moment to come to the door with a tray for Mrs. Reid."

The final telling seemed to have given him strength, for now he put his hands down and there was something like relief in his eyes. When he stopped, there was total silence in the room. The heavy silence of mingled horror and disbelief. Yet we had to believe. There was no doubting Andrew now. The laudanum would be found and his words substantiated—though if he had not spoken, the coroner's verdict would undoubtedly have been death from beating with the instrument of the candlestick.

Brandon moved first. He got up and went out of the room as though he could not trust himself to stay. The weight of the story we had heard lay upon us all, though now I had only pity for Andrew because of the dreadful road he had followed. Pity for Andrew and a slow burgeoning of relief for Brandon, as full realization came home to me. I, too, could stay in this room no longer.

"May I go to Jeremy?" I asked and when the captain nodded I went past Miss Garth, still sobbing into her handkerchief, past Andrew, who did not look at me, and out the door.

Upstairs in his room Jeremy waited and I sat on the bed

310

beside him, knowing that he must be told the truth. Not all the dreadful details, but enough so that he would understand that he was fully cleared and no one would ever point a finger of accusation at him again. He heard me through solemnly.

"What will become of Selina and me now?" he asked when I had finished.

It was Brandon who answered him from the doorway. "I'm going to send you and your sister upriver to your grandmother's for a while, Jeremy. Would you like that?"

The boy nodded, accepting the proposal with quiet satisfaction. I kissed him good night and went into the hallway with Brandon.

"There's a great deal to make up to him for," he said sorrowfully. "I've been blind from the beginning, and a fool to believe the evidence I thought my own eyes had given me. Do you think the boy will ever forgive me?"

"He won't consider that there is anything to forgive," I assured him. "Start with him as things are now. I think he'll want only to go on from here and not look back."

Brandon held out a hand to me. "Come, Miss Megan," he said, and led me into the empty schoolroom, where no fire burned, and sat me down in a chair.

"There are some things that the captain and Andrew Beach don't know," he said. "And needn't know. The true reason behind my marriage to Leslie, for instance."

"I know a little," I broke in. "Miss Garth said it was true that you married her to buy her silence, but there's no need for you to tell me more."

"There is need," he said. "But first let me say that if Leslie shot Dwight—and we know now that she must have—it wasn't because she wanted me. Not then. She had married him for his wealth and promising future. She had notions of flying high in governmental society. But after he managed to involve himself in a scandal of corruption that was about to break wide open, he had a change of heart and intended to make a complete confession. He sent for me to come home and stand by him while he faced what he had to face. Prison, perhaps, and certain disgrace. Leslie couldn't accept that. I can see now that her motive for what she did was clear by her standards. She would never have lived willingly with disgrace, and Dwight told me she had pleaded with him not to throw the matter open. After his death I wanted only to hush the whole thing up and spare my father the truth. There was no point then in making a scapegoat of Dwight, who had been only a weak tool and could no longer speak for himself."

I was beginning to understand. "And later Leslie used that over your head?"

He nodded unhappily. "With Dwight gone she had nothing to gain by secrecy. She could hurt my father cruelly if she spoke out—and all for nothing. If I married her she promised silence. So I bought her silence, but I bought it meaning to make her pay for it for the rest of her life. I did not dream of how heavily I was to pay as well."

He went abruptly to the window, where he stood with his back to me, staring down at the stables. I wanted to go to him, to put my arms about him, and offer the small comfort of my love. But he looked so stern and distant that I did not dare. Yet I must bring him back somehow to things as they were now—to a will to go on from here.

I stepped to the mantelpiece and picked up the pointer Andrew had laid upon it. Lightly I traced its tip along the colored map that hung against the wall.

"Show me," I said—although I knew very well— "show me where Thebes is located."

He turned from the window, smiling gravely, and came to take the pointer from me. "Why do you want to know, Megan?"

"Because you will be going there," I said. "And I don't want to be left here alone." For the second time I spoke the words I had said to him downstairs. "Take me with you, Brandon."

"Do you think I'd go without you?" he said. "When will you marry me, Megan?"

I knew there would be a great buzzing of gossip, but the children would be away with their grandmother and gossip eventually dies.

"As soon as you like," I told him.

How tender he could be, how very gentle. How surely his arms belonged about me, and how strong was the beating of his heart.

But we could not linger for our love now. He had to put me from him and go downstairs where his responsibilities as Leslie's husband must still be met.

When he left me I went into the hall and stood for a long moment, listening to the sound of his steps on the stairs. There were voices below, movement. As I stood in the shadows, Miss Garth mounted the steps slowly, mournfully, and went into her room. She did not see me, and I did not speak to her. I caught the whiff of violet scent in the hallway as she passed.

On the table beside my door was a candle I had left burning and I went to extinguish it. Violets and candlelight— always I would remember those two. "Blow out the candle," Leslie had said to Andrew.

I snuffed the flame with my fingers and went into my room. The scarab pin lay among other trinkets in a bureau drawer, and I took it out to hold in my fingers. Thebes, with Brandon beside me! I would see for myself those great figures of the queen, and all the other wonders. I would be with Brandon under the hot sun of Egypt, where warmth would renew and restore him, where the slow healing would begin that now must come to him. Somewhere there would be a home for us —a place where Jeremy and Selina could come and know that they were loved and welcome.

Though not in this house. Not ever again in this house on Washington Square.

313